"I might not have dated in a while, but I haven't forgotten how to do it."

"It's not..." Beth stopped. This was the best time she'd had in ages, and she wouldn't say anything to spoil it. Besides, *date* was only a word.

And maybe she'd forgotten how to have a good time. The thought ricocheted through her and she pressed her free hand to her chest. She'd been so focused on Ellie and her job that her life had gotten smaller, almost without her realizing it. Joy was right. Beth did need to get out more, and perhaps it was the same for Zach.

However, tonight's good time wasn't about the restaurant, the food or even the dancing. Like when they were teenagers, it was about Zach. Despite the intervening years, there was still a connection between them. So, date or not, what might happen if Beth took a chance and explored it?

Dear Reader,

Montana Reunion is my Harlequin debut. The first romances I read as a teenager were by Harlequin authors, and as a longtime reader of the Heartwarming line, I'm especially excited to join the Harlequin community and share this book with you.

In creating the world of the Tall Grass Ranch and small town of High Valley, Montana, I drew on memories of growing up in western Canada and, in particular, visiting my dad's hometown in ranch country. *Montana Reunion* is also inspired by family vacations in the American state unofficially known as Big Sky Country, a place that means a great deal to me.

Other aspects of the story, such as characters with disabilities and life at Camp Crocus Hill, were influenced by my experience as the mum of a daughter with chronic medical conditions.

I hope you enjoy *Montana Reunion*, a second-chance romance, which is also my favorite kind since I'm a firm believer in second chances in life as well as love.

I always enjoy hearing from readers, so visit me at my website, jengilroy.com, where you'll also find my social media links and newsletter and blog sign-ups.

Happy reading!

Jen

HEARTWARMING

Montana Reunion

—

Jen Gilroy

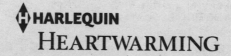

HARLEQUIN
HEARTWARMING

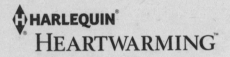

HARLEQUIN®
HEARTWARMING™

ISBN-13: 978-1-335-42660-4

Montana Reunion

Copyright © 2022 by Jen Gilroy

PLEASE RECYCLE
THIS PRODUCT IS RECYCLABLE

Recycling programs
for this product may
not exist in your area.

This edition published by arrangement with Harlequin Books S.A.

For questions and comments about the quality of this book,
please contact us at CustomerService@Harlequin.com.

Harlequin Enterprises ULC
22 Adelaide St. West, 41st Floor
Toronto, Ontario M5H 4E3, Canada
www.Harlequin.com

Printed in U.S.A.

Jen Gilroy writes sweet romance and uplifting women's fiction—warm, feel-good stories to bring readers' hearts home. A Romance Writers of America Golden Heart® Award finalist and short-listed for the Romantic Novelists' Association Joan Hessayon award, she lives in small-town Ontario, Canada, with her husband, teenage daughter and floppy-eared rescue hound. She loves reading, ice cream, ballet and paddling her purple kayak. Visit her at jengilroy.com.

Visit the Author Profile page at Harlequin.com.

For Pam, with love and thanks

Cousin, friend and true horse person

CHAPTER ONE

"IT'S ONLY A SKY. There's nothing special about it." Twelve-year-old Ellie spun away from Beth to roll her wheelchair along a wooden pathway toward a square log building sheltered by pine trees, the welcome center for Camp Crocus Hill.

Except, it was a Montana sky, streaked with soft gold, blue and gray in the early July evening as the sun settled over the distant mountains. A sky as big as Beth remembered and with the same sense of endless possibilities.

She clicked the remote to lock the SUV, slung her bulky purse over one shoulder and jogged to catch up with Ellie, the purple ballet flats she'd traded for her signature heels click-clacking. "This part of the camp looks almost the same as it did the summer your mom and I were here. That big log building behind the welcome center was the dining hall. It likely still is. Sometimes we ate outside." Beth gestured to the picnic tables and barbecue near the building's entrance. "With those big windows, gable roof and wide eaves, I thought it looked like the Swiss chalet in a *Heidi* storybook I had when I was little."

"So?" Ellie braked to a stop and fiddled with a tab on the backpack propped on her lap. "Even if it looks the same, it's not, is it?" She gestured to her wheelchair before tugging on a strand of thick honey-blond hair. "There weren't kids like me here then."

"No, but your mom…she wanted you to come here. For us to come here together." Beth's throat clogged, and the path lined with red-and-white flowers in rustic barrel planters blurred. *Help me, Jilly. You had almost thirteen years to get used to being a mom. I've only had six weeks. How can I help your girl?* As always, only silence greeted Beth's inner plea.

"Whatever." Ellie grabbed a pair of oversize sunglasses from her backpack and stuck them on her face, hiding her eyes but not the sullen tilt to her mouth.

Beth made herself count to three and focus

on the camp's Welcome sign, a vintage barn board nailed to an old wagon wheel propped against a rough-hewn log. Being almost a teenager was hard enough, and Ellie had just lost her mom. Hopefully, things would get easier and time away from home would help. That was why they were here, one of the last promises Beth had made to Jilly.

"Why don't we get checked in, find our cabin and decide what we want to do tomorrow? Or maybe you want to have a snack and head to bed. We've had a long day." Another one in a succession of long days. However, they were here now. This was the safe place Ellie needed to begin to heal from her mom's death and where she and Beth could figure out how to become a family.

"I don't care." Ellie shrugged and hugged her phone like she'd once embraced the pink teddy bear she'd carried everywhere as a toddler. A bear that, along with almost everything else in the pink-and-gray bedroom Beth had decorated for her, Ellie now called *babyish*.

"Look." Beth pointed to a brown horse with a white star on its forehead on the other side of a rail fence beyond the path.

The horse whinnied as if in welcome.

"So? It's a horse." Ellie barely glanced at the animal.

"Yes, but we don't see horses back home in Chicago, do we? Your mom loved horses. She was a good rider too. When she was your age, she won ribbons in shows." Beth made her voice bright.

"Like I don't already know that? She was *my* mom, not yours."

"Of course." Beth pressed her lips tight together. On the long road trip west, she'd tried to engage Ellie in conversation, but the girl had remained silent, earbuds wedged in her ears. Ellie had stared out the passenger window as the flat Midwestern states slipped by, until they'd finally reached these rolling Montana foothills. Camp Crocus Hill was nestled on almost two hundred acres of hilly treed land a few miles from the small town of High Valley. Located in the heart of ranching country, the pretty spot was tucked at the base of the majestic Rocky Mountain range, white-tipped peaks visible in the hazy distance.

As she and Ellie drew closer to the main camp building, Beth sucked in a breath. She and Jilly had met in almost this exact spot the summer they were fifteen, only a few months away from turning sixteen. Both were new campers marooned for four weeks in a place that at first neither of them had wanted to be. From almost that moment, Jilly had been Beth's best friend and one of the few people who'd ever truly understood her.

"Hang on. Let me help." Beth darted forward to grab Ellie's backpack, which had fallen off her lap onto the ground.

"I can do it myself. I'm not a—"

"Hi. Welcome to Crocus Hill." The voice was deep and male.

As Beth jerked her head up, her purse swung outward and whacked the owner of the voice smack in the middle of his jeans-clad knees. "Sorry. Hi." She registered a pair of scuffed, muddy cowboy boots and long legs in faded denim before stumbling to her feet. "Thank you." She took a step back as the man handed the backpack to Ellie.

"No problem. You must be checking in." His voice was as warm as his smile, and he tipped the rim of a battered black cowboy hat.

"Yes." Beth fumbled with her overstuffed

purse. She was a professional woman. A chief financial officer for a fast-growing technology company. And until Jilly died and Beth had become Ellie's guardian, she was always in control. Now, however, the self-assuredness she'd prided herself on had deserted her when she needed it most. Instead, she lurched from one crisis to the next, saying and doing the wrong thing, uncharacteristically awkward.

The man directed his attention to Ellie. "What's your name?"

"Eleanor, but everyone calls me Ellie." An unexpected smile tugged at the corner of her mouth. "Something stinks around here."

"Ellie." Beth's face burned. "You don't—"

"It's okay." The man's laugh made Beth want to laugh too. "That's a ranch for you. I just came from the barn. It's my mom's book-club night and, since you're the last to check in today, she called me to come meet you so she could leave early to pick up a friend. Have you met Princess?" He gestured to the paddock.

Ellie shook her head. "Why is she called that?"

"My sister, Molly, named her. When she

was a kid, Molly loved books and movies about princesses. *Cinderella* was a favorite."

Beth had loved that movie too, back when she'd believed in fairy tales and happily ever after. She suppressed the thought of the romance books on her e-reader, including a few new releases she'd downloaded especially for this trip. They were fiction, a way to relax and escape from the pressures of a demanding job. Her life was fine. There was nothing missing, and now, with Ellie, it was fuller than ever. She didn't need a man to make it complete.

Ellie studied the horse. "I used to like *Cinderella* but I haven't watched it in years. I'm almost thirteen."

"I'm almost thirty-seven, but I still watch it." His laugh rolled out again. "There are way more little girls than boys in my extended family." He turned back to Beth. "I haven't had a chance to look at the list, so I'm sorry I don't know your names or details, but I can help you get checked in and answer any questions."

"Thank you." Beth handed him the sheet of paper with the confirmation email.

He scanned their information and turned

to Ellie. "You and your mom have arrived at a great time, and—"

"She's not my mom, she's—"

"I'm her guardian, Elizabeth Flanagan." Beth spoke at the same time as Ellie. "I emailed the office about the change of plans." She stopped and swallowed hard.

"Of course." The man studied her, and something flickered in the depths of his blue eyes. Compassion followed by puzzlement and a faint glimmer of what might have been recognition.

"Beth Flanagan? From Chicago?" He checked the email again, and his eyes narrowed.

Eyes as blue as a Montana sky in high summer. A whisper of memory stirred and Beth's heartbeat quickened. "I go by *Elizabeth* now." Except, she'd been Beth here and to Jilly and Ellie too.

"Zach Carter." His voice got rough.

The boy who, along with Jilly, had made the month of that long-ago summer the happiest time in Beth's life. For an instant, the world seemed to tilt. "Zach." She forced his name out. "I didn't expect to see you here." Although his family had a ranch half a mile along the main road and it wasn't surprising he'd still be in the area. Still, if she'd known Zach had anything to do with Camp Crocus Hill, she'd have found a different summer camp and never made that promise to Jilly. "It's been years."

"Yes." His voice was clipped, formal and with none of its prior good humor. "Good to see you again."

"Likewise." Her stomach knotted. The boy she'd known was now a man and, except for his eyes and a hint of something in his smile, a stranger. She glanced at Ellie, who stared between the two of them, her expression curious. "Ellie is Jilly Grabowski's daughter. She—"

"Died." Ellie's voice was flat. "That's why I'm here with *her*." She jerked her chin in Beth's direction, and her mouth trembled.

"I'm sorry." Zach's voice was gruff, and his gaze skittered from Ellie back to Beth as his expression softened in sympathy. "I remember Jilly. She was great. There aren't any words."

"No." Beth gripped a handle of Ellie's wheelchair as her heart twisted.

Zach took off his hat and ran a hand through his thick light brown hair, darker now than the tousled sun-bleached blond in the picture Beth still had in an old album. "Come inside, and let's get you settled." He moved toward the single-story log building with white trim, his booted feet making a rhythmic thud on the boards. The automatic door, accessible for wheelchair users, whooshed open as Ellie rolled along the ramp and through the wide opening.

"Thanks." Beth followed them inside, and her arm brushed Zach's bare forearm as she stopped where he stood beside Ellie. She stilled for a fraction of a second, and he did too, his indrawn breath sharp in the sudden silence.

Then she made her feet move and found a chair on one side of the wide wood desk where Zach indicated, his expression shuttered.

Beth had been at Jilly's side as her friend had fought so hard to live—the roller-coaster journey from hope to despair and everything in between until the oncologist had shaken her head and left the curtained hospital room. Beth remained, holding Jilly's frail body in her strong embrace, her friend's sobs muffled against her shoulder. And it was then she'd promised Jilly she'd be there for Ellie, no matter what.

Her gaze caught Zach's and held. For a brief instant, the expression in his eyes catapulted her back to the girl she'd been and the dreams she'd dreamed before her world had imploded and she'd taken another path. A path that had led far away from a life in High Valley, Montana—a path that had now brought her back here, where everything had started.

And yet, although Zach was the first boy Beth had ever kissed and the only one she'd ever thought she'd love forever, they were adults now, and the past was the past.

ZACH'S STOMACH LURCHED as he sat behind the desk in the welcome center and processed Beth and Ellie's check-in paperwork. He struggled to focus on it, not the woman who sat across from him. Her curly dark hair that he remembered was now ironed sleek, and Beth held herself rigid as if the slightest touch might cause her to shatter into pieces.

He clicked away on the computer keyboard. The fact Beth was here again had to be a coincidence. And Ellie. He snuck a glance at the girl hunched in the wheelchair, sunglasses atop her head. Her thumbs darted across the keypad of her phone, and her face was half-hidden by a curtain of honey-blond hair. Now he knew who she was, the resemblance to Jilly was both startling and heartbreaking.

"You're all set."

Jilly had almost lived at the camp stables where he'd worked the summer he'd turned was seventeen, but it was Beth—quieter, more introspective and at first scared of horses—who'd snagged his teenage heart.

He handed Beth a key ring and a large white envelope with the camp's logo, a horseshoe intertwined with a crocus, on the top left corner. "You're in Meadowlark. It's our smallest cabin since there's only two of you. We have twenty-five cabins with different capacities for different size families. As you likely saw on the website, we can accommodate up to a hundred campers at a time. There's a minimum of one staff member for every five campers, and a higher ratio depending on a camper's needs. We pride ourselves on giving individual attention and care."

"How many campers are here now?" Beth's voice was business-like.

Zach glanced back at the computer. "Now that you've arrived, we're at eighty with two more families arriving tomorrow. We'd be full if we hadn't had a couple of late cancellations." Despite the cancellation fee, they couldn't afford to have empty cabins. The familiar worry slid through Zach's mind.

"Apart from fresh paint and more flowers, from what I've seen so far, the camp looks almost exactly the same," Beth said.

Zach nodded. "When my folks bought it, they wanted to keep the name, look and feel as well as the sense of community Camp Crocus Hill stood for. The cabins are still in several interconnected loops beyond the dining hall, but they've been remodeled and upgraded for families, specifically for people with disabilities. We also renamed them since you were here. I've marked your cabin on the map." He passed another sheet across the desk and made sure his fingertips didn't brush against hers. "There's a parking space behind your cabin, and all the camp information you need is in the envelope and on laminated sheets you'll find on the kitchen table. If you need help with your luggage, I can—"

"We'll be fine. Thank you." Beth's voice was as stiff as her posture. Although she'd always been reserved, this elegant woman in crisp dark jeans, a filmy white top and purple shoes with bows on the toes was almost unrecognizable from the girl she'd once been.

"Enjoy your stay." Zach made his tone neutral.

Beth was a guest, and although she and Ellie would be here for five weeks, longer than most visitors, he wouldn't have to see much of them.

"I'm sure we will." Beth's tone was also neutral, her smile looking forced.

"Let us know if we can help you with anything."

Although Zach pitched in at the camp when he could, his priority was the ranch and making it profitable again. He wouldn't lose the legacy entrusted to him by the four generations of his family who'd loved and tilled this land from when it was still the tall grass prairie that had given Tall Grass Ranch its name. Not now and especially not after everything he'd already lost. As he studied the framed watercolor of Camp Crocus Hill that hung on the log wall behind Beth's head, one his older brother had done a few months before he passed, sadness nipped at Zach with the bite of an early frost.

"The camp's activities are listed on the schedule in the envelope. You can be as busy or as relaxed as you want. We have trail riding, short overnight camping trips, nature excursions, as well as art, cookery and singing and drama activities. We've also got a heated swimming pool, and our riding lessons are always popular. You can book those here or online."

"Riding lessons?" Ellie looked up from her phone, a spark of interest in her angry brown eyes fringed by dark lashes.

"Sure." Unless Zach was related to them, he didn't have time for children, and he didn't have time for a relationship either. That part of his life was over. "My cousin's wife, Lauren Carter, is one of our teachers. She was on the US equestrian team for two Paralympic Games. We're real proud of her."

"Wow." There was both respect and admiration in Ellie's voice. "Do you… Could I, like—" she hesitated and worried her bottom lip "—meet her sometime?" The hope in her voice chipped a bit of the ice in Zach's heart.

"Of course. I'll introduce you. If you want, Lauren can even give you a lesson."

"On Princess?"

"Only if she's gentle," Beth broke in and darted a glance at him. "Ellie hasn't ridden before." Her eyebrows drew together in a worried crease under a fringe of hair. She'd been pretty as a teen, but she was gorgeous now and had an air of city polish that made Zach tuck the boots he'd worn to do chores farther under the desk.

"All our horses are gentle, but Princess is the biggest softy of the lot. You don't have anything to worry about." At least, not when it came to horseback riding. Having taken on guardianship of Jilly's daughter, Beth must have plenty of other worries. "If you want, I can help Ellie get started." He gripped the edge of the desk. In addition to qualified riding instructors, they had camp counselors. There were plenty of people to help apart from him, but he'd opened his big mouth and spoken before he'd thought.

"That would be...wonderful." Beth's tense

expression eased. "You were so good with horses. I remember…" She stopped and avoided his gaze, staring instead at the framed photographs that lined the wall behind him. "Didn't some of those pictures used to be in the dining hall?"

"Yes. A few go back to the early days when this camp was founded and then most years until we took over. My mom found them in boxes in a storage room." *Family.* The irony didn't escape him that he was surrounded by families, his big extended one and all the families that came to stay here each summer, but he didn't have one that truly belonged to him.

"That's great." Beth's brown eyes shone, and the warmth in them was like a punch to Zach's gut. How long had it been since a woman had looked at him like that? "Maybe there's a picture of Jilly and me there. Tomorrow, Ellie and I can come back and take a look."

"I have lots of pictures of my mom." Ellie's sullen expression was back. "I keep them in a special album. A *private* album."

Zach studied the girl's bent head. Beneath the anger, she was hurting—the kind of hurt that resonated with a part of himself he'd buried deep. "I don't know how much you miss your mom because I'm not you. However, I know what it's like to lose someone you love, and I've found one of the best ways to keep their memory alive is to talk about them." He picked up a framed photo from beside the computer. "This man here is my dad, and along with my mom, this camp was his dream. He passed a few years ago, but he's still a part of everything we do here."

And his dad's legacy was also the reason Zach was here. Dennis Carter's example was one that both inspired and tethered him.

"I'm sorry about your dad." Beth's voice was soft with sympathy.

"Thanks. He was a good man." And now Zach was torn between following in his dad's footsteps and still being his *own* man—one who'd come back to the ranch, because he'd seen the bigger world, and this little corner of Montana was where he not only wanted but also needed to be.

Unlike Beth, who'd come from that bigger world and had gone back to it and made a success of herself in it. A woman who, in those trendy clothes and with that big-city sophistication, was as out of place in Montana ranch country as he and Princess would be in Chicago's urban canyons.

Beth was the girl who had once turned his teenage world upside down. If that brief, accidental touch after they'd come into the office was any indication, she'd become a woman he wasn't entirely immune to. Yet, apart from one letter, she'd never gotten in touch with him again after she'd returned home. Like a fool, though, he'd checked the mailbox at the end of the lane for months still hoping to hear from her. As he stood and came around the desk to point Ellie and Beth in the direction of their cabin, Zach reminded himself to focus on the present, not the past, and what was, instead of what might have been.

CHAPTER TWO

THE NEXT MORNING, so early the sun hadn't fully peeped over the mountains, Beth eased open the screen door and went out to the wide porch that encircled two sides of the cozy log cabin. Setting a yellow pottery mug of peppermint tea and her e-reader on a low table, she sat in a wooden Adirondack chair topped with a plump blue-and-white-patterned cushion.

When she'd checked on Ellie, the girl was still asleep, her expression relaxed, one hand cuddled against her cheek. So Beth had a few hours before she had to try to be a mom again—the first job she'd ever failed at, and failed spectacularly too.

Still in her pajamas, she tucked her bare feet under the chair and snuggled into the cream-colored fleece blanket she'd grabbed from the sofa before coming outside. Although it was July, the morning air was cool, as well as fresh and still. In her life before Ellie, Beth would have been at the gym now. With her headphones on, she'd exercise while catching up on emails and podcasts before diving into a day that often didn't end until the sun disappeared behind the concrete high-rises again.

Beth went to pick up her e-reader and stopped. She didn't need to escape into a book when all this beauty surrounded her. Besides, it had been ages since she'd stopped to savor a sunrise.

Although two similar, white-trimmed log cabins sat on either side of theirs, each cabin was sheltered by trees. This home-away-from-home had privacy and everything else she and Ellie needed. And the swimming pool and main buildings, including the dining hall, the one Beth remembered, were a short distance along a paved path.

As they'd settled in the night before, Beth had been reassured by hearing children's voices and laughter nearby. They wouldn't be isolated, and if Ellie needed it, the hospital was only fifteen minutes by car.

A bird called, and in the distance, water lapped. It was likely the creek where Zach had once taken her fishing, which ran through part of the camp. Although Beth hadn't liked fishing, she'd liked spending time with him, and the two of them had talked about everything on those long-ago summer afternoons. Apart from Jilly, and unlike her absent and embittered parents, Zach was one of the few people in Beth's life who'd ever truly listened to her—and she'd grown in confidence that summer, not only figuring out who she was but also who she could be, at least before everything changed.

She sipped her tea and stared at the sky as the colors changed from soft gray to pink and faint gold as daylight bathed the cabin, trees and tubs of container flowers in pearly light. A horse nickered, and Beth straightened, putting the mug back on the table.

Highlighted by the sun, a man on a chestnut horse came around the corner of the cabin, a familiar battered black cowboy hat with a white band tilted over his eyes. Like any other ranch hand, he wore a long-sleeved blue plaid flannel shirt, jeans and the requisite boots, but together with the hat, something about the way he sat on his horse was instantly recognizable.

Beth clutched the blanket to her chest and darted a glance at the cabin door. Zach had seen her in a swimsuit, and her pajamas covered more of her than it had. Still, she'd been fifteen, not thirty-five. However, if she dashed inside, she'd make something out of nothing and an ordinary situation more awkward than it needed to be. She plastered on a smile and waved in greeting.

"Morning." He rode to the edge of the porch. "You're up early." Zach sat tall in the saddle, almost an extension of the animal, as relaxed on horseback as he was off it.

Beth hugged the blanket tighter. "Ellie's still asleep, but I wanted to get a start on the day." Mostly because she couldn't face lying in bed any longer, worries circling in her head like a horde of pesky mosquitoes.

"And did you?" Zach's amused gaze slid to the bottom edge of the blanket, where Beth's bare feet stuck out. Her toenails were painted hot pink and patterned with daisies from the pedicures she'd booked for herself and Ellie before they left Chicago. She'd hoped it would be something fun for them to do together.

"Did I what?" Her face got warm, and she

covered her feet, the blanket slipping at her neck to expose her pink pajamas patterned with panda bears.

"Start your day." He gave her a crooked, almost boyish grin.

"Yes. I was admiring the...view." The words got stuck in her throat as she stood and moved to the porch railing. Zach was tall, well over six feet to her five feet five, but on horseback he loomed over her and put her at even more of a disadvantage.

"Me too." His gaze took her in from top to toe and seemed to linger for a brief instant on her mouth. Then his grin broadened as he slid off the horse and tethered it to an iron ring on the porch. "I had to check a line of fence, but early morning is my favorite time of day."

"Mine too." Beth wrapped the blanket around her shoulders like a shawl. She was never ill at ease around men, but she talked to them at work, the gym or social events, not on her porch in her pajamas. Not that her Chicago condo had a porch, only a balcony she rarely used. "What's your horse called?"

He patted the animal's neck. "Scout. He was born here on the ranch. I got lucky. A horse like him comes around once in a life-time."

Maybe men were like horses. If you missed your chance at a good one, you didn't get another. Beth moved closer to Scout and patted his neck like Zach had, the gesture instinctive. "I'd forgotten how pretty it is here." Or maybe she'd made herself forget.

"Montana's the best place in the world."

"Have you been many other places?" She could make small talk with him as if he was any other guy.

"Beyond the western US, Europe mostly. After college, I played hockey in Germany for ten years. Hockey in the winter, and the ranch in the summer. It was a great life." His voice had an unexpectedly bitter note.

"You must have been good. At hockey, I mean." Despite Beth's pink-panda pajamas, they were having a normal adult conversation.

"Good but not good enough to play at the highest level professionally, at least in North America. I could have stayed in Europe to play a few more seasons, but my dad died, and well... I'm a full-time rancher now. Along with my family, of course. Most of us are still here." His expression changed again and became impersonal as if he'd shared something too intimate. "What's the situation with you and Ellie?"

"Jilly had an aggressive cancer, and when she found out it was terminal, she asked me to raise Ellie. Except for an older cousin, Jilly wasn't close to her family, and Ellie's dad was never in the picture so… I said yes. On top of some vacation I was owed, I took an unpaid leave of absence from my job, and here we are." And each day from the time Beth woke until she went to bed again at night, she floundered like a swimmer out of her depth without inflatable armbands to keep her afloat.

"Not a lot of people would have done what you did for Jilly, and Ellie." In Zach's expression, respect mixed with something else warmed Beth inside. The feeling gave her a greater sense of achievement than paying off her mortgage or buying her dream car, the sporty two-seater with a convertible top that now sat in her underground-parking garage while she drove Jilly's SUV.

"Of course they would. Jilly was my best

friend. I loved her and Ellie too, so agreeing to be Ellie's guardian wasn't even a choice."

"You always have a choice." His voice was grim. "I hadn't thought about Jilly in years, but hearing she's gone… When Ellie said her mom had died, it got to me, you know?"

"Yeah." Beth's throat tightened. "Before she passed, Jilly told me I should make the most of the moments because once they're gone you can't get them back. At the time, I didn't know what she meant, but now…" She patted Scout again. "This summer, I want to make some special moments with Ellie, but I'm not married and I never had kids, and now I have one who is almost a teenager. I don't know how to be a mom." The confession slipped out, and she bit her lip, wishing she could take the words back.

"You're doing the best you can. It's all you can do." Zach's expression was compassionate, and Scout leaned into Beth as if in silent support. She'd forgotten how intuitive horses were, or maybe it was only this horse—and this man.

"I guess so." Except, apart from at her job, Beth's best had never been enough. It hadn't kept her parents together, and it sure wasn't helping her these days. And now, with her job on pause and without her regular routine and the familiar comfort of numbers, spreadsheets and charting a financial strategy, she was more lost than she wanted to admit. "Ellie likes you." At least she'd smiled at Zach in a way she hadn't done since Jilly's death.

"I try to connect with all our guests."

"I'd like to connect with her too. I just don't want to seem as if I'm trying to replace her mom. I only want to be Ellie's friend." But even on a good day, Beth couldn't get a handle on anything other than, at best, stilted conversation and, at worst, outright resistance and aggression. "Ellie and I had fun together before Jilly got sick. They lived in an apartment in a Chicago suburb, so I got together with them all the time. Since Jilly's death, though, it's been different. It's natural Ellie's angry, but I don't know how to help her."

"All you can do is be there for her. Grief takes…time." Zach's mouth twisted before he looked away, at the cabin, instead of her.

"Do you have children?" She could picture him with a brood of little ones, like steps on a staircase, and a wife working in partnership with him on the ranch. A woman who'd grown up in ranching country and knew this way of life from birth.

"No wife or kids." His tone was short, and he avoided her gaze. "I should get going. Although I wasn't scheduled for early chores, the ranch doesn't run itself."

"Of course." Beth pressed a hand to her throat.

He untethered Scout and swung into the saddle. "Trust your instincts. Like with horses." Zach rubbed the animal's neck, his fingers strong and capable. "With horses and kids, like most things in life, if you trust your instincts, you won't go far wrong. And if you make a mistake?" He gathered the reins. "You can start over again."

Except, it wasn't so simple, at least not for her. There were times, she thought, when no matter how much you wanted to, you couldn't start over because things were too broken to fix. Or even if you tried, you kept making mistakes. Beth swallowed and made herself smile. "Thanks. I'll remember that."

Zach waved in farewell as he and Scout

moved around the cabin toward the thick stand of trees that edged this side of the camp.

Beth stood on the porch until they disappeared from view, watching the treetops sway in the light breeze. Jilly and Zach were right. She needed to make the most of the moments this summer, and although Beth couldn't change what had happened or bring Jilly back, she could still change her own future. Starting over, like Zach said. Starting now.

JOY CARTER SET the breakfast table in the spacious ranch-house kitchen, counting each place setting as the sun streamed through the big window that framed her favorite view. Those rolling fields, a palette of gold and green that stretched toward the horizon, were her bit of heaven on earth. And from when she'd first visited Tall Grass Ranch as a child to when Dennis had carried her over the front doorstep as a bride and the forty years since, she'd planted deep roots here.

She set the last plate at the end of the long farmhouse table, opened the screen door and stepped outside to ring the brass bell that hung from one end of the porch. Jess, the arthritic sable-and-white collie, nosed her knee.

"You've already had your breakfast, so don't give me that look." Joy patted the top of the dog's head.

"Mom?" Zach's voice echoed from the kitchen, and her mouth curved into a smile. Home, family and everything that made her life what it was were all here. Her three sons, Zach, Bryce and Cole, all lived nearby, and now her daughter, Molly, was home from college in Bozeman for the summer. Joy had lost her husband too soon, and there had been other losses, but she was still here, and the remaining family they'd made together would go on beyond both of them.

"Out here." She returned to the kitchen and studied Zach, his back to her as he washed his hands at the utility sink. Had she done the right thing? She straightened one of the breakfast plates and linked her hands together. "Did you get the fence fixed okay?"

"Yeah. It was a smaller job than I figured." Zach dried his hands on a towel and turned to face her, the sun highlighting new lines on his face. The older he got, the more he looked like his dad, but instead of causing

Joy pain, that familiarity to her beloved Dennis was comforting.

"I expected you back earlier. I was worried." On a ranch, if you weren't worrying about the weather, animals or crops, you worried about accidents. Her chest got tight, but Zach wasn't Dennis. Her son was healthy and whole.

"Sorry." Zach dropped a kiss on the top of her head and moved toward the counter with the big bowl of pancake batter she'd made earlier. "I got held up."

"Oh?" Joy made her expression neutral as she took bacon from the fridge and joined him beside the stove. "Was there another problem?"

"No." He half turned away from her to coat a large skillet with oil and switch on the heat. "I rode back through the camp and got talking to a guest. Beth Flanagan. Remember her?"

Joy smoothed the *Super Mom* bib apron the kids had given her for Mother's Day. She couldn't tell him. She'd promised Jilly—and herself—she'd see this plan through. "Vaguely."

"She was at camp here that summer I

worked in the stables. She and Ellie Grabowski checked in yesterday. I looked at the file after they'd gone to the cabin. Beth is now Ellie's guardian. When they arrived, I thought Beth was Ellie's mom. Ellie corrected me, but you should have told me Ellie's mom passed."

If she'd told him, Zach would have gotten someone else to check Beth and Ellie in. "I forgot. My memory... Those hormones, you know. Brain fog."

"I got them settled as best I could. Beth's doing a good thing for Ellie." Zach ladled pancake batter into the skillet.

"Is Beth the girl you used to be friendly with?" Joy put several slices of bacon in another pan and avoided Zach's gaze.

"Yeah." His voice was low.

"She was a nice girl from what I remember." Unlike someone else. Anger slicked through her at how her son had been betrayed. Thanks to that woman whose name Joy still couldn't bring herself to say, Zach had lost his trust in people—and most of his hope for the future.

"Beth's sure a city girl now." Zach flipped a pancake, his expression unreadable. "You should have seen her shoes. Purple things with little bows on the toes. She wouldn't last five minutes on a ranch. Who wears shoes like that around here?"

"Lots of women, at least when they're not working in a barn." He'd noticed those shoes enough to describe them to her. Hope flickered in Joy's heart. Maybe Jilly's idea would work. If Joy didn't try, she'd never know, and she'd do anything to help her son. "Besides, look at me. I grew up in a city and settled into ranch life fine."

"You grew up in Missoula. It's hardly the same as Chicago. Besides, you spent every summer in High Valley and had family here. You were almost a local." Zach's smile was stiff as he set pancakes onto a warming dish and added more batter to the skillet.

"Still, you never know if—"

"Stop trying to fix me up with every woman you come across. I'm happy on my own." Zach softened his words with a one-armed hug. "Thanks to Bryce, you've already got grandkids. Molly and Cole will likely have kids someday too. What more do you want?"

"Don't change the subject. We're not talking about your sister and brothers." She put cooked bacon on a plate lined with paper towels to drain. "As for what I want, I want you to be happy. You make everyone else happy, but I worry you forget about yourself." She was his mom, and she worried about her kids, no matter how old they were. "Someday, when I'm gone, you'll be rattling around in this house alone. Do you want that?"

"I'll have dogs." He glanced at the collie sprawled in a patch of sunshine next to the table. "Besides, this house is for a big family. Even though I haven't finished renovating it, I'm happy in great-grandma and great-grandpa's old place. When that time comes, and it won't be for years yet, Bryce or Cole or Molly can live here."

"You're my oldest child." Her *oldest living child*, Joy silently corrected herself, the ever-present pain of loss stabbing her ribs. "This house should be yours, the way it's always been."

"But it doesn't always have to be that way." Zach's voice was sharp. "I don't—" He stopped as boots thudded on the porch and voices rang out. "Everyone's here. You go sit, and I'll dish up."

Joy rested a hand on his tense back, but Zach didn't turn around. Her son was too much like her: determined, unyielding and slow to forget or forgive. But that meant, out of all her children, Joy knew best how to reach him.

She pulled out her chair at the far end of the table and sat as Molly, Bryce, Cole and the two ranch hands clattered into the kitchen, teasing each other with a good humor that came from respect, friendship and long familiarity.

And as she pulled out the napkin and spread it on her lap, she studied Zach. He started serving breakfast, but the sadness in his eyes hadn't gone away. He was still young, and even if she hadn't promised Jilly, she had to show her son that he needed to make changes in his life before it was too late. Jilly, may she rest in peace, had given Joy a necessary push. Now it was Joy's turn to push Zach and maybe even Beth too. Because that was also what a mom did.

CHAPTER THREE

THAT AFTERNOON, BETH gripped the water-color pencil and glanced around the bright art studio. The last time she'd been here, it was a cramped, dark room in the camp's activity center across from the dining hall. Back then, it had only been used on rainy days and had held a Ping-Pong table, shelves stacked with books and board games and squashy beanbag chairs. Now, however, it was painted a light cream, and a bank of tall windows had been cut into one wall opening onto a deck that overlooked fields and mountains.

Sunlight flooded the airy space, and easels were set up here and there along with wheelchair-accessible tables. At the front of the room, the art teacher, who'd introduced herself as Sarah, sat on a low stool and talked to Ellie and another girl around the same age.

Beth sat in the back with several other

adults, in an art class for the first time since junior high, with instructions from Sarah to *discover her inner creativity*. Whatever that meant. She gripped the pencil tighter.

Ellie was fine. She didn't need Beth here. In fact, since she'd gotten up, and from breakfast through to swimming in the pool, during lunch, and until now, Beth's attempts at conversation had been met with stony silence. She wanted to be around, though, in case Ellie *did* need her. She wouldn't hover, but, for the next thirty minutes until the art class ended, she'd be a quiet, supportive and accepting presence. Ellie's psychologist had suggested several books about parenting teenage girls, including one focused on coping with the death of a parent. Beth had read all of them and was now trying to put the advice into practice.

"You hold that pencil any tighter and you'll snap it in two." A woman at the table next to hers gestured with a smile. "Some days are harder than others, aren't they?"

Beth nodded and unclamped her numb fingers to set the pencil beside the open drawing pad, the creamy expanse of white paper taunting her. Everyone else was drawing or painting, but she was stuck.

"I'm Kate Cheng." The woman waved a paint-spattered hand and smiled at Beth from behind trendy tortoiseshell-framed glasses. "That's my daughter, Lily, with your Ellie. Since Ellie's new, I asked Lily to sit with her."

"She's not my..." Beth stopped. Ellie wasn't her daughter by birth, but Beth was all Ellie had. "Thank you. That was kind."

"No problem." Kate's sleek black hair, cut into a blunt bob, bounced. "This is our third summer here, but we're locals now too. Lily and I love this area so much we moved to High Valley from Seattle last year. We couldn't miss camping at Crocus Hill, though, because it's our special mom-and-daughter time."

Beth's stomach knotted. She'd never had that kind of time with her own mom, and she'd likely never have it with Ellie. "I'm Beth Flanagan." The old name popped out before she thought of it. "We're from Chicago." *Elizabeth* belonged to Chicago too, and that life was on hold. "I came to this camp when I was a teenager, but now, with

Ellie... I'm her guardian. Her mom died six weeks ago."

"That's rough." Kate's dark eyes softened in sympathy. "Do you have other kids?"

Beth shook her head. "No husband either."

"Wow. This must be hard for you too. I'm a single mom, but I have an older son who's at college. I'm a special-education teacher, and although some people say that makes it easier, it's different when it's your own child who has special needs. Lily had cancer and had to have part of her leg amputated. She's fine now, but it was touch-and-go for a while."

"I'm so sorry." Beth swallowed. Cancer impacted—and often destroyed—a lot of lives, whether young or older.

Kate's expression turned serious. "I was angry at first, but after a while, I decided I could spend time regretting what Lily and I had lost or instead be grateful for what we still have. That change in mindset made a world of difference." She gestured to her sketchbook and the abstract profusion of colors splashed across the page. "I'll never be great at art, but there's something about playing with colors and textures that makes me feel like a kid again. If you give it a try, you might be surprised."

Beth studied the art supplies scattered across the table and set the pencil aside. When she was a kid, she'd enjoyed using markers. She pulled the marker package toward her, chose a green one, took off the cap and drew a thick squiggle in the middle of the blank page.

"In art or anything else, the first step is always the hardest." There was a smile in Kate's voice. "But now you've done it, who knows where you might end up? The first summer we were here, this camp was life-changing for Lily and me. The first few days, though, I was sure we'd be packing up and heading home early."

"Lily didn't like it?" Beth took another marker and added a yellow swirl beside the green.

"That's an understatement. She fought me every step of the way until, well, she didn't. She made friends with the other kids and bonded with the counselors. By the time we left, she was a different girl, almost like she was before she got sick but more confident and wiser somehow. You see, here she wasn't different or defined by her disability, and she took that understanding of herself out into the world with her."

"After a minor injury playing soccer two years ago, Ellie was diagnosed with the first of several rare chronic illnesses. They're primarily neurological and mostly invisible." And because until recently Beth hadn't lived with Ellie, she hadn't truly grasped what life with those medical conditions involved. "On good pain days, Ellie can walk independently, but she uses her wheelchair to help with mobility when she needs to. However, she hasn't been out of her wheelchair since her mom died. I don't know what to do." Beth added blue, pink and purple to her picture.

"When it comes to the general public, there's not a lot of awareness about invisible disabilities. Most people don't understand what an ambulatory wheelchair user is either. How can someone be disabled and use a wheelchair but they're also able to walk in certain circumstances?" Kate's expression was kind. "I get that question in my work. The answer, of course, is that every person is different. They know when they need their wheelchair and when they don't and it changes from day to day. Even hour to hour."

"I didn't understand ambulatory wheelchair use either but Ellie is teaching me." And Beth was trying to learn as fast as she could.

"That's good." Kate gave Beth an encouraging smile. "Based on my experience, maybe—and this is only a guess—Ellie feels safer in her wheelchair. Everything in her life has changed, so she uses her wheelchair even when she might not need to because it's the one thing that's a constant. Her mom's passing would have thrown her whole physical and emotional system into an upset too, so she's likely not as steady on her feet, even on what would for her be a good day. Talk to the staff. They're trained to help. As for you?" Kate patted Beth's hand. "All you can do is make sure Ellie knows you love her and will be there for her, even if she pushes you away."

"*All* she does is push me away." But Beth wouldn't give up, no matter how long it took. "Thank you."

"You're welcome." Kate grinned. "Moms

need other moms, and no matter how you got there, you're a mom now too."

She was, and maybe in Kate she'd made a mom friend she hadn't known she needed. "Most of the time, I don't know what I'm doing."

"I still don't, and counting my son, I've been at it for nineteen years." Kate laughed and dabbed more color on her painting. "As soon as I figure I've got a handle on motherhood, everything changes again. All you can do is focus on the moments. That's what my mom says, although she says it in Mandarin."

Beth's mom had a new life with her second husband in Atlanta and was only a fleeting presence in Beth's life. She couldn't talk to her mom, but like Kate had said, maybe she should stop regretting what she didn't have and focus on what she did. She dumped the remaining markers out of the package. "My best friend, Jilly, Ellie's mom, talked about focusing on the moments too." Beth's eyes smarted. Jilly was gone, but Beth had to move forward like she'd promised.

"Kids help you with that, and so do friends." Kate's tone got flat. "My ex-husband's a fun, successful guy, but he couldn't handle it when

Lily got sick. That was when I found out what marriage should be and who my friends were. He's still in Seattle living the life he always did, but when our son left for college, I searched for a teaching job and got licensed here. I needed to change my life, and Lily was all for it. We've made new friends here, ones we can count on, and although I'm not dating yet, when I do, it will be a man who will stand by me in good times and bad. Someone who's honest, dependable, loyal and believes in family. Like him." Kate gestured with her paintbrush.

Beth looked where Kate pointed. "Zach?" While she and Kate had been talking, Zach had come into the studio. In worn jeans and a white T-shirt, he approached Ellie and Lily, showing them something in the palm of his hand.

"You bet. He's good with kids and horses, and that tells me a lot about what kind of man he is. Most of the time he works on the ranch, but whenever he's here, the kids follow him around like he's Santa Claus with a sack of toys. Unlike a lot of people, he treats everyone the same, including the children and teens, and they need that. Every year, a few moms make a play for him, but he's

oblivious. If there was any kind of spark between us, I'd be tempted too, but there's not."
Kate laughed. "He's a good friend and Lily's
adopted uncle, that's all. Funny, I didn't have
a thing for cowboys until I came here. Now
they sure have a certain appeal."

Zach talked with Lily and Ellie, and the
girls giggled before he drew something on a
piece of paper that made them laugh harder.

Beth's chest got warm. She didn't have
a thing for cowboys, did she? Back in Chicago, she'd dated guys who had jobs like
hers. They wore suits and polished shoes,
played golf and collected fine wine. Guys
who were focused on making money and
rising to the top and who didn't always consider what it might take or who they might
hurt to reach their goals.

And guys who might not make the time
for Ellie. The realization hit Beth hard. Like
Kate's ex-husband, they were men who were
about the good times but who wouldn't be
there for her when she—or Ellie—needed
them. Like her own dad too. Her mouth got
a sour taste.

More kids clustered around Zach, and

Ellie raised an arm and waved at Beth. "Zach found dinosaur fossils. Come see."

For the second day in a row there was a real smile on Ellie's face and, instead of her typical scowl, the kind of excitement and interest Beth had almost forgotten.

"Come on." Ellie waved again, and Beth smiled in return, the backs of her eyes smarting. Ellie might not need her, but she *wanted* her. And this was one of those fleeting, special moments to cherish.

TWO DAYS LATER, Zach led Princess out of the barn and into the fenced paddock at the side of the camp. The horseback riding area lay beyond the main camp and closer to the ranch. A stunning snow-topped mountain range edged the far horizon. "You take extra care with Ellie, you hear? She's a new rider."

The horse turned to him, and he could have sworn she bobbed her head in agreement.

Zach adjusted the saddle and neared the gate at the far end of the paddock, where Beth and Ellie waited outside the fence. Ellie sat in her wheelchair dressed in the camp's riding clothes, morning sunshine glinting on her fair hair. Beth stood behind her and swung a riding helmet from one hand, her stance protective. She wore faded jeans and a strawberry-pink top that hugged her slender figure. On her feet, a pair of sneakers gleamed so white they must have come straight from the store.

"All ready for your lesson?" He greeted Beth and returned Ellie's smile. It was an ordinary lesson, and he was helping out at the camp like he often did. *Not usually on such a busy day for ranch work, though.* He pushed away the little voice in his head. "While we're waiting for Lauren and the side walkers, do you want to brush Princess? It will help you get to know her a bit." He pulled a soft brush from the bag slung over his shoulder.

"Sure." Ellie's face glowed.

"Side walkers?" Beth's expression was puzzled.

"They're the people who walk alongside the horse with the rider. Everything we do here is PATH certified and accredited. Professional Association for Therapeutic Horsemanship International." He opened the gate, and Beth and Ellie joined him in the paddock. "We offer a range of equine-assisted therapies and activities for young people and adults with special needs, all by trained instructors." Zach gave Ellie one of the carrot fingers he'd cut earlier and showed her how to give it to Princess, her hand out flat, palm up.

"Oh, that's good." Beth's tense expression eased.

"She likes carrots." Ellie's smile almost split her face in two, and Zach's heart caught.

Unlike adults, most kids were easy to please and were all about small joys. "She sure does, but she shouldn't eat too many of them at once." He rubbed the brush along Princess's neck. "She's already been groomed, but she likes it when we use this brush on her. Here, you give it a try."

Ellie reached out for the brush, but hesitated before she took it from him.

"Come closer." He tethered Princess to the fence.

Ellie rolled her wheelchair next to the horse and put the brush on Princess's side. "Like this?"

"Almost. Brush in the direction of her hair.

May I put my hand on top of yours to show you?"

Ellie nodded, and the tip of her tongue poked out from between her lips as she concentrated.

"That's right. See? She likes you." Zach indicated with his chin as Princess turned her head to study them.

"I like her too." Ellie's voice was low.

Zach took his hand away and let Ellie brush the horse on her own. "If you want, you can come into the barn to help with grooming one day after your ride. My sister, Molly, handles that job, and she can teach you."

Ellie shifted forward in her wheelchair to reach higher on the horse's coat. "Okay."

"You're doing a great job." Beth's voice was thick. "Your mom would be so proud of you."

Zach swallowed the unexpected lump in his throat. He already knew life wasn't always fair, but at her age, Ellie losing her mom was especially unfair. "Molly has lots of books about horses. If you ask her, I bet you could borrow some."

"Wouldn't that be nice, Ellie? You love to

read." Beth's voice was bright, and over El-lie's head, she gave Zach a tremulous smile, one where relief mixed with gratitude.

"I guess." Ellie was intent on Princess.

"It's okay." He mouthed the words. And for a brief instant, he was as comfortable with Beth as he'd been all those years ago when he taught her to ride and took her fishing in the creek—and she'd taught him about places and people a world away from High Valley, Montana.

Beth's gaze held his until the paddock gate rattled, breaking the connection between them.

"Here's Lauren and the others who'll help with your lesson, Ellie." He made himself smile at the two camp counselors and Lauren as he introduced them.

He took the grooming brush from Ellie so she could put on her riding helmet and then he fumbled with Princess's lead rope. His hands were all of a sudden unsteady, the roar in his ears masking Ellie's excited, awe-filled chatter at meeting a Paralympic athlete.

Once Ellie was safely in Princess's saddle, Zach led the horse away from the fence toward the center of the paddock. However, he turned back for several seconds, half expecting to catch Beth's gaze again.

Instead, though, she was focused on Ellie, smiling and encouraging the girl when she wasn't taking pictures with her phone.

When not on Ellie, Zach's focus should be riding out to check the cattle in the far pasture, a job that would keep him away from the ranch for the rest of the day, until evening chores. Instead, his attention was fixed on Beth and how her sweet smile lit up her face, and the soft wind ruffled her dark hair. His face got warm, and he pulled his hat further over his forehead.

"All set?"

He turned at Lauren's voice. Her gray eyes twinkled as she glanced between him and Beth.

"Yeah, sure." He led Princess in a slow circle as Lauren, and the counselors who walked at either side of the horse, talked to Ellie.

"I'm riding a horse." Ellie's voice squeaked as they rounded the corner of the paddock closest to the red barn with white trim.

"You sure are, honey." From her perch atop the fence, Beth took more pictures.

Zach figured she didn't remember the things he did the month they'd spent together that summer long ago, and she hadn't felt that spark between them either.

"This is the best day ever."

"What?" He blinked. Strands of dark blond hair stuck out from beneath Ellie's helmet, and her eyes shone. He forced himself to keep his attention on her and not Beth, the other girl he'd taught to ride in this same paddock. Beth waved at them and he waved back.

"I said it's the best day." Ellie laughed, and Princess nickered.

"It sure is." His heart got full, and he tilted his face to the sky. Even though he hadn't done anything special, and Princess hadn't gone faster than a slow walk, it *was* the best day, at least the best one he'd had in way too long.

Zach stopped Princess near where Beth sat on the fence. She'd been joined by Molly, his younger brother, Cole, Zach's mom, and even Jon Schuyler, the veterinarian from town that Zach had called to check on a pregnant mare.

Beth laughed at something Jon said, and Zach's heart gave an uncomfortable thump.

Zach didn't have any claim on Beth, so what was with that unexpected flicker of something that might have been jealousy?

"If Zach has time, do you want to go around again?" Lauren's voice yanked Zach out of his thoughts.

"Can I? Please?" The hope in Ellie's voice tugged at his heart.

"Of course." Zach cleared his throat. The cattle and everything else could wait. He glanced at Beth, and she looked at him with a soft, trusting expression before she turned back to his mom and Molly.

The woman Zach had promised himself he'd stay away from could still pull him toward her with the same ease as he lassoed a calf. He shook his head as he led Princess and Ellie on another circuit of the paddock. A busy, successful woman like Beth wouldn't want anything to do with him now. What they'd shared as teens would always be a good and special memory, but it was the past. And after July slipped into August, Beth would be gone again, back to Chicago.

More laughter rang out from the group by the fence. Above the rest, Zach heard Beth's sweet chuckles. He thought of the bells he fixed to the sleigh that the ranch's draft horses pulled each December in High Valley's holiday parade.

Zach caught his mom's gaze and her knowing expression that said she hadn't missed how he was drawn to Beth.

His face got hot, and he stared at his boots as he led Princess around the corner near the barn again. He'd made his choice, and he was happy with it. His life was here, and his responsibilities were too. Nothing Beth said or did would change anything, Zach least of all.

CHAPTER FOUR

"THE BUTTERFLY EARRINGS and matching pendant, please." Several days later, in the nearby small town of High Valley, Beth pointed to a glass display case at the craft center. The local silversmith's designs were laid out on a nest of black velvet. "They're beautiful."

"Thank you." A dark-eyed woman, her shoulder-length gray hair held back from her face with a turquoise-and-orange beaded clip, took the pieces Beth had chosen out of the case and tucked them into two small boxes. "Along with dream catchers, butterflies are my most popular design. If these are gifts, I can wrap them for you."

"Yes, please. That would be great." Beth handed over her credit card and darted a glance out the half-open window of the historic brick building that signage indicated had been the local train station. Her back to Beth, Ellie sat on the porch, once the station platform, and stared at High Valley's wide main street, where locals mingled with summer visitors.

The woman smiled as she wrapped the boxes in pale green paper and tied them together with white and darker green ribbon in a curly bow. "Are you staying at Camp Crocus Hill?"

"Yes." Beth returned the woman's warm smile. "I'm Beth Flanagan."

Since Ellie needed some extra clothes, a morning free from camp activities was the perfect time to come into town and explore. And Beth needed a breather from the place that was so closely linked with her memories of Zach and what they'd once meant to each other. He'd never given any indication he remembered that connection they'd shared as teens, but Beth felt a sizzle of attraction whenever he was near.

"I'm Rosa Cardinal." The woman put the boxes in a brown paper bag with the store's name, Medicine Wheel Crafters, and a stylized dream-catcher logo. "Joy Carter and I are friends from way back. You must be Beth and Ellie from Chicago."

"We are." Beth glanced out the window

again, but Ellie hadn't moved from that spot on the porch. "Ellie's thirteenth birthday is at the end of July, while we're here, and I want to make it special for her. This necklace and earrings are for her birthday."

Yesterday, when they'd spotted a butterfly hovering over a patch of purple asters behind their cabin, Ellie had been captivated, and Beth remembered reading somewhere that butterflies represented change, as well as hope and life. Maybe this present could symbolize the new family she and Ellie were making.

Rosa reached across what had once been the railway station's ticket counter and patted Beth's hand. "You let Joy know what you need and we'll all help. A party or whatever feels right for you and Ellie. You've got a few weeks yet."

"Thank you." Beth swallowed. She'd forgotten how interconnected this place was, the ranching community linked with the nearby small town of High Valley and Camp Crocus Hill too. "It's hard, you know?"

"I can't even imagine." Rosa's expression softened, and her brown eyes were kind. "I raised three kids of my own and fostered almost forty others, but every kid is different, so you have to let them guide you. I'm teaching at the camp next week. It's an art workshop with craft projects that are easy for beginners. Here." She took a business card from beside the cash register and gave it to Beth. "When Ellie was in the store with you earlier, she told me she likes crafts. If there's something in particular she's interested in learning, call me so I can bring whatever supplies are needed. If Ellie wants, she can call me herself too."

"Thanks." The tightness in Beth's chest eased. The more interesting activities she could expose Ellie to, the better. The more good people too.

"Butterflies have been important to me since childhood. My dad is Haida from the Pacific Northwest, and my mother's Ojibway from Canada. They both taught me that butterflies symbolize transformation, as well as grace, harmony and balance. That's what I try to capture in my designs." The smile lines on Rosa's face deepened.

"You certainly do. Your work is gorgeous." In addition to the jewelry, Beth had admired Rosa's delicate watercolors, weaving and beadwork, all inspired by elements of the natural world. "How did you end up in Montana?"

"I met my husband when I was visiting family near High Valley. It was love at first sight for both of us. He already had a good job in this area, and since I'd just graduated from college I moved here to be with him." Rosa's eyes twinkled. "We celebrated our fortieth wedding anniversary last month."

Murmuring congratulations and thanking her, Beth took the bag and left the store. Once, she'd have said she'd fallen in love with Zach the first time she saw him but they'd been kids. Now, as an adult, she was more practical. She fixed her face in a smile as she went onto the wide porch. The welcoming space was dotted with rustic outdoor furniture and painted flowerpots stuffed with trailing greenery and summer blooms. "Ellie?"

"What?" Ellie barely glanced away from her phone.

"High Valley looks like a real Western town, doesn't it?" She gestured to the boardwalk and mix of old brick and timber-frame buildings that lined both sides of the wide street, the sky an overarching blue bowl.

"It's almost like the movies." Dial down the perky, she told herself. With her already well-honed teenage radar, Ellie would guess Beth was trying too hard.

"Whatever." Ellie's shoulders hunched so far inward that the wheelchair seemed like an extension of her body. After her riding lesson with Lauren and Zach, and the time she'd spent in the barn helping Molly groom Princess, Beth had been so hopeful that Ellie had turned a corner, but this morning her sullen expression had returned.

"We could have an early lunch before going back to the camp. The Bluebunch Café looks like a fun place to eat." And Beth had already confirmed that it was wheelchair accessible. "Bluebunch is a type of wheatgrass. It grows all over Montana. I learned that when I was here before." She pointed to the other side of the street where a blue awning extended across the front of a two-story, buttermilk-yellow timber building. The restaurant's name and a wheatgrass graphic were outlined in silver on the blue. "We got the clothes you need, and we have lots of time before the basketball game this afternoon." She gestured to the bag on Ellie's lap that held several pairs of new shorts, T-shirts, as well as a cute denim skirt and a red-and-white polka-dot swimsuit.

A so-called real mom would have known what her kid needed before they left home, but Beth was learning as she went, including how many changes of clothes Ellie went through each day. "Or, if you want, you could look in the craft store again." She'd made an excuse to get Ellie to wait outside while she bought the jewelry after clocking the longing in the girl's eyes when she'd spotted the silver butterfly pieces. "What do you think?"

"Lunch would be okay." Ellie's hands tightened on the handles of the paper shopping bag, and her lower lip worked. "Did my mom like it here?"

"She did, although we spent most of our time at the camp and didn't come into town often." Beth sat on a slatted wooden chair beside Ellie. "High Valley has changed a lot since then." At least on the surface, with new businesses, including the craft center, several restaurants that boasted menus as varied as ones in Chicago, and an upscale Western-living interiors store. In other ways, though, the small town was the same, with the drugstore and bank that had been here when Beth was a teen, as well as the family restaurant offering rancher-sized steaks, and the small natural-history museum.

"I wish my mom was here." Ellie's voice broke. "She was great at helping me pick out clothes and…everything."

Beth scooted her chair closer and wrapped Ellie in a hug. "I wish your mom was here too, but she's not, so we have to try to do the best we can. And I need your help." She made herself say the words that would make her vulnerable.

"You do?" Ellie's voice was muffled against Beth's shoulder.

"Sure. I don't know anything about being a mom. Your mom will always have her special place, but I want to give you everything she would have. I want to care for you like she did." *And love you too*, although it was too soon for Beth to say so.

Ellie brushed a hand against her tear-stained face. "I don't know how to be or who I am without my mom."

Beth didn't either, but maybe they could learn together. "It will take time, but don't forget that in a lot of ways, your mom is still with you, with both of us. She'll always be in both our hearts, yours most of all." Beth brushed tears from her face too. "Why don't we start with lunch and see how it goes from there?"

"Okay." Ellie straightened and moved away. "The Bluebunch Café has local ice cream. See?" She pointed to a folding A-frame sign on the boardwalk. "Mom sometimes let me have ice cream for lunch."

"Only ice cream?" Beth dug in her purse for tissues for them both.

"Well…not exactly." Ellie blew her nose, and then one side of her mouth turned up at the corner. "We could start a new tradition, though."

"Why not?" Making a new family meant making new traditions. Beth stood and drew in a breath as a tall man with light brown hair exited the bank next door.

"Look, there's Zach." Ellie's voice hummed with excitement, and before Beth could say anything, she'd swung her wheelchair toward the ramp and made her way toward him. "Hey." Ellie waved, and Zach turned, his gaze focusing first on Ellie before glancing past her to Beth.

Her heart skipped a beat at the expression in his eyes and how his mouth curved into a smile. She smoothed her hair and tugged at the hem of the casual navy-and-white-striped T-shirt dress she'd paired with tan wedge sandals. It was Ellie that Zach was pleased to see, not her. She couldn't let herself think a smile meant anything important.

"Beth." As they met on the boardwalk, his voice wrapped around her, its rich timbre as warm and comforting as the melted chocolate on her favorite hot fudge sundae, a treat she hadn't had in far too long.

"Zach." She cleared her throat and tucked a stray strand of hair behind her ear. With a pair of glossy cowboy boots, he wore black dress pants and a white button-down shirt, more formal than his ranch clothes, but behind the easy smile, his blue eyes were troubled.

"We're having lunch at the Bluebunch Café, and Beth said I could have ice cream. For my whole lunch. Want to come with us?" Ellie asked.

The hope and excitement in Ellie's voice stuck with Beth. Did all kids' moods change so fast, or was Ellie more mercurial than most? Although Beth had never met Ellie's father, a man Jilly rarely spoke of and who'd been killed in a car accident before Ellie was born, what qualities had he given the daughter he'd never known? And did Ellie need a good man's example to help her grow to adulthood?

"I... Beth?" Zach turned to her again.

It was her call. His expression made that clear. "Okay, sure." She took a breath. "You're welcome to join us for ice cream for lunch." And she wouldn't spoil or diminish Ellie's happiness by insisting she pair the treat with something healthy like a salad.

"Thank you." Zach's tone was oddly stiff. As Ellie checked for traffic and wheeled forward again, Zach took Beth's elbow. "Potholes." He gestured to a crater in the pavement between a parked pickup truck and a motorhome with a South Dakota license plate. "It was a bad winter and spring with freezing and thawing and then freezing again. The town is still working on patching all the holes in the streets." His gaze lingered on her wedge shoes.

"Oh. Thanks." His hand on her arm sparked a pleasurable tingle that radiated from the tips of her toes to the top of her head.

"Here we are." As they reached the other side of High Valley Avenue, where Ellie waited, he took his hand away, and Beth shivered at the sense of loss.

"You can have more than ice cream. It's new and fun for Ellie and me to try, that's all." She moved closer to Ellie and looped her hands around the wheelchair handles.

"It's good to try new things." Zach's mouth quirked into a teasing grin laced with something else that made the heat in Beth's body ignite again. "Ice cream for lunch sounds fine."

It was only lunch, and Zach didn't want to disappoint Ellie. As Ellie pressed the button for the automatic door to open, Beth followed her into the busy café with Zach behind. The buzz of conversation stilled and heads swiveled in their direction.

Yet, if it was only lunch, why did it all of a sudden feel like so much more?

FROM ACROSS THE small table, Zach studied Beth as she stuck her ice-cream spoon into the empty hot fudge sundae bowl. "Good?" He pushed away the thought of the never-ending chores waiting for him at the ranch.

He'd planned to head there straight after his meeting with the bank manager, but stopping for lunch with Beth and Ellie had been a good break he hadn't known he needed. As long as he kept it casual, maybe he needed to make more space and time for this kind of fun in his life.

"So, so good. This is a great place." Beth grinned back and looped an arm around Ellie, who'd chosen a banana split with three flavors of ice cream and eaten it faster than Zach had thought possible for such a petite girl.

"The Bluebunch Café was new last year, but it's already a local favorite. Hang on." He grabbed a paper napkin from the holder and leaned forward to dab a bit of chocolate sauce from Beth's cheek. "All gone." He crumpled the napkin and dropped it beside his plate, his fingers warm. Although the gesture had been teasing, at her sharp intake of breath, he'd stilled and his heart pounded, something inside him he'd thought was gone forever sparking into life.

"Thanks." Beth wrapped her hands around her water glass and avoided his gaze. "Are you finished, Ellie, or do you want something else? More milk, maybe?" Her voice wavered, and she held the glass tighter.

"No, but…hey…" Ellie waved across the café. "There's Lily and Ms. Kate. Can I go say hi?"

Lily and her mom waved back, and Zach returned the greeting. He liked Kate, and Lily too, but Kate was a friend, nothing more.

"Sure." Beth smiled at Kate and her daughter. "I'm waiting for my tea, so take your time."

"Great." Ellie took her napkin off her lap and grabbed the shopping bag she'd left under her wheelchair. "I want to show Lily my new clothes."

"Hang on." Beth put a hand on Ellie's arm. "If you need your wheelchair, I can help—"

"It's fine. It's a good pain day so I don't need it for such a short walk. I have enough spoons."

"Spoons?" Beth's expression was puzzled.

"Zach can explain." With the bag bumping against her hip, Ellie made her way to the other side of the café. In her jean shorts and purple T-shirt, she looked like any other girl her age.

"A lot of what Ellie deals with is new for

me." Beth pushed back her chair as if poised to go after Ellie. But then Ellie reached the other side of the café and sat in a chair next to Lily, her back to them.

"You're learning as fast as you can." Zach made his tone reassuring to try to ease Beth's worried expression.

"I'm trying to." Beth studied Ellie for a few more seconds before she turned back to him. "I've never heard Ellie mention 'spoons,' though."

"Spoons is the terminology that some people in the chronic-illness community use to explain how much energy they have. They call themselves *spoonies*." Zach made himself focus on the explanation instead of the memories of his big brother. "Each spoon represents energy, so on a good day, a person has enough spoons to do the things they want. On a bad day, not so much." He stopped as the teenage waitress filled his cup with coffee and gave Beth a mug and teapot encased in a cozy, knitted in a strawberry pattern. "Thanks." He acknowledged the girl as she moved away. "Ellie monitoring her energy levels in terms of spoons is healthy. It's also a way of separating *who* she is from her illnesses and not letting her medical challenges define her."

"I see." Beth poured tea into her mug, steam and the scent of the sweet, aromatic blend rising between them. "Before Jilly died, I only saw Ellie for a few hours every couple of weeks. Either those were good days or she managed to hide what she experiences. Probably a mix of both." Beth's expression was still troubled. "Her diagnoses and treatments continue to evolve. Sometimes Ellie can manage her chronic pain and other symptoms effectively. But when she has a bad day, she needs her wheelchair or additional mobility aid."

"She seems to be coping well at the moment." Zach cradled his coffee cup.

"Yes, but until now, Ellie's never, at least since her mom passed, been out of her wheelchair outside the house. Kate suggested I talk to one of the camp counselors so I did. The counselor said I needed to be guided by Ellie, which I have. But *spoons*? I had no idea. It makes sense, though. I wish…" She worried her lower lip.

"You wish that a girl of Ellie's age didn't have to think of spoons at all except as something to eat ice cream with?" Zach reached across the table and covered one of Beth's hands with his, the gesture instinctive but also new. "Me too, but since Ellie does..." He swallowed the unexpected lump in his throat. "Whatever her energy levels, she'll persevere and have a good and long life." Unlike his brother.

Yet with all the challenges that had come with having cystic fibrosis, Paul had lived his best life and maybe Zach needed to learn from his example—and Ellie's too.

"Yes, but..." Beth's mouth worked, and she squeezed his hand tight. "Why couldn't Ellie tell me about spoons herself?"

"Maybe because for her it's something she takes for granted." Like Paul, which was why Zach had only mentioned his brother to Beth in passing. He hadn't told her about Paul having cystic fibrosis either because his brother didn't like people talking about it. Besides, Paul had been away visiting their mom's folks for the month Beth and Jilly had stayed at the camp. And honestly, Zach had wanted to focus on Beth. "Hey, she's excited to see her new friend. She didn't want to waste time explaining or potentially losing the moment."

"But you got it?"

Her fingers wrapped around Zach's were warm, and her hand fit in his like it belonged there, just as it had all those years ago. "Although I worked in the stables that one summer, my real involvement with Camp Crocus Hill began when my parents bought it. They wanted to make it accessible for those with disabilities, so I learned a lot then." He made his shrug nonchalant to belie the emotion surging through him. The familiar grief for his brother, but mixed with the realization that maybe he could open up to Beth, at least a bit, and still keep things casual.

"As part of developing the camp, I've also taken workshops, other training and asked questions. Kate's been a great help. Lily too." He nodded in their direction.

"Most of the time I don't know where to start." Beth's voice was low. "I thought I knew Ellie before Jilly died but I didn't, not the things that mattered most. I'm scared of making mistakes."

Like Zach had thought he'd known how to be a rancher before his dad passed, until reality hit and he'd discovered how his dad had shielded him, shielded all of them, from some of the hardest parts of the job. "If you don't make mistakes, how will you learn? That's what my folks always said." Right now, he was holding to that advice. "Besides, you can always start over, remember?"

"Right." She squeezed his hand once more and then picked up her mug of tea. "I'm trying."

"That's all you can do." Like he was trying with the ranch.

Although he wanted to, it didn't feel like the right moment to bring up his brother's death. For that kind of private conversation, Zach needed time and a quiet space with only the two of them. He could get Beth's fresh take on something else, though.

"Look, I need… You know about financial stuff and accounting, right?" He'd looked her up online, and it was another reminder that the two of them lived in much different worlds.

"Yes." She set her mug on the table. "Along with my undergraduate degree in finance, I have an MBA, and I'm the chief financial officer for a small technology company."

He winced. "I saw. Impressive."

"The internet?" She gave him a teasing smile.

"Yeah."

"Likewise. Your hockey career is pretty impressive too." Her smile broadened, and she chuckled.

He glanced around, but nobody was paying attention to them, and the couple who'd sat at the next table, his dentist and her husband, had gone to the cash register to pay. "I need some advice. Help, actually." There, he'd said it, and getting the words out hadn't been as hard as he'd expected because there was no judgment in Beth's expression, only concern.

"In what way?" Her voice was even, her patience clear.

"It's the ranch. I was at the bank talking to the new manager and...well, we're struggling. It's not like we're going to lose the place." At least not yet, but the bank manager had been honest, and if her projected figures were right, by this time next year the situation would be grim. "My dad was great at a lot of things, but he wasn't as good a business manager as he might have been, and the books are…" He hesitated, trying to find the words to tell Beth what he needed while still being loyal to his father, the man Zach had always looked up to and wanted to be like.

"I expect that ranching has changed a lot over the years, certainly from when your parents started out." Beth's brown eyes were serious. "From economic changes to new technology and changing government regulations, it must be hard to keep up with it all, along with everything else ranching families have to do."

"Yes." Zach let out a long breath. Beth didn't know the half of it, or that his dad had resisted even small changes, but she'd saved him from having to explain the extent of the mess he'd inherited. "I promised my dad and mom too that I'd keep the ranch going, but I don't know where to start. Like you with Ellie, maybe."

"So you'd like me to help in some way? Look at the financials, perhaps?"

"If you could. The bank manager wasn't much help, but she was only the messenger. It's not her job to figure things out. It's mine, but I don't know what to ask, let alone who or how. I know you're on vacation, but if you'd be able to take a look, I'd pay you. Or give you a reduction on the camp fee, whatever you want."

"Don't worry about it." Beth shook her head as she drained her mug of tea. "We're friends, or at least we used to be." Her face went a pretty pink making her look more like the girl he'd known. "I'd be happy to help, at least when Ellic doesn't need me. She's my priority."

"Of course." He liked how Beth put family first. A code his folks had modeled and taught Zach to live by too. "For someone like you, it likely won't take long to see where things are at, but I don't want to worry my mom or brothers. And Molly is still at college. I want her to finish her senior year, and she's talking about graduate school too."

If they discussed financial stuff, and since Beth still considered him a friend, maybe they could talk about other things too. Like why she'd broken off contact all those years ago.

"I'm happy to help. Despite what the bank manager said, you must have options. It might take a bit of time to find them, that's all."

The confidence in Beth's voice gave Zach

hope. "Thank you. This situation is only between us, right? My family, they can't…" He gripped the table edge. His dad had never admitted there was a problem so the problem had gotten worse, and if Zach didn't swallow his pride and ask for help, he might have to start selling land, something he swore he'd never do.

"Even if I hadn't taken an oath of client confidentiality, I wouldn't ever talk to anyone else. The ranch and the camp are special. I don't want them to change, except for the better. I'll do everything I can to make sure they survive. You have my word."

Some of the crush of worry in Zach's chest lifted. "Thank you. We should get going. The ranch—I have things to do. You must too."

"I do. After I say hi to Kate and Lily, the camp's laundry room is calling my name. I didn't pack enough clothes for Ellie." She gave him a teasing smile. "Would it work for me to meet with you when she has her swimming lesson tomorrow morning? Apparently, it's embarrassing to have me by the pool, so I'll be free."

"Sure. I can pick you up or—"

"I remember the way to the ranch."

"Great. My office is at the front. It's the small door in the big red barn. I'll be outside at ten to meet you."

"Sounds good." Beth got to her feet. "Maybe we'll see you at the movie night later? Like with the spoons, Ellie can talk to you in a way she can't to me, and whenever you're around she's happier."

"I can drop by." He hadn't planned to, but apart from checking the horses before bed, it wasn't as if he had anything else on tonight. Beth was helping him, so anything he could do to help Ellie was a fair exchange. Besides, it would be friendly. His gaze drifted to Beth's body-skimming dress and her slim ankles in another pair of those impractical but ever-so-appealing shoes, before he forced himself to look back at her face.

Friends. Yeah, right. Her smarts intrigued him, and her beauty meant he couldn't look away. His heart was clamoring for more, but he'd silence it. And he'd be fine. They both would.

CHAPTER FIVE

BETH DROVE THE SUV she still thought of as Jilly's along the winding gravel lane that led from the highway to the center of the Tall Grass Ranch. The Carter family had a big spread, and both sides of the lane were edged by pastureland but, as Beth remembered, the main house and barns sat well back from the road that linked the town of High Valley with Camp Crocus Hill.

Although now white instead of its previous soft gray, the sprawling wooden ranch house still sat behind a picket fence at the top of the lane. The porch was festooned with hanging flower baskets that overlooked a large garden edged with more flowers.

A sable-and-white collie barked and wagged its tail as Beth pulled into a parking spot by the red barn. She waved at Zach, who stood in front of a small door and checked the clock on the dash as she turned off the vehicle. Ten o'clock. They were both right on time.

She drew in a steadying breath. In jeans, boots and a red plaid shirt, Zach was dressed for ranch work, but the casual clothes hugged his body better than any of the tailored suits her male colleagues or dates wore. She grabbed her bag and keys and got out of the SUV, stopping to pat the dog, who nosed her ankles below her navy capris. While Ellie was at her swimming lesson, Beth was here for an hour to help Zach with the financials, nothing more. She shouldn't be noticing his fitness or anything else.

"Meet Jess." Zach joined her beside the SUV. "She's my mom's dog, and although she stays close to the house, she still keeps an eye on everything that goes on here." He gestured to another dog, a black-and-white border collie, who bounded out the open barn door. "Here's Sadie coming to welcome you too. Sadie's mine, and she's still almost a pup." He grabbed the dog's collar to keep her from jumping up. "Are you still okay with dogs?"

Beth patted Sadie. "Yes, absolutely." What did it say about her life that, although she loved dogs, she'd never had time to have one of her own?

"Do you live at the main house?" She glanced toward it and waved at Zach's mom, whom she'd chatted with at the movie night. Joy stood on the porch in jean shorts, a floral T-shirt and a pink floppy hat that covered her blond bob. She held a watering can in one hand and had a basket of garden tools at her feet.

"No, it's only Mom and Molly there now. I have a place a few miles away along the main road. It's the house my great-grandparents lived in back in the 1940s before they built the new one here. I'm renovating it, but since I'm doing most of the work myself, it's slow. My brothers help when they can, but they have their own stuff to take care of." His smile slipped, and the troubled expression she'd spotted at the café the day before was back.

"I only have an hour, so we'd better get started." The ranch's financial situation. That was why Beth was here. Although she wouldn't charge Zach for this consult, he was still a client, and she needed to focus on work.

"Right." His tone became businesslike.

"Come through." He stepped back to let her go through the door to the office and followed with Sadie, who, her tail wagging, darted by Beth. "All of us have a work space here, but I got my dad's desk." He gestured to an alcove away from the main area where Sadie already sprawled in a tartan dog bed next to a vintage wooden office desk topped with modern computer equipment. "Here." He pulled a chair around from the other side of the desk so Beth could sit beside him.

"Thanks." She sat and set her bag by the chair. Beneath the soaring beamed ceiling, what must be the original wooden barn floor was covered with stacks of paper, agricultural magazines and beige file folders.

"Do you want a coffee or tea?" He indicated a coffee machine and kettle on a stand beyond his desk. "There's also bottled water, juice and sodas in the fridge."

"Water would be great." As Zach went to the small fridge, Beth glanced around the room again. He needed an office manager, although even a high-school student who needed summer work could help bring order out of this chaos.

"I'm sorry about the mess. It's not usually

this bad, but for the meeting at the bank I had to find some papers of my dad's. His filing system was…interesting." Zach set the bottle of water and a glass beside Beth on top of the desk, not meeting her gaze.

"Rule number one, don't apologize." Beth's heart squeezed. Between the daily ranch work and trying to run the business side, it wasn't surprising Zach was struggling. She worked long hours too, but her job wasn't 24/7 every day of the year. She also only worked to support herself and now Ellie, not to provide the livelihood for an extended family.

"Is there a rule number two?" Amusement quirked one side of Zach's mouth as he clicked the computer keys to log in.

"Only that since I'm here to help you like you're helping me with Ellie there's no judgment." It must have taken a lot for him to ask for her help. "After the movie last night, all Ellie could talk about was how you promised to show her where you found those dinosaur fossils. She's also excited that you're going to help with one of her riding lessons again this week. Thanks to you, she's gotten comfortable with horses in only a few days. When we first got here, I never expected her to get on a horse, let alone love it like she does."

"Lauren's done more than me." Zach still clicked the computer keyboard.

"Don't be so modest. Ellie hugged me before bed last night, and even before Jilly died Ellie wasn't a kid who hugged a lot. You're making a big and positive difference in Ellie's life, so thank you."

"You're welcome." When Zach turned and finally met her gaze, the troubled expression was gone, replaced by a teasing that was both familiar and new. "You can show your appreciation by working some magic on our financial situation."

"I'll try." She grinned and teased him back. "I might need something stronger than water, though. Do you have chocolate?"

"Of course." He dug in one of the desk drawers and produced a big paper bag. I've got a selection of milk, dark and white chocolate bars made by a chocolatier in town, as well as their chocolate raspberry and butterscotch fudge. He shook the treats out of the bag and onto the desk. "Take your pick."

"Wow. I thought I was a chocoholic, but you have a chocolate drawer?" Beth's chest fluttered as she leaned closer to accept a milk chocolate and almond bar. She was attracted to him even more than she'd been all those years ago.

But back then, so much had been different. Her parents had still been married, for one. She hadn't yet learned that promises could be broken as easily as hearts. "Where do you want to start? Monthly expenses?" She peeled away the wrapping from the chocolate bar.

"That's as good as any." Zach took a piece of chocolate raspberry fudge and stared at the screen, and Beth tried to focus on the spreadsheet he'd opened.

"Beth?"

She started at Zach's voice. "What?"

"Is our financial situation even worse than I thought? The way you're staring at that spreadsheet is scaring me."

"No." For maybe the first time in her adult life, she'd looked at a spreadsheet without seeing it. "I'm thinking about options, that's all." A necessary lie. Numbers. That was what she was here to assess. Not how good Zach smelled—fresh from the shower with spicy soap, mixed with the scent of a Montana summer morning, an enticing blend of sweet grasses and sunshine.

"There are probably government grants or some other kind of funding you could apply for." Not a lie, and one of the options she'd explore for any client.

"I've been thinking I should find out what the US Department of Agriculture offers to ranchers. I haven't had time, though."

"I can look into that for you and at least make a start." Although Beth didn't know about agriculture, she knew about government grants, and she was good at her job and took it seriously, almost as seriously as she took her responsibility to Ellie. She glanced at Sadie, who'd settled in her bed. Ellie might like a dog, and in Chicago there were dog day cares for when Ellie was at school and Beth at work. She could hire someone to help with a dog, like she already hired a cleaner.

"Show me how you track your monthly business expenses, and we'll go from there." Get back to business and numbers. In a lot of ways, numbers and dogs were the same. They didn't lie or cheat, and unlike her dad and the few other men she'd dated, they also didn't make promises they never planned to keep.

"Okay." Zach clicked more keys, his strong hands workmanlike, the knuckles dusted with light brown hair. The day before, when he'd taken her hand at the café, it had felt even better than it used to.

Beth set the half-eaten chocolate bar aside and linked her fingers together beneath the desk. This was a vacation, nothing more. Zach lived here, and she lived in Chicago. She couldn't let herself start something with him that had no chance of going anywhere.

Besides, Ellie had just lost her mom. She didn't need any more changes in her life. Beth couldn't risk getting hurt again for her own sake, not to mention Ellie's.

A WEEK LATER, Zach tilted his head to let the afternoon sun warm his face. Although it was only just after lunch, he'd already done a day's work and earned some time off. At least, that's what he'd say if anyone asked why he'd joined this trail ride with Ellie, Beth and a few of the other campers.

As he rode Scout, the horse's feet sure along the trail that ran beside the pasture nearest Camp Crocus Hill, a saddle creaked, and Zach turned. Coming up beside him, his mom rode Cindy, the seal-brown mare his dad had given her for their wedding anniversary the year before he passed. "Beth and Ellie are in the last group." Beneath her white cowboy hat with strands of blond hair blowing in the breeze, his mom's smile was amused. "You should go back and check on them, don't you think?"

"Why?" He made his tone casual. "Beth must have gone trail riding when she was here before, and Ellie has two side walkers and a teacher looking out for her." Zach fixed his gaze on the far horizon, the mountains rising out of the foothills in a muted haze, like one of his older brother Paul's watercolors.

Although painting had always been a hobby, in the last year of Paul's life and as his body had failed, his art had become so much more. Maybe in all those paintings his mom had framed and hung throughout both the ranch house and camp, Paul had been trying to capture the places that had meant the most to him. So that those familiar scenes, almost unchanged since the ranch's early days, would also be a reminder of him.

Zach tightened his grip on Scout's reins.

Although selling land would be the quickest way out of their financial situation, he couldn't sell any part of his legacy. A new owner might change this landscape that he loved, and his dad and Paul had loved too. Zach was determined to not let that happen.

"I'm sure Beth and Ellie would like to see you." His mom patted Cindy's neck. "Why else did you come on this trail ride today? It's not as if you don't have other things to do."

"Maybe I needed a break." Even to his ears, the excuse was false.

"Beth is sure helping us out with that mess in the office."

"She's given us great options." Options Zach would never have found on his own. Besides cutting some costs, even if only a few of those options came through, the Tall Grass Ranch would be safe for the next generation.

"Beth's wonderful with Ellie too, even though she was thrown into motherhood under such tragic circumstances. Ellie's a sweet girl and so smart. Rosa said Ellie picked up that craft project she taught the kids right away, and when I led the baking class,

Ellie was the best at decorating the cupcakes we made. You're not getting any younger, you know."

Like he needed the reminder. His mom had picked out not only a wife for him but one who came with a ready-made family. "I know what you're saying."

"I'm not sure you do." His mom's tone was firm. "Where else are you going to meet a nice woman near your age here? Most of them are married, and the ones that aren't…" Her mouth got tight. "You need a woman who wants to build a home and family with you."

"Don't go there." He tried not to think about the woman who'd been his fiancée, what Dani had really wanted—and what she hadn't.

"Why not ask Beth to have dinner with you? I'd be happy to stay with Ellie for an evening."

"I'll think about it, okay?" If for no other reason than to get his mom onto another subject. "I don't hear you bugging Bryce, Cole or Molly to settle down."

"Molly still has to finish her nursing training, and she's looking into that master's program. That's where her focus is. As for Cole,

I doubt he'll ever settle. He's not made that way, but you are. And Bryce?" His mom's voice hitched. "So soon after Alison's death, he's not ready. His kids aren't ready either."

Zach's body got heavy. Alison's death, only eighteen months after Zach's dad, had been another big loss for Bryce and his two young children especially. "We all miss Ally."

"We do, but her death is another reminder that life is short. I don't want you to regret—"

"I won't." He'd learned regrets were pointless.

"Zach." Ellie's voice reached him on the warm summer breeze. "Wait up."

Was Ellie conspiring with his mom to bring him and Beth together?

"Well?" His mom grinned and urged Cindy into a faster walk. "When opportunity knocks, you don't want to wait around." She laughed over her shoulder as she caught up with the camp counselor who rode at the head of the line of trail riders.

Opportunity, or something more intentional? In the past week, opportunity—or Ellie—had brought Zach and Beth together several times each day, and they'd reconnected almost as if no time had passed, finding a grown-up version of the friendship they'd shared as teens and before there had been anything romantic between them. Much of that time together had been spent poring over every part of the ranch's finances, when Ellie had a swimming lesson or groomed Princess with Molly. But at Ellie's request, Zach had also dropped by the camp most evenings to play a board game, work on a jigsaw puzzle or watch a movie.

And for the past three mornings, Zach had swung by Meadowlark cabin when Ellie was still asleep and Beth was on the porch with her e-reader and mug of tea. Although they hadn't talked about anything important, he looked forward to those brief chats when the sun had peeped over the horizon and the day was new and filled with possibilities.

As he eased Scout off the path to wait for Beth and Ellie, who brought up the rear of the trail-riding group with Lily, he forced himself to admit the truth. Although he had happy memories of the girl, he liked Beth even more as a woman. One who, if he wasn't careful, he could let himself like too much. Even as the alarm went off in his mind, he made himself smile at Ellie perched atop Princess. "Having fun?"

"Yes, but it would be even better if they didn't have to walk beside me." Her dimpled grin at the two side walkers took away any criticism in her words. "I want to go faster."

"You need to learn to walk before you run, remember?" At Ellie's far side, Beth grinned too, her dark brown hair curling under her riding helmet. "Or, in this case, trot or canter."

"I know." Ellie let out a heavy sigh. "But Lily can go faster. She's only going slow because of me. Princess wants to go faster too." She patted the horse's glossy neck. "Please?"

"Ellie's doing great." The younger side walker, Becky, a high-school student who'd worked at the camp for the past two summers, confirmed what Zach had already seen in the paddock a few days before. Ellie was a natural on horseback, like Jilly had been.

"Okay. A bit faster." He nodded at Becky and the other side walker while gesturing to the riding instructor by Lily. "You okay to stay with them?"

"Sure." Chris, who, when he wasn't teaching riding at the camp, was on his college's rodeo team, tipped his hat and darted a glance at Beth.

"Be careful." Beth gripped her horse's reins and glanced between Ellie and Zach.

"Even if I fall off, there are lots of people to catch me." Ellie rolled her eyes and made the kind of face Zach remembered from when he was a teenager.

"You'll be fine." The fact was, he reminded himself, you had to trust kids and give them space to learn, even if they made mistakes. "Not too fast, though," he added, because Zach understood where Beth was coming from and the all-encompassing urge to protect someone you loved.

Another eye roll from Ellie. "Since Beth hasn't been on a horse since she was here with my mom, she said her butt would be so sore after today she might not be able to walk for a week. She's the one who needs help, not me. You should give her some tips, Zach."

"Ellie." Beth's face went pink, and Chris put a hand to his face as if stifling a laugh. "I didn't say a week. I'll be fine."

Ellie waved and squeezed Princess's sides as she moved ahead with Chris.

"Kids." Zach held back a laugh. "They tell it like it is. No filter."

"I'm out of practice on horseback, that's all. I could have stayed at the camp with Kate, but I wanted to be with Ellie."

"Even though she might not show it, Ellie likes having you around." Scout nickered as Zach eased the horse onto the trail beside Beth, who rode Daisy-May, the gentle Appaloosa Zach had picked out for her. "Kids are like horses. You need patience for the challenges. All horse people know that."

"I'm not a horse person." Beth sat stiff in the saddle. "Not like you or Jilly."

"So? Who asked you to be a horse person? Kate's not a horse person either, and it's not a big deal to Lily or anyone else."

"Kate's not a horse person because she's so allergic to horses she can't get within twenty feet of one without needing a megadose of antihistamines. It's not the same."

"No." Okay, bad analogy. "Equestrian expert or not, with your support, Ellie will learn how to be her own person and achieve things in her life. That's all that matters."

"How did you get to be so smart?" Beth's tight stance relaxed.

"Because I..." Zach's throat constricted. He'd compartmentalized his life back then so that the time he spent with Beth was separate from his family and whatever was happening at home. When he hung out with her, he was able to be carefree, even if only for a few hours. "If I have life smarts, it's mostly because of my parents and older brother, Paul."

"I'd forgotten about him. You and your mom must have wondered why I didn't ask about Paul." Beth's expression was sheepish. "You hardly mentioned him that summer but now I remember. He was in Missoula staying with your grandparents. What's he up to these days?"

Zach cued Scout to a stop, and Beth did the same with Daisy-May. The summer air was still, and Ellie and the rest of the riders had dipped behind the hillock where the trail led along the creek. Bees hummed in a patch of sweet clover, and far overhead a hawk soared on the thermals, a black dot against the vivid blue sky. Zach's palms got damp, and he loosened the reins to rest his hands on the saddle horn. He and Beth were alone. This was the moment he'd been waiting for. "Paul passed when I was in college. He was twenty-three."

"I'm so sorry." Beth reached between the horses and took his hand.

"It wasn't an accident." Not like Zach's dad. "Or cancer." Not like Jilly and Bryce's wife, Alison. The beginning of a headache pressed against Zach's temples. "Paul had cystic fibrosis. Nowadays, a child with cystic fibrosis could live into their forties and beyond, but when Paul was born he wasn't expected to live much beyond his teens. However, thanks to medical research, new drugs and better treatments, he reached his twenties." Although Zach had learned to live with Paul's death, he'd never gotten over it and likely never would.

"The reason why Camp Crocus Hill is now for children and youth with special needs is because of Paul?" The compassion in Beth's voice made the lump in Zach's throat grow bigger. He prided himself on being independent. Apart from his family, he didn't need anyone else, and even with his family he often avoided talking about emotional things. Instead, he buried feelings deep, but something about Beth drew those emotions to the surface, and it wasn't as hard, or scary, as he'd expected.

"The camp is in Paul's memory. It was something we—my mom and dad at first, but all of us now—do for his legacy. Paul loved kids but never had a chance to have any of his own. He also loved Montana and the ranch, so before he passed he said he wanted any and every kid to be able to experience this kind of life." The backs of Zach's eyes burned. "Although we had to let Paul go, because of the camp it's as if part of him is still here. If Mom and Dad hadn't bought the camp, the ranch would be in better financial shape, but for Paul and my folks too, somehow I have to make all of it work."

"Here, help me down." Beth handed him Daisy-May's reins.

"Sure, but…" By reflex, Zach swung off Scout and then grabbed Beth's arm as she slid one leg over Daisy-May to dismount. For a brief instant, he held Beth close, the warmth of her body and sweet-apple scent of her hair making him tremble. Her denim-clad knees grazed his as he set her on the ground, and despite himself, he held her for another few seconds before letting go. "What is it?" He made himself step away and looped both sets of reins over a low-hanging branch of a nearby ponderosa pine.

"You look like you need a hug." Beth closed the distance between them again, and her arms went around his neck as she pulled him into an embrace. "Why didn't you ever tell me about Paul?"

Zach relaxed against Beth as he hugged her back, taking the comfort she offered. "I respected Paul's wishes that we didn't always need to be talking about him. But that didn't stop me worrying about him. Besides, when I was with you, I wanted to focus on us, not my brother. What we shared was special."

"It was." Beth's voice shook. "I think I understand about Paul." Beth hugged him tighter, and Zach absorbed not just her closeness but the feelings for her he'd tried to make himself forget. "Paul would be proud of you and what you and your family have done at Camp Crocus Hill."

"I hope so. I don't mean to make him sound like a saint. We argued like all siblings do. If he'd ended up running the ranch instead of me, we'd have continued to clash because we both liked having our own way." Zach blinked hard as the vast land, sky and woman in his arms blurred together. "Paul never felt sorry for himself, though, and he always pushed hard to reach whatever goal he set. Ellie reminds me a bit of him, so I want to help her, like I did with Paul."

"Me too." Beth's voice was thick. "We're doing it together."

And maybe helping each other too. The words she didn't say hung between them.

Scout gave a high-pitched neigh and bumped Zach's shoulder.

"You're missing your friends, are you?" Scout stood like the well-trained horse he was, waiting for Zach to give the signal for them to move on, but Daisy-May had loosened the reins from the branch and munched a patch of grass ten feet away. "Unlike Scout, the moment I'm distracted Daisy-May tries to see what she can get away with."

"Like Ellie." Beth's laugh was shaky.

"Like most kids." Zach's voice trembled too. "We should catch up with the others."

"Yeah." Beth stepped away. "Thanks for telling me about Paul."

"Thanks for listening." And comforting him in a way Zach hadn't known he'd needed. That was the thing with grief: it was never truly gone and came back to hit you when you least expected. Beneath his hat brim, he rubbed a hand across his brow.

While the sting of Paul's death was softer now, he also carried a different, more personal kind of pain, one that a hug couldn't take away. One too deep to share with Beth or any other woman who might want him and a family of her own one day.

CHAPTER SIX

JOY HESITATED OUTSIDE the camp's laundry room tucked in a wing of the main building beyond the kitchen. Since she couldn't make Zach see sense, and he'd avoided her after that trail ride two days earlier, she had to talk to Beth too. Since Ellie was at a drama workshop, and Kate had said Beth was doing laundry, this was the chance Joy had been waiting for. She glanced through the window at the top of the laundry-room door and then pushed the door open. Apart from Beth, who sat in front of one of the dryers, the place was empty.

It was either a sign or Jilly helping from beyond the grave. The thought of Jilly strengthened Joy's resolve. She was doing what Jilly wanted for Beth and Ellie, and what Joy wanted for Zach. Even the ranch hands saw how Beth and Zach looked at each other. Now, and with a little help from Ellie, Joy had to encourage them to take that next step.

"Hi." Joy walked across the laundry room, her sneakers soundless on the white-tiled floor. "It never ends, does it?"

"Hello." Beth put an e-reader on the laundry-folding table by her chair. "What never ends?"

"Laundry." Joy took the chair on the other side of the table. "I remember those days. With a husband and five kids, I got through a lot of laundry." Yet, she often missed that time when all her family had been safe at home together.

"It's only me and Ellie, and I bought her some more clothes, but I've never done so much laundry in my life."

"Why don't you ask Ellie to help?" Joy edged her chair closer to the table as she considered how to proceed. Like Joy's childhood pony, Beth was skittish and needed careful handling. "It's good for kids to learn how to do chores. Besides, if they do some of the work themselves, they appreciate your efforts more." Maybe she needed to apply that principle to getting Zach and Beth together. After today, she should step back and make them work for what they both needed, even if they didn't know they also wanted it.

"You're right, but Ellie's on vacation."

"And you're not?" Joy made her tone firm. "You need to look after yourself so you can look after her." And going on a date with Zach would be the perfect first step.

"True, but…" Beth stopped and worried her bottom lip. "I want Ellie to like me."

"She already does, but Ellie also needs to respect you enough to understand that vacation isn't all fun and you expect her to do her part to keep family life running smoothly. Every kid will try to push boundaries. Part of your job is to push back."

"Most of what Ellie does is push boundaries." Beth's expression was sheepish. "You think asking her to help with laundry will make a difference?"

"I do. It sure did with my Molly. For a while, when she was about sixteen, her life was a nonstop fashion parade. If she wanted to change her clothes five times a day and leave her discarded outfits on her bedroom floor, she had to wash those clothes too. Once she understood I meant what I said, the fashion show soon stopped."

"I'll try." Beth's voice held new resolve. "I have to do something, and not only about laundry. Most days, and with the mess Ellie leaves behind, our cabin looks like a tornado has hit it."

"A chore list with small rewards worked with my kids." Apart from Zach. Joy's heart squeezed. He'd always been happy to help around the house, even after a full day of ranch work, but he was the one who hid his feelings the most too.

Joy straightened and glanced at the dryer's timer. The cycle was almost done so she had to do something while she had Beth's attention. "If you want to make Ellie more self-sufficient, why not leave her with me for an evening and go out for a meal with Zach?"

"What?" Beth's mouth dropped open. "Ellie's the reason I'm here. Besides, I can't go out with Zach. I'm not dating at the moment."

"Dinner with a friend isn't a date." Except, it could turn into one. "You and Zach are friends, aren't you?"

"Yes, but Ellie's my priority." Beth stared at her flip-flops, a cute pink pair with white flowers that Joy would have liked for herself.

"It's not good for you to be so focused on Ellie without having a break, and Zach never takes time off." Beth's peasant-style white top was cute too. Joy didn't plan to be invisible in life or fashion, no matter what her age. Yet, since Dennis's death, and with her sixtieth birthday looming, she'd lost parts of herself and didn't know how to get them back. She should ask Beth for some styling tips and help buying a few new clothes too. Beth's look had caught her eye several times. "How long has it been since you went out with a friend?"

"Not since a few months before Jilly died."

"You're long overdue, don't you think?"

"Maybe, but Zach wouldn't want to go out to dinner with me." Beth fiddled with one of her silver and turquoise hoop earrings, one of Rosa's designs.

Joy suppressed a snort. In her own way, Beth was as stubborn as Zach. "You both have to eat, and you'd be helping me and Ellie if you and Zach went out for dinner one evening." It was mostly the truth and what was the harm of a little white lie for a broader good?

"I would?" Beth raised an eyebrow, her expression skeptical. "How?"

"Zach's birthday is the day after Ellie's. When we were making cupcakes, Ellie told me she'd like a joint party and to make it a surprise for him. I promised I'd help her organize it. If you and Zach go out, Ellie and I can plan." Although Joy had suggested the idea, Ellie was keen so there was no harm done. Besides, Zach hadn't celebrated his birthday in years. Along with Ellie, if anyone deserved a party it was him.

"I want to make Ellie's birthday special. It also makes sense she'd want to celebrate with Zach. She looks up to him. I've been worrying about what to do for her birthday. It will be her first birthday without Jilly, and that's going to be hard."

"Problem solved. Rosa and Kate are on board to help, and so is Molly. She's gotten close to Ellie when Ellie helps her groom the horses."

"Rosa and Kate offered to help with Ellie's birthday, but I wasn't sure they meant it. I hardly know them or you or Molly either."

Like Zach, Beth was independent, but both of them needed to learn to accept help when it was offered. "Here in ranch country we don't say things we don't mean. Helping each other out is called being neighborly."

"Okay." Beth gave a tip-tilted grin. "Thank you."

"I'll make a reservation for you and Zach

tomorrow night at Ruby's in town. It's the best place to eat in the evening around here." Unlike the family steak house that had existed since Joy went on her first date with Dennis, Ruby's had an intimate, romantic vibe. "Usually on Saturday nights in the summer they're booked up, but I know the owner, and she'll find me a table." As in fishing, Joy wasn't taking any chances. She'd hooked Beth, and now she needed to reel her in.

"What if Zach doesn't want to have dinner with me? I can ask him, but he might say no. I can't tell him it's because you and Ellie want to plan a surprise birthday party for him."

"Leave Zach to me." Joy had already done the hardest bit. Zach might grumble, but if Joy told him it was part of a surprise Ellie was planning and she needed his help to get Beth out of the way, he'd come around. In only a few weeks, Ellie had him wrapped around her little finger and had pulled Zach out of himself in a way Joy had never managed to. And when her son was with Beth and Ellie, there was a lightness in his eyes that hadn't been there for years. "Remember, you'll be helping Zach and Ellie too."

"Of course." The dryer timer dinged, and Beth got to her feet. "Thank you for letting me know."

"My pleasure." Although Beth didn't know it, Joy was also helping *her*, and it wasn't only to do with Jilly's idea. "Everyone deserves a happily ever after, don't you think?" She glanced at Beth's e-reader.

"Sure, but it's only dinner." Beth's cheeks went pink. "Zach and I aren't…you know. We're friends, nothing more."

"Of course." Or not. Although Zach didn't know Joy knew, he wasn't dropping by Beth's cabin early every morning and chatting with her on the porch only to be friendly. And Beth having coffee ready and one of the cinnamon buns Zach liked set out on a tray was a whole lot more than friendly too. "I'll let you get on with folding laundry. I've already interrupted your reading. Ellie says you like romance. Those books got me through some of the hardest times in my life. You're welcome to check out the bookshelf in the family room at the house. I keep my favorites there. Maybe we like some of the same authors."

"Maybe." Beth grabbed a white plastic laundry basket from the end of the table, her cheeks the same deep red as Joy's garden tomatoes when they were ready to pick.

Joy suppressed a laugh. Like the best romance heroines, Beth was a strong, confident woman. And unlike Dani, who'd been dishonest about so much, Beth would be perfect for Zach. Somehow, and although Zach and Beth had to find their own way to be together, Joy had to make sure both of them saw what was right under their noses.

BETH WAS IN Zach's truck heading toward High Valley. Although it wasn't a date, it sure seemed like one. She laced her fingers together on top of her white clutch purse. *News flash.* She was only here to help Ellie and Joy. Zach too, although he didn't know it. She couldn't let herself make this evening into something it wasn't.

She glanced at Zach's profile. Like everything else he did, his driving was confident but relaxed. Beneath a black felt cowboy hat, his hair was damp at the temples like he'd showered before picking her up, and he'd paired a blue shirt the color of his eyes with crisp dark jeans and polished black cowboy boots. With any other guy she'd dated, the hat and boots would be props but they were part of who Zach was and this place too.

Beyond the half-open passenger window, the rolling landscape slid by, the long, golden evening shadows extending across the land as the sun dipped toward the western horizon. Although Chicago was supposed to be home, Beth would miss Montana. She and Ellie had less than three weeks left here, and the time that had at first seemed infinite was shrinking in on itself.

"It's too bad you won't be here for the county fair in early September," Zach said. His shirtsleeves were rolled up to his elbows and as he drove he rested one tanned forearm outside the truck's open window. "I bet Ellie would love it."

"She would." Beth glanced out the window again where a cluster of signs for High Valley businesses indicated they were almost in town. For a city girl, Ellie had taken to Western life like she'd been born to it and now spent every free minute with the horses and in the barn. Although she still used her wheelchair, Beth trusted her to know when she did—and didn't—need it.

"Maybe you'd like the fair too."

Was that vulnerability Beth glimpsed in Zach's expression before he looked back at the road? "It sounds like fun. Kate and Lily told us about it." When they left Camp Crocus Hill, Ellie would miss Lily, and Beth would miss Kate. While nobody would ever take Jilly's place, in only a short time Kate had become a closer friend to Beth than anyone back in Chicago. "They promised to send us pictures." Except, pictures wouldn't be the same as being there.

The truck slowed as Zach signaled to turn right into High Valley Avenue near the craft center and Bluebunch Café. People strolled along the boardwalk, enjoying the early evening warmth. In Chicago, Beth never strolled, but here she walked more slowly. She ate more slowly too, savoring her food. And maybe most importantly, she was herself here, not who everyone at work expected her to be.

"Kate and your mom said this place is good." She gestured to the restaurant sign, *Ruby's Place*, the name in slanted teal script on a dark board hung from a wrought iron stand. It was a redbrick building fronted by an almost-full parking lot at the corner of High Valley Avenue and Jackrabbit Road.

"It is. A hundred years ago the building was a general store and more recently an insurance office, but when Ruby bought it, she fixed it up as a modern restaurant with a Western feel." Zach waited for a silver truck to pull out of a spot, and after waving to the other driver, who waved back, he parked and shut off the engine. "Ruby and my mom are friends. That's why Mom was able to get us a table here at short notice. You must be wondering why I asked you out."

"I guess so." Beth smiled, knowing already.

"I'm not supposed to tell you, but Ellie's planning a surprise, and she needed you out of the way. You have to pretend to be surprised."

"I will." Beth's chest got tight as Zach got out of the truck and came around to open her door. Although he didn't know the real reason, they were both doing this for Ellie.

Zach grinned as he gave Beth his hand to help her navigate the distance from the running board to the ground. Although she could have managed it herself, there was something nice about having him look out for her—a kind of consideration she could get used to. "What my mom and Ellie don't know is that I also wanted to spend time with you away from the ranch."

"You did?" Beth's hand fit in his, warm, safe and right as they walked the short distance from the truck to the restaurant's main entrance.

"Sure, we're friends." He squeezed her hand as Beth's heart twisted. "Although, the way my mom and Ellie were going on, you'd think this was a date. Out of the blue, my mom came by my place earlier to iron my shirt, and before I picked you up Ellie texted me to ask what I was wearing and to be sure to use aftershave. Between the two of them, you'd think I was seventeen, not thirty-six."

Beth laughed as Zach held the restaurant door open for her and took off his hat. "Ellie was the same with me. She means well, though, and your mom does too." Except, and despite the party planning, maybe both Ellie and Joy wanted there to be something between Zach and Beth that could never happen.

The restaurant hostess, a dark-haired teenage girl who taught the beginner swimming classes at Camp Crocus Hill, greeted them and led them across a spacious dining room to a table for two tucked in an alcove by a cream-painted wall. A group of framed black-and-white photos hung above the table, Western buildings interspersed with landscape scenes.

Zach hung his hat on a hook and pulled out Beth's chair for her to sit before taking his own seat, then thanked the hostess as she set menu cards on the table. The hostess filled their water glasses and apologized that owing to a big party their server would be delayed in coming to take their order.

In between the hostess leaving and the server arriving, Beth had to clear up any confusion. "Your mom thinks Ellie needs to be more self-sufficient, so when we chatted in the laundry room yesterday, she said she'd be happy to stay with her if I went out for an evening. Your mom has so much more experience with kids than me." Beth grabbed a menu and pulled it toward her, pretending to study the specials.

"That makes sense. Besides, we can both

do with a night out. Between the ranch and working on my house, I don't take much time off."

"I don't either. I'm usually busy with work, and then Jilly got sick, and now with Ellie I don't have time." Beth made her tone light. Could she hide behind the menu? No, too obvious. The last time she'd gone out with a man alone, not as part of a group, was well over a year ago, maybe even longer. Too long for her to admit to Zach or anyone else, but long enough that she'd forgotten how to make this kind of small talk.

"How long has it been since you've been on a date?" From the other side of the small table, Zach studied her.

"I don't remember." How had they started talking about dates when they weren't on one? And had he somehow read her thoughts?

"I haven't been on a date in eighteen months."

"Oh." Beth set the menu aside. Although Zach's expression was sheepish, it was amused too. "Me neither." She didn't need to be embarrassed about her own dating history. They were in the same boat. "Dating hasn't been a priority for you?"

"No." His tone was curt, and his amused expression slipped. "I was engaged, and it didn't work out, so since then I haven't… Well, my brother Cole calls me a lone wolf."

"I'm sorry." It wasn't surprising that Zach was closed off but also so sensitive to Ellie. He'd had too many of his own losses.

"It was for the best. Dani and I weren't suited, not for a lifetime together." He scanned his menu again, but not before Beth glimpsed the pain that lurked in the depths of his blue eyes.

Beth clenched her hands in her lap. "If things weren't going to work out, and no matter how much it hurt, it would have hurt a lot more if you'd gotten married and broken things off. Or if you'd had children." She stopped. She never talked about her parents, and she wouldn't start now.

"You're right. Dani wasn't the person I thought she was, so any love I thought I had for her wasn't a true love." His voice was gruff as he pointed to his menu. "Have you decided what you want? I usually have a steak, but the rainbow trout is good, and there are a couple of vegetarian options."

"The trout is fine." Beth recognized a subject change. Unless Zach wanted to tell her, whatever had happened with his fiancée was none of her business.

"I'm sorry to keep you waiting. Ready to order?" The twentysomething female server wore black pants and a matching T-shirt beneath a white apron with the restaurant's logo in teal and had her dark brown hair in a high ponytail.

"Sure." Beth gave her order for the fish, and Zach ordered his steak with, at her nod, a glass of the house white wine for Beth and a local craft beer for himself.

And while they waited for their meals and then ate, they talked about easy, friendly topics like movies, travel, her job and the time he'd spent playing hockey in Europe. As if by mutual albeit unspoken agreement, big emotional things were best left alone.

Beth folded her napkin and set it beside her empty wineglass. The evening had been fun. "This is the best meal I've had in months." The food had been well and simply cooked, less pretentious than most of the restaurants she usually ate in. "As for that dessert? I've finally met my chocoholic equal.

I might have to jog beside the truck part of the way home."

"I have an idea." Zach put his fork on the empty plate that had held the s'mores bars they'd decided to share, marshmallows, graham crackers and chocolate prepared in an upscale version of the campfire classic. "Let's work dessert off another way. Want to go line dancing?" He grinned and signaled for the check.

"Line dancing?" A woman Beth worked with had taken a class last winter and asked Beth to go with her, but Jilly was sick, so line dancing, or anything else, had been out of the question.

"There's a place across the street that used to be a saloon. It's popular with tourists, but a lot of locals go too."

"I've never gone line dancing before, but I'm willing to try it." If Jilly were here, she'd already be on her way across the street, pulling Beth with her. Now it was up to Beth to be adventurous on her own. "I don't have boots, though."

"For your first time, you don't need them. Those blue flats you're wearing will be fine. How many pairs of shoes did you bring on this trip? Almost every time I see you, you're wearing a different pair." Zach's eyes and voice teased her. Was Beth imagining Zach's intent expression, focused on her as if the crowded restaurant didn't exist?

"Shoes are a luggage category all their own. I never count how many pairs I travel with." She teased him back. It didn't mean anything that he'd noticed her footwear. Her work colleagues teased her about her shoe collection too.

Zach paid the server, waving away Beth's offer to split the cost of their meal. "Come on, then." He grabbed his hat from the hook and held out his arm. "I might not have dated in a while, but I haven't forgotten how to show a woman a good time."

"It's not…" Beth stopped. This was the best time she'd had in ages, and she wouldn't say anything to spoil it. Besides, *date* was only a word.

And maybe *she'd* forgotten how to have a good time. The thought ricocheted through her, and she pressed her free hand to her chest. She'd been so focused on Jilly, Ellie and her job that her life had gotten smaller, almost without her realizing it. Joy was right.

Beth did need to get out more, and perhaps it was the same for Zach.

However, tonight's good time wasn't about the restaurant, the food or even the line dancing. Like when they were teenagers, it was Zach. Despite the intervening years, there was still a connection between them. So, date or not, what might happen if Beth took a chance and explored it?

CHAPTER SEVEN

"KEEP YOUR WEIGHT on your toes, and swivel your heels out and back together." As the last notes of "Achy Breaky Heart" faded away, a country line-dancing classic by Billy Ray Cyrus that Zach's parents had danced to back in the day, he demonstrated the movement to Beth, who copied him. "You've got it."

"Line dancing is more complicated than I thought." Beth pushed her hair back from her flushed face.

"You're having fun?" His breath caught at her animated expression and sparkling eyes—unguarded, joyful and fully in this moment with him.

"As Ellie would say, *it's the best ever*, but I need another soda." She fanned her face with her little purse and glanced around the dance floor, packed with singles and couples, some sporting cowboy hats like him but others, like her, not.

"I'll get you one at the bar if you can find us a table." Although it was almost midnight, and Zach had early chores tomorrow morning, he didn't want the evening to end.

He scanned the surrounding tables, which, like the dance floor, were also packed. His night out with Beth hadn't gone unnoticed, but so what if they'd set the town grapevine humming? They were both unattached adults, and whatever anyone else thought didn't matter. As the music started up again, he spoke into Beth's ear. "There's an empty table over by the old metal saloon sign."

"I'll wait for you there." Beth patted his arm and made her way toward it.

She had a great walk, purposeful but with a nice little sway. In a blue-and-white floral dress that skimmed her knees and left her arms bare, she had a great figure too. He was reminded of it each time they'd gotten close while dancing.

"Hey, you."

As he got in line for the bar, Zach turned at the familiar voice. "Cole." What was his brother doing here? He liked fast horses, faster cars and party-loving women. Line dancing in High Valley wasn't his usual Saturday-night style.

"Beth's popular, isn't she?" Cole grinned and slapped Zach on the back.

"What do you mean?"

"Take a look." Cole gestured toward the saloon sign that hung on the wall next to the table where Beth sat.

"So? She's talking to people." The table that had been empty moments before was now surrounded by a group of men, as well as women, and Beth sat in the center like a homecoming queen with her court. Zach's heart squeezed. It wasn't surprising that Beth was popular. Everybody at Camp Crocus Hill liked her, and since she and Ellie had taken a few trips to town, people here had gotten to know her too.

"If I'd seen Beth first, you wouldn't have had a chance, bro."

"Says you. She's too old for you, anyway." Despite Cole's teasing, Zach stiffened.

"Beth's not that old. She's younger than you. Besides, some women like younger men."

Was Beth one of them? Although they'd talked about Dani, Beth hadn't said anything about guys she'd dated. Especially not ones who might have taken her line dancing at a country bar. He'd thought Beth was having a good time and that he was a good judge of character, but after Dani he couldn't be sure. Dani had put on a convincing act, and he'd been the fool who'd fallen for it. Was Beth putting on an act pretending to enjoy line dancing too? "I didn't expect to see you here." He made himself focus on Cole, the only one of his siblings who looked like Paul, a thick piece of dark blond hair flopping over his eyes.

"I thought Jade would be here, but she's not." Cole's smile slipped.

Zach drew in a breath. He didn't want to overstep, but he was a little concerned for Cole. Although he hadn't met his brother's latest fling, Jade sounded too much like Dani. If Cole couldn't return to riding rodeo after the injury that had brought him home this summer, would Jade stick with him? Or, like Dani, would she want a different life? "Jade must have gotten busy."

"Yeah." Cole's shoulders slumped. "Don't get that worried big brother look. Jade and I aren't serious about each other. I don't do serious, remember?" Cole's laugh was forced. "Beth's a nice lady. She and Ellie were at the barn yesterday when I was fixing the baler. We talked for a while. Although, at first, I thought Beth would be snobby, she's not. She has a good sense of humor too."

"You mean she laughed at your jokes?" Zach teased to cover that Cole had hit too close to the truth.

"You should think about settling down." Cole pulled his hat farther over his forehead.

"Have you been talking to Mom?"

"No, but Beth is the first woman you've been out on a date with in years."

Eighteen months wasn't *years*, but Zach wasn't going to argue the point. "It's not a date, but even if it was, Beth lives in Chicago."

"So? That's only geography."

"That geography is almost half a continent." He turned to the bartender and ordered another club soda with lime for Beth and a cola for himself before paying their tab.

"I watched you dancing with her. If it wasn't a date, you'd have taken Beth back to the camp right after dinner. Dinner was all Mom asked you to do. But no, here you are dancing the night away, even though you have to be up for chores at the crack of dawn, and despite Beth stepping all over your fancy boots. You even look happy." Cole ordered himself a beer and handed over a twenty. "If you find someone who makes you happy, go for it."

"Paul used to say that." Dani had made Zach happy, at least for a little while, but he'd never been comfortable with her like he was with Beth. And Cole was right. Not only was this a date, it was the best one Zach had been on in years, maybe ever.

"Paul had more sense than all of us combined. You especially."

"That's a low blow." Zach took his drinks. "Ever since I came back here, I've worked as hard on the ranch as you or anybody else. I'm doing everything Dad did and more."

"No, you're not." Cole took a long swallow of beer. "Dad worked to live. Whereas you, as the saying goes, are living to work. What happened to Dad could happen to any of us. One minute you're going about your day, and the next… you're not."

Zach tried not to think about that moment.

If only he'd been with his dad, maybe the tractor accident wouldn't have happened, but instead, he'd been playing hockey half a world away, oblivious. "Most jobs have risks."

"Sure, but life should be fun, at least some of the time. For you, it's not."

"I have fun." Zach was having fun tonight, wasn't he? "I don't know what you're talking about."

"I think you do." Cole grinned and tipped his hat. "I also think that if you let yourself, you could have a lot of fun with Beth. A lifetime, even. She's the kind of woman who'd be there for you."

"How can you be sure?" Although not like Dani did, Beth had still disappeared from his life once before.

"When you date as much as I do, you know when one of the right ones comes along. Beth's solid, and she's loyal. You only have to see her with Ellie to know that. She also isn't bad to look at."

"She's gorgeous, and you know it."

"Yeah, but if I said so you might deck me." Cole's laugh rolled out like Paul's once had. "But other guys might not think that way." He gestured to the table where the man who owned a ranch adjoining the Carter spread, a newcomer from Wyoming, sat beside Beth. "If you're smart, you won't let her go."

Zach *was* smart, but Beth was too, and he couldn't ask her to settle in a place like High Valley. But what if she wanted to? He'd never know unless he let himself take a risk.

"Enjoy the rest of your evening. It's a nice night with lots of stars. Real romantic." Cole shoved Zach's shoulder like he'd done when they were kids. "You could take the long way home."

"Back off." Zach steadied the glasses he held. "As for you, don't do anything I wouldn't."

"Then I'd have no fun at all." Cole waved at a woman with long blond hair and moved toward her as Zach made his way to Beth.

Brothers. Zach loved his family, but in some ways, Beth was lucky she was an only child. As Zach neared the table, her face lit up. How long had it been since someone had looked so happy to see him?

"Sorry I took so long. There was a line." And his brother was too chatty.

"No worries." Beth took her club soda with a murmured thank you, and with a glance at Zach, the Wyoming rancher and everyone else clustered around her moved away. "If Cole's here on his own, he could sit with us. We talked in the barn yesterday. He seems lonely."

"Cole? Never."

"You can be around people and still be lonely." Beth sipped her drink.

True. Maybe Zach was lonely too. Horses were good company, but he needed more in his life. "You had lots of company while I was getting our drinks." He made his tone teasing to mask a flicker of jealousy.

"People here are friendly, but I'm new in town and with you." Her eyes twinkled. "That's bound to spark conversation, but I ignored the more personal questions."

"Good." Zach didn't want to think about what kind of personal questions Beth might have been asked. For much of the year, High Valley was a small, isolated town, and because of that, friendliness could also be nosiness.

"I bet you wouldn't lack company either. If you wanted it." Something glinted in Beth's expression that wasn't teasing. Although he hadn't dated in a while, Zach wasn't immune to a woman being interested in him, especially if he was interested in her.

"I've had a good time tonight. Would you like to—"

"Hang on a second." Beth stilled and rummaged in her purse. "My phone." She hit Answer. "Joy? What's wrong?"

Zach's breath caught in his chest as he set his drink aside and fumbled for his truck keys. Especially at this time of night, his mom would only be calling for one reason: Ellie.

"We're on our way." Beth disconnected and turned to him, her expression anguished. "Your mom and Ellie are at the hospital. Ellie got out of bed, fell and hit her head on the dresser before she landed on the floor. Your mom heard her fall but couldn't get to her in time, and when she found her, Ellie was unconscious. When she came around…" Beth's voice held a sob.

"Ellie will be okay." Zach wouldn't let himself think otherwise. He shepherded Beth to the door and into the starlit night, his body numb. "We'll be at the hospital in ten minutes. The doctors are great, and between them and my mom, they'll look after Ellie until you get there."

Beth grabbed Zach's hand and held on.

"The last time I was in a hospital, Jilly... she... I lost her. I can't lose Ellie too."

"It's not the same. Ellie had a little accident, that's all." At least Zach hoped that's all that it was. "With everyone looking after her, she'll soon be her usual self."

And he'd look after Beth. Not because he needed to. He'd look after Beth because he wanted to. And there was a world of difference between the two.

BETH STRETCHED IN the padded armchair that Zach had moved into Ellie's bedroom in the middle of the night. Bright sunlight poked through a gap in the curtains, so it must be late morning, but Ellie slept on, tucked under the pink-and-white patchwork quilt, her worn pink bear cuddled under one arm. A bear that Beth didn't know Ellie had packed until the girl had asked for it after they'd returned from the hospital.

Beth had slept sitting up, so she was stiff, but Ellie was fine, and that was all that mattered. Beth stumbled to her feet, her legs tingling as she tiptoed from the bedroom.

In the living room, the blue gingham curtains had been opened to let in the day, and the navy sectional sofa was empty. The folded tan blanket topped with a pillow on the pine trunk that served as a coffee table were the only signs that Zach had been there. He'd spent what had been left of the night on the sofa like he'd promised.

Beth hugged herself. Joy had been great, but it was Zach who'd insisted on staying here in case Ellie needed to go back to the hospital. Zach who'd checked on Ellie hourly with Beth like the doctor told them to. And Zach who'd helped Beth stay strong for Ellie, who'd looked so young and frail in the hospital bed, an IV attached to one arm.

She moved into the small galley kitchen to boil the kettle and yawned as she checked the clock on the stove. Almost noon. If not for Ellie, and even after sleeping the morning away, Beth could sleep for most of the afternoon too.

"Beth? Where are you?" Ellie's voice echoed from the bedroom, high and childlike.

"Right here." Abandoning her plan to make tea, Beth went down the short hall to Ellie's room. "How are you doing, Sleeping Beauty?"

"Okay." Ellie still had the quilt tucked to

her chin, but the pink bear was now a lump under the blankets. "When I woke up, you were gone, and I didn't know where you were."

"I was only in the kitchen. I'd never leave you on your own, honey." Beth sat on the end of the bed and patted Ellie's legs through the covers before pulling her hand away as Ellie winced. "Sorry, I forgot." Chronic pain was invisible, and even a gesture meant to comfort could hurt.

"It's okay." Ellie's voice was flat. "I'm sorry too."

"Sorry for what?" Beth scooted higher up the bed and smoothed Ellie's tangled hair away from her pale face. "You don't have anything to be sorry for."

"I ruined your date with Zach."

"You didn't, and it wasn't a date." Except, he'd been about to ask her something when Joy called. "You're more important. I was scared you were badly hurt. You could have had a concussion. You haven't fainted since we got here."

"I have, but I didn't want you to know." Ellie looked everywhere except at Beth. "Besides, I don't usually fall, or if I do, I know

I'm going to, so I can make sure I don't hit anything. Before I went to bed, Mrs. Joy said to call her if I needed to get up, but I didn't. I wanted to be like other kids."

Ellie's voice hitched, and Beth's heart turned over. "You're you, and I wouldn't trade you for any other kids. I can see why you didn't want to call her, though." Being almost thirteen was almost like being an adult.

"She's nice and all, but…" Ellie traced a pink patchwork square with an index finger. "I want my mom."

"I know." Beth wanted Jilly too, never more than when she'd stood in the hospital the night before and memories of her friend's death had flooded back. "I'm not your mom, but you can talk to me about anything. Or you can call your psychologist in Chicago or talk to a counselor here." So many people to reach out to, but not the person Ellie wanted most.

Ellie jerked her chin. "I hate having things wrong with me that hardly anybody has ever heard of. I like being here, but when I go home I'll be the kid who's different again. I hate that too."

Beth thought she'd known what POTS, postural orthostatic tachycardia syndrome, was, but reading about it was different from living with someone who had it. She'd also thought she'd known about the joint dislocations and subluxations that came with Ehlers-Danlos syndrome, EDS, until she'd seen Ellie's dislocated shoulder the night before. And then there were the gastrointestinal problems, the chronic pain associated with CRPS, Complex Regional Pain Syndrome, fatigue and disrupted sleep. All the things Ellie lived with, a kid who, otherwise, seemed fine.

"We don't have to go home yet." Beth seized on the easiest part of what Ellie had said. Except, Ellie was right. Their time at Camp Crocus Hill was limited. Beth's time with Zach was limited too. "You're doing so well here, and when we go home it will be a new start. You'll go to a new school, and the teachers there are supposed to be great. Your mom chose that school especially for you."

"What if it isn't better? What then? Maybe the kids will be mean to me like they were at my old school."

"If they are, I'll find somewhere else for you to go." A muscle in Beth's jaw got tight.

"What if I faint at school?"

"The ER doctor adjusted your medication so once you've been on the new dose for a few days, as long as you keep hydrated, your blood pressure shouldn't drop as suddenly. Besides, if you need to, you can use your wheelchair at school like you did before. At the new school, though, you won't be the only one."

"But what if my wheelchair is the only thing people see? And if they see me walking, they'll think I'm faking needing a wheelchair? That happens too."

"Then they're not the people you want to be friends with, right?" Beth covered Ellie's hand atop the blanket. "Whether you use your wheelchair or not is nobody's business but yours. Have you and Lily talked about this? Maybe you've had similar experiences?"

"There's not much time left for talking. Lily's going home tomorrow." Ellie's lower lip wobbled.

"She and her mom live in town, so we can still see them."

"It won't be the same."

"No, but it can still be good. Lily and Kate are coming on the overnight camping trip, and they'll be at your birthday party too."

"I guess." Big tears oozed out of Ellie's eyes, and she brushed at them with a corner of the sheet.

"It will be okay, sweetie." Beth wrapped her arms around Ellie in a gentle hug. If it wasn't okay, she'd try to make it so, and she knew Zach would help. "But you have to promise to tell me if you faint or anything else is wrong. Like you told your mom."

"I didn't always tell my mom. I didn't want her to worry. She didn't want to die and leave me."

"I know." Beth hugged Ellie closer, a sterile hospital smell mingling with a whiff of strawberry body lotion. "But your mom wanted you to go on and live your best life. You're so good at riding, swimming and art, and you're learning new things everyday here. I'm proud of you, and your mom would be too." Beth took a deep breath. "I'm not your mom, but I want to do everything I can to help you have that good life."

"You do?" Ellie snuffled against Beth's

shoulder. "Even though having me messes up *your* life?"

"Never think that. Having you makes my life better." It was true. With Ellie, Beth's life was busier and more complicated, but it was also richer, more loving for a start. "You're my family, and we're a team. The dynamic duo."

"That's weird." Although Ellie's voice was still choked with tears, she laughed.

"Okay, you come up with a better name." Beth laughed through her own tears. "Do you want some lunch? I have enough groceries to make a sandwich here, or if you feel well enough, we can go to the dining hall. You need to take it easy today, but after lunch we can work on a puzzle, watch a movie, play a board game or draw. Whatever you want."

"I want to do something with Zach." Ellie levered herself to a sitting position.

"He's working today, honey." Even though, like her, he'd been up most of the night, Zach had still gone to do chores. Ranch work didn't stop because it was Sunday.

"After work, then." Ellie clutched her bear. "He said I could call him anytime."

Beth would do anything Ellie asked, and maybe Zach would too, but what would happen when they were back in Chicago and Zach wasn't there? Her insides got cold. And what would happen if Beth made a habit of depending on Zach like she had last night, and he let her down, let Ellie down too?

CHAPTER EIGHT

Two days later, Zach finished cleaning Scout's saddle and stored it on the empty stand in the deserted tack room. Late-afternoon sunshine filtered through the high windows casting a golden light over the saddles, bridles, reins and other equestrian equipment. He rubbed the back of his neck and breathed in the scent of leather, crisp hay and horses. He'd worked since four thirty this morning, so he should go home or even head to the camp and help his mom in the office for late check-in, but apart from meals, this was the first time he'd stopped all day.

Yet, whether he was in the fields, the barns or the office tackling the plans Beth had suggested, he couldn't stop thinking of her, or Ellie either. And when he returned to his empty house, it was Beth's sweet face he wanted to welcome him from the front porch. It was Ellie's chatter he missed as he ate his solitary meal, the girl always asking questions about horses and the ranch.

Beth and Ellie would have good ideas about how to make his house a home too, adding the cushions, curtains and ornaments that didn't seem like much but made a place cozy and comfortable.

From the barn, a horse nickered. Princess. Although she was in the stall closest to the tack room, Zach would still have recognized that soft sound as hers. It was how Princess greeted someone she liked. Molly had finished mucking out the stalls ten minutes before, so she'd likely forgotten something. Zach moved toward the tack-room door.

"Hey, girl." Beth's voice was quiet, but it carried in the empty barn. "Would you like a treat?"

Princess snuffled, and it was followed by a crunching noise.

"Thanks for being so good with Ellie. It's like you know what she needs even when I don't."

Hidden behind the half-open door, Zach's stomach fluttered.

"Ellie loves everything about you." Beth's voice was muffled as if she was leaning into

Princess's neck. "She'll miss you when we go home. I'll find her a therapeutic riding program in Chicago, but it won't be the same."

Princess would miss Ellie too, but not as much as Zach would. As for Beth, that would be a whole other level of missing. He gripped the doorframe near where the brooms and brushes were stored on wall hooks.

"Do you want to help at Ellie's birthday party? She's—"

Zach grabbed for a broom, but it fell to the floor with a clatter.

"Who's there?" Beth called out.

"Only me." He came into the barn's wide central aisle by Princess's stall. "I didn't mean to scare you. I was ready to leave, but you started talking and, well, horses are good listeners."

"Yes." Close to Princess's head, Beth's face was as pink as the T-shirt she wore with faded jeans and battered boots like a pair Zach's mom had. "Ellie's doing makeovers with Lily and one of the camp counselors. It's a mom-free zone, and Kate had to go into town so... Not that I'm Ellie's mom, but you know what I mean."

"It's fine. You're welcome in the barn anytime." Although her jeans were too clean, Beth looked as good in ranch clothes as she did in everything else. "Is Ellie okay now?"

"She's fine." Beth patted Princess, and the horse nestled closer. "We talked, and I know more how to help her when she has a POTS episode or any other medical issue. Ellie had a telephone session with her psychologist in Chicago too, and she's promised to ask me or anyone else if she needs help. She forgot to hydrate, and the bulb in her night-light burned out, so she got disoriented in the dark. It was bad luck she hit her head when she fell." Beth's shoulders sagged. "I want to keep her safe, but I guess I can't, at least, not all the time."

"No one can do that. Expectations you have for yourself have to be reasonable too. It's one day at a time, remember? Be grateful for the good days, and when you have a bad one, as my dad used to say, *It's like mud season. You can either complain or get through it.*"

"Good advice."

Zach patted Princess and chuckled. "I learned a lot from my folks' example. My dad especially had plenty of sayings. As a kid, I didn't pay much attention, but now things he said come back to me."

"You're lucky." Beth's tone was flat, and her face got the same shuttered expression as the day she and Ellie had checked in at the camp, as if she needed to keep the world, and him, at a distance.

"You were saying something to Princess about helping with Ellie's birthday?" Zach kept his tone conversational. He wouldn't push Beth to talk about her family, but he'd listen if she wanted to.

"Yes." Her mouth curved into a smile. "Ellie wants to have Princess at her birthday, and your mom said we can use the picnic area near the front paddock for a party. Could we put ribbons in Princess's mane and tail and get a special treat for Ellie to give to her?"

"Sure. Princess would love a banana, and I can braid ribbons in Ellie's favorite colors. If you want, though, we could do something even better."

"What?" Beth drew in a soft breath, and Princess nudged her shoulder.

"Come see." Zach led Beth to the far side of the barn to what had once been a carriage house and opened the door to let her go through first. "What do you think?" He pointed to a small horse-drawn buggy parked between an antique sleigh and a vintage farm wagon.

"Wow." Beth's eyes shone. "You mean you'd take Ellie for a ride?"

"Absolutely. My brother Bryce's kids love it when Princess and I take them for a buggy ride."

"These things belonged to your family?" Beth ran a hand across the buggy seat and one shiny black-painted side.

"For several generations. They were in bad shape before my dad restored them. We don't use them much these days except in town parades or for other special events."

"They're gorgeous." Beth walked around the buggy before inspecting the wagon where Zach's dad had painted *Tall Grass Ranch* in red letters. "Ellie will be thrilled. I want to keep it a surprise for her." Even in the muted light of the carriage house, Beth's excitement was palpable.

"Sure." Zach's pulse raced. Unlike Dani, Beth was easy to please, and here was still the unpretentious girl he remembered. "Want to take the buggy for a spin?"

"Now?" Beth's mouth dropped open.

"Why not? There's still a couple of hours of daylight left, and we won't go far. If you have time, that is."

"Since it's Lily's last night here, Ellie's having a sleepover at Lily's cabin. I need to be back to help Ellie get settled and say good-night, but that's not for a few hours."

"Well?" Zach held out his hand, and Beth took it, her touch sending a tingle across his palm and up his arm. A tingle that felt good, right and like, maybe for the first time ever, he'd finally come home.

BETH HUGGED HERSELF as Zach scrambled into the buggy and sat on the narrow seat beside her. Although it could have been a scene in one of her favorite historical romances, it wasn't. Zach was taking her for a buggy ride to be friendly. She wouldn't let herself think it meant something important when it didn't.

He'd already opened the main carriage-house doors and hitched up Princess, so when he made a clicking noise and flicked the reins, the horse pulled them out of the barn. "You're sure we're not too heavy for her?"

"She's fine. She's used to pulling this light buggy. For the big sleigh or the heavy farm wagon, I use a team of draft horses." Zach drove the buggy around the barn, past the field that bordered Camp Crocus Hill and then by the ranch house, waving at his mom, who sat on the garden swing shelling peas.

"Where are we going?" Beth waved at Joy too while keeping her other hand on the buggy's frame. The black padded seat was comfortable, and a black canopy overtop shaded them from the westerly sun, but it was a bouncier ride than she was used to in a car.

"I want to show you something. It's not far, only around a couple of bends in the creek where we used to go fishing." Zach gave her a tip-tilted grin and took a right along a narrow gravel path before the ranch's driveway met the highway.

"Those were good times." Even as she grinned back, Beth turned away and gripped the side of the buggy harder. Those times were gone, and she was on vacation. Nothing that happened here was part of her real life. Yet, as Princess's hooves clip-clopped along the path lined by sweet-scented fields, an expanse of sky tinted blue, gold and pink spread out in front of them, this life seemed more real than anything she had Chicago.

"Has a guy ever taken you for a buggy ride?" Zach's shirtsleeves were rolled up to his elbows, his forearms tanned, light brown hairs glistening in the sun.

"No." Beth's mouth went dry. "I haven't dated that many guys, at least not seriously." Even the few she'd dated for longer than a couple of months had never made her feel like Zach did. Not as vibrant, or as happy to be alive, or that the world was a better place because the two of them were in it together.

"Why not?" Zach stared at a point between Princess's ears, his strong profile etched by the sun's rays as it dipped toward the distant mountain peaks. "An attractive, smart woman like you must have plenty of opportunities."

He thought she was attractive? And smart? Her breath got short. "Not so much. I never wanted to date anyone at work, so after college I didn't meet a lot of single men." She didn't try to meet them, though, because she was wary. Love led to loss, at least for her. "By the time I turned thirty, most of my friends were married and some had kids, so except for Jilly, who was on her own with Ellie, I didn't fit with the group like I used to."

"I get that." His voice had a bitter edge. "Most of the guys I grew up with or played hockey with are married with kids too. My brother Bryce was married, but his wife passed from cancer like Jilly."

"Your mom told me." Beth studied the vast landscape. Although the size of it made her feel small, she didn't feel alone here, at least not the way she did in Chicago. "Bryce's kids were at the camp for a couple of activities last week. Ellie was great with them. She seemed to recognize they were hurting too."

"Kids are smart that way. Horses are as well."

The path dipped toward the creek, where water lapped against rocks with a soft splash, and birds wheeled above a patch of birch trees. Edged by wild roses, white daisies with yellow centers and other plants that Beth couldn't identify, the farm track narrowed into a grassy lane. Princess slowed to a walk as Zach guided her along the creek bank until the path went uphill again, and the panorama of pinkish-gold sky reappeared, the sun lower now and casting long shadows on a field where a herd of red-and-white cattle grazed.

As the buggy rolled to a stop, Beth blinked. "What's a New England covered bridge doing here?"

"My grandfather Joe Carter—I forget how many *great*-s back—built it. When he was only eighteen, he and an older brother came west from Vermont hoping to find their fortune in the gold mines."

"And did they?" Princess stood quietly as frogs croaked, and birds dipped and wheeled, buffeted by warm air currents.

"No, but they stayed in the area and became homesteaders. Then Grandpa went back east to get married. His bride was a girl from Vermont he'd grown up with. The family story is that for her first few years here, Grandma Laura hated Montana so much she always threatened to go back to Vermont." Zach's low chuckle warmed Beth at the same time as it made her tingle. "Since Grandma

Laura missed New England, Grandpa Joe built her this covered bridge to remind her of home."

"That's so sweet." Beth leaned forward to take a closer look. Painted red with white trim, the bridge spanned the creek at its widest point. "It's been here since then?"

Zach nodded. "With a few improvements. Every other summer, we have a big family picnic and repaint it. When the roof part caved in after a bad storm in the late 1990s, my dad and his brothers rebuilt it, but the bones are still there. Grandpa Joe made that bridge to last, like his marriage to Grandma Laura. The two of them were together for almost seventy years."

"That's amazing." Beth's parents' marriage had lasted less than twenty years, and many of her college friends had divorced before celebrating even their tenth wedding anniversary.

"Joe and Laura raised nine children here." Zach gestured away from the creek. "Their house is long gone, but you can still see where it was because there's a dip in the ground where they dug the cellar. The Tall Grass Ranch started here."

What would it be like to be so rooted in a place? Although Beth had grown up in Chicago, neither of her parents were from there, and she'd only returned to the city after college because of work and Jilly. Zach had roots and family going back well over a hundred years in this little corner of Montana. "How could you leave here to play hockey in Europe?"

He clucked to Princess, and the buggy rocked forward before turning in a wide circle. "I left the first time because I got a college hockey scholarship, but maybe I had to leave home to truly know what I'd miss."

Beth's heartbeat sped up. She'd known what she'd miss when she'd left Montana all those years ago, but until now, she'd pretended she hadn't. Would she make that mistake again? "We're not driving across the bridge?"

Zach shook his head. "Not tonight. I didn't bring a lantern, so we need to get back to the barn before sundown." He gave her a teasing smile. "Do you know that covered bridges are known as *kissing bridges*? In my family, the tradition is that when couples are on that bridge, they have to kiss." He drove with one hand and slid an arm around Beth's shoulders. "When I kiss you, I don't want to rush it." His smile broadened as Princess broke into a trot.

"Oh." Beth smiled. She didn't want to rush a kiss either. Yet, she and Ellie only had several weeks left here.

"I like you, Beth. I like you a lot. I always have." Zach's voice was low and as he drew her into the curve of his body. "And I like what we have now. With Ellie, and you, and me."

"I like it too." Beth nestled into Zach's shoulder, the sky outside the buggy a palette of reds, pinks and oranges until it met the edge of the rolling land that seemed to go on forever.

She wouldn't analyze whatever was happening between her and Zach. Not even if she might be falling in love with him as an adult instead of that teenage crush. She'd enjoy this moment. The two of them together behind Princess, the sweet summer air brushing her face and the vast western landscape cradling them. No matter what happened in the future, and after a lifetime of always striving for something more and better, what Beth had right now, right here, was perfect.

CHAPTER NINE

"ALL FIXED." THE MORNING after he'd taken Beth for the buggy ride, Zach slid the drawer in the welcome center's desk in and out.

Outside, in Zach's line of sight through the window, Beth and Kate chatted while Ellie and Lily hugged. Kate and Lily were going back to their house in town so it wasn't as if the girls wouldn't see each other again, but they'd been saying goodbye the whole time that Zach had been fixing the desk.

"Your dad would be happy we're still using this desk." His mom's smile was bittersweet. After his father's death, his mother had gone on with her life, but some of the light had gone out of her eyes, and there was a sadness to her smile that not even Bryce's kids could wholly take away.

"Dad built things to last." A philosophy the man had lived by and taught his kids too. Whether the furniture he built, the ranch or relationships, his dad had been there for the long haul, and Zach had tried to follow in his footsteps. Maybe that was why, although he'd had opportunities even before Dani, Zach hadn't settled down with anyone. He wanted the kind of long marriage his folks had and wouldn't accept anything less.

"Although I appreciate your help, I could have fixed the drawer myself. You're busy with haying, and your dad taught me to be handy. He gave me this toolbox too." His mom patted the scarred red metal box on top of the desk. "When we were first married, I could barely change a light bulb, but with his help I learned."

His folks had been a team in every sense of the word, complementing each other like a pair of well-matched horses in harness. Zach's heart squeezed as he glanced out the window again. The light wind lifted Beth's dark hair, and as she pushed it away from her face, her expression was animated as she said something to Kate.

"I was in the main barn so it wasn't far out of my way, but call me whenever you need help. Besides, when is there a time that isn't busy?" This year, though, the weather had been so warm that haying season had started early, and on top of the regular chores, they all were working longer than usual.

"That's ranch life."

"It is. Anything else need fixing while I'm here?"

"You do." His mom's blue gaze was steady, her expression serious. "You've fallen for Beth, haven't you?"

"We're friends." Zach fiddled with the screwdriver. His mom was too sharp. "I have to get to the field."

"You took Beth out in the buggy in the middle of haying season because the two of you are friends?" His mom's voice had a knowing inflection.

"The work will get done." He avoided her gaze.

"It always does, and that's not what I meant." His mom laid a hand on Zach's arm. "You work too much."

Because work helped him avoid thinking about things he didn't want to think about. "How else are we going to make two thousand bales of hay by early August?"

"Make hay while the sun shines?"

"Exactly." Zach tried to stifle his grin.

Maybe he was making another kind of hay. He looked for opportunities to spend time with Beth and took advantage of them when they presented themselves. Beth and Ellie's cabin was ten minutes out of his way, so he had no reason to pass it on his way back from the far pasture, but he'd ridden by their cabin three times already this week. He'd taken Beth for that buggy ride to the kissing bridge because when he'd finally found her on her own, he'd hoped to kiss her. Instead, afraid of the intensity of his feelings, he'd made an excuse about needing to get home.

And he'd jumped at the chance to fix this desk drawer because it might give him a chance to see Beth, even at a distance. He stuck his hands in the front pockets of his jeans. He'd be thirty-seven on Sunday, but he was behaving like a teenager, and his mom had caught him out.

"I've never seen you look at a woman the way you look at Beth. It's wonderful, and you're lucky. She is too." His mom's voice softened.

Except, Zach didn't feel lucky. Instead, like a teenager, he was churned up, most of the time not knowing whether he was coming or going, hardly able to keep his mind on ranch work because of thinking about Beth. He couldn't talk to his brothers, Molly or the ranch hands, and most of his friends were well along the path of married life. And although he didn't want to talk to his mom, maybe she was the only one who could help. "What am I going to do?"

"What do you *want* to do?" She moved to the window, and Zach joined her. Kate was in the driver's seat of her SUV now, while Lily leaned out the front passenger window still talking to Ellie. Beth stood a few feet away scrolling on her phone.

"I like Beth." He more than liked her. If he still believed in love, he'd have said he was falling in love with her, but true love couldn't happen in only a few weeks, at least, not for him. "But she's going back to Chicago. I can't start something with her."

"If you don't start something, wouldn't you always regret it? You won't know if you don't take a risk."

"You're probably the most risk-averse person I know. Dad always said that while he was the accelerator, you were the brake stopping him from doing something foolish."

Like Zach should talk. Except for Dani, he'd always looked before he leaped, and with her, the one time he didn't he'd fallen and lost not only his heart but a lot of his self-respect too.

"True, but if you're always risk-averse, you can miss a lot of what's good out there." His mom grinned. "I should know. When your dad asked me to marry him, I said I had to think about it. To be honest, I almost said no."

"What?" From all Zach had heard, his folks had a great love story, childhood sweet-hearts who'd never had eyes for anyone else.

"Oh, yes." His mom looped an arm around Zach's tight shoulders. "I loved your dad, but at first, I wasn't sure I could marry him. I didn't want to tie my life to a rodeo cowboy, but he promised me that after a year on the circuit he'd settle down to ranching."

"I never knew." He'd always thought of his dad as a rancher, but he'd also never asked him what dreams he might have given up.

"That year, when your dad was away and I was pregnant with Paul, was one of the hardest of my life, but your dad kept his promise, and here we are. He needed to try rodeo life, and because I loved him, I let him go. I was so scared he'd get hurt, but instead I lost him on an ordinary day, in a barn I can see from my kitchen window, in a freak accident."

Zach's throat got tight as he leaned into his mom, the woman who'd nurtured him since birth but who maybe he'd never truly known. "I'm sorry."

"It taught me that most of the things you worry about will never happen, while things you couldn't have imagined break your heart and turn your world upside down." His mom's voice trembled. "If you could have something special with Beth, don't worry about what might be. If I'd said no to marrying your dad all those years ago, I'd have missed out on hurt, but I'd have missed out on happiness too. You don't get one without the other, so sometimes you have to take a risk and listen to your heart instead of your head."

What if you were too scared to risk your heart? His folks' situation wasn't the same as his and Beth's. "I'm glad you took a risk on Dad. If you hadn't, none of us would be here." He hugged his mom tight.

"I want you to be happy." His mom's voice

was muffled against Zach's chest. "If Beth makes you happy, find a way to make things work, and don't let her go."

Outside, Kate's SUV pulled out of the loading zone, and Beth gave Ellie a hug before they made their way toward the dining hall.

As he held his mom, Zach's thoughts got more and more complicated. He might not want to let Beth go, but she'd already left once, and chances were, she would again. At seventeen, he'd been hurt but not heartbroken. But now he knew what true heartbreak was, he couldn't tempt it. Beth might not think so, but she was a natural with Ellie. As such, it stood to reason that, like Dani, she'd want something he couldn't promise to give her.

"ZACH SHOULD BE here by now." Beth checked her phone for the second time in as many minutes and glanced around the shaded picnic area behind the camp's welcome center. "The party's about to start." Tables loaded with food were lined in rows interspersed with lawn chairs and blankets, and together with Joy, Molly and Rosa, Beth had tied purple and green balloons and streamers to trees and bushes. She wanted everything to be perfect for Ellie's thirteenth birthday and Zach's surprise party too.

"He'll be here." In the camp chair next to Beth, Kate's tone was certain. "It's haying season. Zach could be running late for any number of reasons. Not that I know a binder from a baler, but one of the first things I learned after moving here is that cutting and baling hay is a lot of work."

The kind of work Beth didn't understand but had heard enough to know it could be dangerous. "Zach texted me half an hour ago. What if something's happened? He doesn't know this party is for him too, but he'd never disappoint Ellie by not showing up." Unlike Beth's dad, he was a man who kept his promises.

"Zach wouldn't disappoint you either." Kate jumped up and caught a purple balloon that had come loose from one of the weeping willows that edged the picnic area.

"You think?"

"I hope that's a rhetorical question." Kate grinned as she tied the balloon to the back of Beth's chair. "Zach's head over boot heels for you."

Beth glanced around again, but nobody else was nearby. "I like him too, but it's a crush. A summer thing." At least that was what she told herself, because otherwise, what would she do about it? Besides, Zach might not have a thing for her if she ever told him the real reason she'd broken off contact all those years ago.

"Liar." Kate studied Beth from under her red bucket hat, and her dark eyes twinkled behind her glasses. "Fate has us meet from a thousand miles away. That's a rough English translation from Mandarin, but it means that love is fate or karma, so it's meant to be."

"Do you believe that?"

"I do, actually." Kate's expression was serious, the teasing wiped away. "Even though my marriage didn't work out, I have two great kids, and they were meant to be. Also, for lots of us, there are different loves at different times in our lives. I also believe that fate brings us together with people for a reason."

"Like Ellie and Lily?" The two girls laughed as they helped Joy stack plates on a table near the barbecue, where Bryce was getting ready to cook hot dogs and burgers.

"Yes, and us too." Kate's smile slipped. "As soon as you and Ellie leave, I want to book a trip for Lily and me to come see you in Chicago."

"That would be great. You're welcome anytime." Along with unconditional support and acceptance, Kate's friendship had helped give Beth a new way of looking at the world, one she needed.

"You'll have to come back to High Valley too. Next summer to the camp for sure but what about Thanksgiving or Christmas?"

"We'll see. I—"

"See what Mrs. Rosa gave me?" Followed by Lily and Rosa, Ellie rolled to a stop in her wheelchair in front of Kate and Beth and held out a glittery purple gift bag topped with green tissue paper. "She made a butterfly dream catcher to match the necklace and earrings you gave me. She also taught Lily and me a butterfly game she played when she was little." Ellie touched the jewelry she'd put on when she'd unwrapped her presents from Beth at breakfast.

"It's beautiful. And you're beautiful too."

Beth took the dream catcher in its nest of tissue from Ellie and pulled her into a hug, her heart full as Ellie hugged her back, her arms tight around Beth's neck.

Was this how a mom felt? Love and pride mixed with the need to protect your kid, no matter what? *Thank you, Jilly.* By taking guardianship of Ellie, Beth had thought she was helping her friend. Instead, Jilly had given her the most precious gift Beth had ever received.

"Look!" Lily squealed.

"What? Where?" Ellie slipped out of the hug.

"It's Zach. With Molly and Princess, see?" Beth pointed as she tucked the dream catcher back into the gift bag and put it on the nearby present table.

"Princess, she, Zach... I... Wow. I thought we were the ones giving him a birthday surprise." Ellie took off across the picnic area in a blur of wheels, Lily following.

In the lane by the paddock, Zach sat high on the buggy seat with Molly beside him. Harnessed to the buggy, Princess had purple and green ribbons in her mane and tail and a wreath of wild flowers around her neck.

As Beth followed the girls and Kate, tears pricked her eyes. Polished to such a high sheen that the black paint gleamed in the afternoon sun, the buggy was decorated with purple and green ribbons too, and a *Happy 13th Birthday, Ellie* banner hung across the back.

"Hey." She reached one side of the buggy as Ellie, Lily and a group of excited campers surrounded Molly, who'd jumped out of the buggy and stood at Princess's head, holding the horse's bridle. "It's fantastic. Thank you for doing all this. Ellie will never forget her thirteenth birthday, and for all the right reasons."

Zach pulled his hat farther over his eyebrows, a faint pink flush coloring his face, rough with beard stubble. "I didn't do it all by myself. My mom, Molly and my brothers helped too." He jerked his chin toward Bryce, who stood with his two children near Molly, and Cole, who'd come out of the paddock, a roll of green ribbon sticking out of his shirt pocket. "I'm sorry I'm late. The baler broke again. Cole got it fixed, but that put us behind."

"But you still did this for Ellie and me too." Beth pressed a hand to her throat. "Thank you, all of you."

Her gaze connected with Zach's and held, his blue eyes warm and gentle, the smile lines fanning out around them, lines that hadn't been there when he was a teen but now added character. He had a dependable face, the kind that would only become more attractive as he aged, each new line representing a good life lived. She moved closer as he bent and tucked a strand of windblown hair behind her ear. "Beth, I—"

"Does the birthday girl want to go for a ride?" A cheer went up at Molly's words.

Zach jerked his hand away from Beth's face. Her legs trembled, and her cheek tingled where his fingers had brushed against it when he'd touched her hair.

"Can I, Beth?" At Beth's side, Ellie's voice was high and excited.

"I can take you and Lily together if you want." Although Zach's smile was for Ellie, the intimate look in his eyes was for Beth. "After your ride, everyone else can have a turn too."

"Of course." Beth dragged her gaze away from Zach to focus on Ellie. "But don't you need to say something first?"

"Thank you." Ellie stood and held out her arms for Zach to lift her up. "And surprise!"

"What do you mean?" He darted a glance at Beth, his expression puzzled.

"This party is for you too." Ellie bounced on the seat. "Happy Birthday!"

"You helped me plan the surprise with Princess for Ellie, while we were all planning a surprise birthday party for you too." Beth gestured to the sign Joy and Bryce had strung between the tops of the log poles that marked the entrance to the picnic area.

"You didn't guess, did you?" Ellie's face shone.

"Not at all." Zach gave Ellie a one-armed hug. "It's a great surprise, and even though my birthday's not until tomorrow, it's much better to share yours today. Thank you."

As everyone, led by Joy and Rosa, began to sing "Happy Birthday," Zach's gaze met Beth's and held it once again. For an instant, it seemed as if time stopped. And Beth not only felt like a mom but like they were a family too. Not the kind of family she'd grown up in, but a new and better one: a real family, and maybe even one she could count on.

CHAPTER TEN

THE CAMPFIRE ZACH had built in the blackened, rock-edged pit crackled. Red-orange flames glowed against the backdrop of a summer sky hung with stars. With Ellie's hand on top of his, he turned the marshmallow on its roasting stick and glanced around the circle of faces.

As well as a small group of campers and their families, his mom and Bryce and his kids were here, along with Kate and Lily. Beyond the camping area, cattle grazed on Tall Grass Ranch land that stretched as far as he could see, a legacy that, thanks to Beth's help, he had a better chance of keeping.

Until now, he'd thought that these overnight camping trips, a highlight of summers at Camp Crocus Hill, couldn't get any better, but he'd been wrong. Sharing this trip with Beth and Ellie was the best ever.

"Is the marshmallow done yet?" Ellie

squeezed his hand, her touch warm and trusting.

"What do you think?" He pulled the stick away from the hot coals to show her.

"It's nice and brown. Not like the other one. I've never seen a marshmallow burn up before." Her giggle twisted Zach's heart. Like every kid who came to Crocus Hill, Ellie had challenges, but while they were here, she and her peers could enjoy life and just be themselves, like Paul had wanted.

Ellie took the roasting stick and turned away from the fire to the camp counselor who was helping the kids make s'mores.

"What are you thinking about?" Zach eyed Beth, who sat on a blanket on Ellie's other side, her chin in her hands as she stared into the dancing flames.

"Nothing and everything." Her smile was soft. "Mostly, though, how much I missed things like this."

"No campfires in Chicago?" Zach added another log, and the fire's flames shot higher into the summer night.

"There must be, or at least at summer camps nearby, but camping trips have never been part of my life there."

"Where do you usually go on vacation?" The mellow firelight brought out reddish tints in Beth's dark hair and gentled the planes of her face.

"I don't often take time off, at least not much beyond long weekends. I fly to New York to visit friends from college, or I once combined a business trip to San Francisco with a city break and a few days in California's Wine Country. Jilly and I took Ellie to Disney World in Florida for Christmas when she was seven, but beyond that, not much. Sad, huh?" Her laugh was forced.

"It's not too late to change." Zach didn't take many vacations either, but that was ranching life. Still, the ranch would function without him for a week if he took off, but he didn't have anyone to go with—which was also sad.

"True." Beth stared into the fire and avoided his gaze. "Kate has invited Ellie and me to come visit for Thanksgiving."

"You should." Zach's heartbeat sped up. He glanced around the campfire again. While he and Beth had been talking, the others had wandered off, either to make s'mores or stargazing with a counselor who was a keen amateur astronomer. "Walk with me?"

"Where?" Beth glanced around too. "And what about Ellie?"

"Ellie's fine. She's with my mom." He gestured to his mom. She'd joined the group making s'mores and was telling a campfire story Zach remembered from childhood. "As for a walk, only down to the creek."

"Okay." Beth got to her feet. "I'll let your mom and Ellie know." She made her way around the campfire, her figure trim in gray cropped leggings, sneakers and a purple T-shirt with the Camp Crocus Hill logo in white. Although Beth looked great no matter what she wore, Zach liked her best in these casual clothes with her hair curled around her face and, tonight, a cute pair of cat-eye glasses.

After asking one of the camp's staff to keep an eye on the fire, Zach looped a sweatshirt around his shoulders, grabbed a flashlight from the box of camping supplies and joined Beth outside the circle of light. "All set?"

"Yep. Ellie's having such a great time she won't notice I'm gone, but your mom knows." She waved at Zach's mom before turning to face him. "It's good Ellie's becoming more independent, but I want her to know I'm around too. Is that weird?"

"No." Zach laughed as he and Beth linked arms. They walked over the rough ground, away from the camping area where canvas tents were set up in a big circle around the center firepit, horses tethered beyond. "You sound like a mom." Although the only mothers he'd known were his own, the wives of his friends and Bryce's wife, Ally, all of them were protective like Beth. They wanted their kids to fly while keeping them close as long as they could.

"I'm not a mom, though. Not really." Beth's voice was hesitant. "Whenever Ellie says I don't do something the way Jilly did, she's right, and it's like I'm failing her. Failing them both."

"You and Ellie are moving beyond that, though, or it looks that way. That's significant." Zach led Beth between two tents at the far side of the circle and then full darkness enveloped them, the beam of his flashlight casting silvery light across the grass. "Don't be so hard on yourself."

"I always have been." Beth took her arm

away from his, and her voice got small, almost regretful. "You must have wondered why, after that one letter, I never wrote you again."

"You were busy. It was a summer romance, and when you went back to the city, you forgot about me. We were kids. It wasn't a big deal." Although it had seemed like a big deal at the time, Zach had moved on.

"Yes, it *was* a big deal." The breath she exhaled was a whisper on the night air, the campsite sounds faint in the distance. "Ever since Ellie and I got here, I've been trying to find a way to tell you the truth."

"You don't have to. It was a long time ago." Yet, with Beth at his side, walking across the land they'd explored as teens, it seemed like no time at all.

"I want to. I cared about you a lot. You were the first boy who ever kissed me. You were special. What we had together was special."

"Agreed, it was." Beth hadn't been his first kiss, but she was the girl he'd always remembered. The way she smiled at him had lit up his world, and in some ways, it still did. "It was a different time. Nowadays, kids have all kinds of ways of keeping in touch. Back then, I didn't even have an email address, and the only computer I could use was at school." His folks had raised five kids, including one with complex medical needs, while trying to keep the ranch afloat. Beth, meanwhile, had had an email address, her own computer and everything else that went along with being an only child from a wealthy family.

"It wasn't because of technology that I didn't keep in contact." Beth stared at her feet, tall grass brushing against their legs as they took a path away from the pasture to the creek. "Things happened so fast between us, and although we thought we loved each other, I didn't know what love was. I was still only fifteen. I didn't turn sixteen until November." And by then, her parents were separated and on the way to divorcing.

"I'd just turned seventeen but I still thought you were the one for me." Zach's stomach churned, and his insides went cold. Beth wanted to tell him the truth, so he owed her honesty in return, at least as much as he felt he could share. "When you didn't write me anymore it hurt, but you'd gotten over what I thought we'd shared, so I had to as well. In a way, you did me a favor. My senior year, I focused on school and earned a hockey scholarship to the University of North Dakota. I was the first one in my family to go to college, and it gave me a chance to learn and see more of the world." But maybe all that getting over it had brought him back to where he'd started, here with her.

"I wanted to keep writing to you, but there was a lot going on in my life." Beth's voice was laced with hurt. "I thought it was better to try to forget all about you, us and this place." In the velvet darkness, her arm swooped out to encompass the big landscape, the two of them specks of humanity in the vastness.

"Apart from anything else, we were friends. Maybe I could have helped you with whatever was going on." He cleared his throat. Losing her friendship was what had hurt most of all.

"I didn't think you could have. Your parents and your family were great. Whereas with my parents, I thought everything was fine, but my dad… The day I got home from camp he moved out. He had this whole other life my mom and I didn't know about. He traveled a lot for work, my mom did too, but I always thought we were a family, and when I found out we weren't, I didn't know who I was either."

"Oh, Beth." Zach slid an arm around her hunched shoulders. "You still could have told me." Except, he hadn't told her about Paul. Although in different ways, both of them had been who they thought the other person wanted, too scared to be who they truly were. He was still too scared, but how could he tell her the whole truth when she was leaving again in a couple of weeks?

"I wanted to tell you, but somehow I couldn't." Her voice wobbled. "I was so hurt and ashamed. I pushed Jilly away too, but because she lived in Chicago, she turned up at my house and wouldn't take no for an answer."

"What happened with your parents?"

"My dad moved to California to be with his girlfriend and her kids. A few years later, he married her, and they had a son together. I've only seen my dad a couple of times since. I tried to help my mom, but I couldn't, so when I went to college, I didn't see her much either. Jilly and then Ellie were my family. My mom remarried too, and she's got a new life in Atlanta, so when Jilly died…" Her shoulders shook.

"You were alone." They stopped by the spot at the creek where Zach's dad had built a wooden bench, a small brass plaque on the back in Paul's memory. "It had never occurred to me." He took a deep breath. "I'm guessing you felt abandoned, and because you were hurt, you turned in on yourself. Like you couldn't trust anybody."

"Yes." Her voice was thick. "How do you know?"

"Because I felt that way too. When Dani broke our engagement, she didn't do it in private. She left me at the altar. Literally." He pushed the words out. "I was waiting for her at the front of the church, everybody was there, and she didn't show. Instead, she asked her mother to tell me the wedding was off. At least you wrote me a letter." He shook his head, clicked off the flashlight and sat on the bench, patting the space beside him. Crickets chirped, and water lapped against the rocks, the familiar sounds grounding him.

"But why?" Beth sat beside him, the moonlight, almost a full moon, bathing her face in a silvery hue.

"At the last minute, Dani decided she didn't want to live in Montana. She didn't want to be married to a full-time rancher either. We met in Europe. She was from Florida but worked on an American military base in Germany and modeled part-time. We met at a bar after she came to one of my hockey games with her friends." He took a deep breath and looked at the sky. "Ranching was fun for a summer but not forever." He'd told Beth part of the truth but not all. That last truth, that he carried the cystic fibrosis gene and didn't want to have children since he might pass it on, he hadn't told anyone, not even his mom.

"I'm sorry." Beth moved closer, her warm breath brushing his cheek. "You must have been so hurt. Lost your faith in people, in love."

"A bit." A lot. "For a while, I even avoided going into town. I sent Bryce instead." While there must have been gossip, Zach never heard it, but worse than any talk was the pity in people's eyes. He'd been the guy who'd had everything and lost it. "These past few weeks with you and Ellie have been fantastic. Now that I know what happened with your folks and why you didn't keep in touch, I understand."

Unlike Dani, Beth hadn't dumped *him*, she'd retreated from everyone. And with the kind of marriage his folks had, he could see why Beth wouldn't have wanted to tell him about her parents. She'd been rich in money, but he'd been rich in what truly mattered—the love of family.

"I missed being friends with you."

"I missed being friends with you too." Except, he'd also missed loving her and imagining the future they might have had together.

"I missed not only being friends but everything." Beth's voice broke.

Zach tugged her into his arms, her body fitting against his. He traced the soft curve of her cheek. "May I take these off?" He touched the rim of her glasses.

"Yes." Her voice was low. "I usually wear contacts, but they wouldn't be good for camping."

"I like you in glasses, but right now…" He slid them off her face and set them on the bench at his side. "I want to do this." He dropped kisses across her cheeks and the side of her eyes and, when her eyes drifted closed, on her eyelids too.

Maybe he was a fool, but showing Beth how he felt was good. He missed everything they'd once shared too, and although they couldn't have forever, they still had right now. He drew back, she opened her eyes and he gazed into their soft, dark depths. And then he covered her mouth with his.

BETH STILLED. ZACH was kissing her, and it was as exciting as she remembered. No, it was better. She wrapped her arms around his neck and kissed him back. She wouldn't overthink whatever *this* was. Instead, she'd simply enjoy it.

"Okay?" He moved back a fraction of an inch and gave her a teasing smile.

"More than okay." She smiled back. "You're still a good kisser."

"Only *good*?" His grin broadened before he kissed her again.

"Okay, *excellent*." She murmured the words against his mouth, a soft vibration against her lips as he chuckled. Not that she'd kissed a lot of guys, but nobody had ever kissed her like Zach did. She nestled into his chest, his heart beneath his shirt a steady thump against her ear. "Thank you."

"For what? Kissing you?" His voice rumbled above her head. He had a great voice, not too deep but mellow and comforting.

"Well, the kissing *is* great." And she wanted to do more of it. "But I said thank you because you didn't judge me. You could have."

"No, I couldn't." His fingers tunneled up the back of her neck and into her curls. "If I judged you, I should judge myself too. I could have made more of an effort to contact you and find out what was going on."

And then Dani must have hurt him even more. Beth winced, and Zach's hand in her hair stilled. "I didn't know who or what to trust, and we'd only known each other a month. It seemed like my parents had lied to me about our family for almost my whole life."

"Is that why you never married?"

"Maybe. I told myself I never met the right man, but I also always tried to keep things casual, because if I let someone into my life, they could hurt me again." Except, although she hadn't planned it, Zach *was* in her life, and she didn't know what to do about it.

"Whatever we have here feels good, Beth."

"It does." The wind picked up, and she shivered even as she held him tight. She was Beth here, not Elizabeth. She didn't have to be Elizabeth yet. "While I'm here, I'd like to…" She stopped, her mouth all of a sudden dry.

"Like to what?" His voice got husky.

"I have feelings for you." If she didn't tell him how she felt about him, she'd always regret it. She paused, catching his familiar scent of crisp soap and saddle leather mixed with a spicy tinge of woodsmoke from the campfire.

"I have feelings for you too. A part of me always has since we first met. I thought those feelings were gone, but they aren't."

"I'd like to see what we have between us." Her heartbeat sped up. A lot could happen in a few weeks, and maybe by always being cautious she'd missed out on much of what life had to offer.

"I'd like that, but I…" He wrapped a finger around a curl of her hair. "My life is here. It has to be."

"It's okay." She made herself give him a bright smile. "I understand." She had Ellie and her job in Chicago. Except, even before Jilly died, that job seemed less important than it once was, and here in Montana it was less important still. She wanted to work and needed to carn money to support herself and Ellie, but now Beth wanted to make memories and the most of the moments too, not only this summer but always. "So where do we go from here?"

"I don't know." His voice held hope. "I want to take you line dancing again and show you some of my other favorite places here." He looked into her eyes, his expression searching. "I want Ellie to be part of some of those things too."

"Yes." Because Ellie was the biggest part of Beth's life. "But what if—"

"No *what if*s right now. Be in the moment, remember?"

"Like we talked about my first morning here." When Zach had surprised her on the cabin porch when she was in her ridiculous pink-panda pajamas.

"Yeah. There you were in the light of a

new day, even prettier than you were before, and I couldn't take my eyes off you."

She hadn't been able to take her eyes off him either. She still couldn't. "Okay, the moments." She wouldn't let herself worry about the future; she'd follow her feelings instead. Zach wasn't her dad. He wouldn't hurt her, at least not on purpose, and she was older now. She wouldn't let herself be hurt.

"Good." His low chuckle made her stomach flip. "I want to take you back to the kissing bridge too."

"I'd like that." She shivered a little.

"You're cold." He rubbed her arms and then drew back. "Wear my sweatshirt." He took it from around his neck and bundled it over Beth's head, the navy garment, like her T-shirt, emblazoned with the camp's logo, swamping her smaller frame. "It's late. We should get back."

"Yes, it's Ellie's bedtime soon. She's excited about sleeping in a tent for the first time." She snuggled into the sweatshirt, wrapping herself in Zach's warmth and scent.

"One more kiss."

As he kissed her again, Beth made herself focus on the magic moment. Held in Zach's strong embrace, the creek water rippling over the rocks, the gentle croak of frogs, the crickets' soft chorus and the stars in the big sky dipping so close she could almost touch them made a memory that, no matter what, she'd treasure always.

CHAPTER ELEVEN

"TIME FOR LUNCH, EVERYONE." Zach jumped off the back of the hay wagon and wiped his hot face with the hem of his shirt. His mom's truck was parked outside the field along a dirt road, and she walked toward them carrying a blue cooler. Although it was only midday, he'd been working here since five this morning and likely wouldn't stop until nine at night. He wasn't the only one, though, and at this time of year, field meals were a necessity, not a luxury.

"Take a look at that." Cole slapped Zach's back and gave a low whistle. "You've got special company, bro."

"What? Who?" Zach turned and shaded his eyes from the sun with his hat brim. Behind his mom, Beth carried another cooler, and the collie dogs, Jess and Sadie, brought up the rear. He was glad to see her.

In the three days since the overnight

camping trip, he and Beth had spent every free moment together, sometimes with Ellie but often alone, mostly talking but a bit more kissing too. And with each sliver of time they spent together, he fell for her a little harder and tried not to think about what his life would be like when she left.

"Beth looks like she belongs on a Montana ranch, doesn't she?" Cole laughed and poked Zach in the ribs.

"Of course she doesn't." Yet, as Beth walked across the field in jeans, a simple white T-shirt, boots and a white cowboy hat she must have borrowed from Molly or Zach's mom, she sure was more Montana than Chicago, including the dogs bounding around her feet.

"Something wrong with your eyes? All Beth needs is jeans that are a bit more worn-in and a few kids and you've got a picture for a family Christmas card right there."

"Stop it. Go help Mom, why don't you?" Zach poked Cole back. Growing up in a big family he was used to teasing but, after Dani, not this kind. Leaving his brother to meet their mom, he walked toward Beth and took the cooler. "Hey."

"Hey yourself." She laughed. "*Hey* or

hay?" She gestured to the hay field and scattered workers.

"Both." Zach brushed dirt off his jeans. He couldn't kiss her here, not with an audience, but he sure wanted to. "This is a nice surprise." He carried the cooler to the edge of the field and set it in the shade of one of the wagons.

"Ellie's taking a jewelry-making workshop at Rosa's studio, so I was free." Beth gave him a dimpled smile. "Your mom called and asked me if I could help her out, so why not?"

Although his mom could always use help with field meals, her bringing Beth out here likely wasn't accidental. He glanced at his mom in another patch of shade with Bryce, Cole, Molly and the rest of the crew, and she gave him a little wave.

"We made ham sandwiches with cheese and topped with greens from your mom's garden." Beth took the lid off the cooler and handed Zach a sandwich parcel wrapped in waxed paper. "There's cut-up carrots too, as well as apples, potato chips and date squares. I made the date squares." She continued taking food out of the cooler. "Drinks and a chocolate treat for you, Mr. Chocoholic. Keep it with the ice so it doesn't melt." With a teasing smile, she passed him a chilled water bottle and Zach's favorite chocolate and raspberry fudge made by High Valley Treats in a container with an ice pack. "Back at the house there's beef and sweet potato stew in the slow cooker, homemade crescent rolls and a bunch of other stuff for dinner later. Your mom's planning on feeding twenty."

"Some guys from a neighboring ranch promised to drop by later to help us finish. We do that for each other from time to time." Zach grinned back and sat on the ground, patting the space beside him. "Join me?"

"Okay, but I've already eaten." Freckles that hadn't been there a few weeks ago dotted Beth's nose. "Before today, the most I've ever cooked for is five people, and I thought that was a lot. When Ellie came to live with me, even cooking for two was a big change. I went from half a grocery cart every two weeks to a full cart every week. I can't imagine how your mom managed with five kids."

"We grew or raised a lot of our food. Still do." Zach bit into the sandwich and shook his head at the two dogs flopped in the shade and eyeing his meal. "When I was little, I wanted to name the cows. That's a bad idea when you end up eating some of them."

Beth winced. "I never thought of it like that. So the beef in that stew in the slow cooker…"

"Yep." He tried not to laugh.

"I won't tell Ellie. She may be a teenager in years and likes to seem grown-up on the outside, but I'm learning that in a lot of ways she's still a kid." Beth tilted her head back against the wagon. Having her this close was distracting Zach from his meal. "Because of my parents, even if I got married I never thought I'd want kids, but maybe I was wrong. I didn't think I'd know how to be a mom, but Ellie's teaching me."

Zach's stomach twisted, and he slugged water, the homemade sandwich tasteless in his mouth. "You'd be a great mother. Ellie's lucky to have you, and any other kid would be too." Beth deserved to have kids of her own, and given she was in her midthirties, if she wanted them, she'd want them soon.

"Thanks." She tucked her knees under her chin and hugged herself. "After the divorce, both my mom and my dad remarried, and they have stepkids. Like I mentioned, my dad had another child with his new wife too. My half brother will be fifteen this fall, but I barely know him."

Zach didn't miss the hurt in her voice. From the sounds of it, her folks had made new families that didn't include her. "That's hard. I'm sorry."

"Don't be." Beth held herself rigid. "I chose my own family." Her smile was too bright. "Try a date square? I found the recipe online. I used to like to bake, but these days I don't have time for it."

"Sure." He took the sweet treat from the lidded plastic container she held out. Beth should have the kind of life where she had time for things she liked. He should too. Starting with taking a real break for meals, even on a busy day. "These are great."

"Thank you." Her cheeks went pink.

"Smart and you can bake. You have so many talents." He took another date square before unwrapping the fudge. "Somebody from the government came back to me about that agricultural grant you helped me apply for. They said my application was under consideration and I should get a response soon. If we're eligible for money, I hope it's enough to cover a few equipment upgrades."

"That's great you won't have to wait too long to hear." She pushed the hat back on her head. Although Zach had never pictured Beth in a cowboy hat and this one was too big, it sure looked cute on her. "Whether you get an agricultural grant or not, I've also been thinking that you need to look at supplementing the ranch's income with other things besides the camp."

"Like what?" He needed to focus on the ranch, not on how much he wanted to kiss her.

"Any number of things. Lots of ranches host special events like weddings or—"

"Not weddings." Despite the sweetness of the chocolate, Zach's mouth had a bitter taste.

"Okay, I can see why weddings would be hard." She patted his hand, her gentle touch soothing. "What about miniconferences or retreats? I've looked at the schedule, and apart from summer, the camp cabins aren't being used. Your mom said they're winterized. You also need to advertise Camp Crocus Hill more widely."

"You're right, but how? Nobody in the family has that kind of experience. To do those things we'd need to hire someone, and that would take money."

"Okay." Beth tapped her hands against her denim-clad thighs. "To start, what about promoting animal sponsorship among your existing camp families? That could be an easy win, because there must be a lot of kids like Ellie who want a horse but for whatever reason can't have one. Some of those families would likely be interested in sponsorship. If Ellie had her way, I'd be keeping Princess in feed, tack, treats and veterinary care for the rest of that horse's life."

"That's a great idea." Zach hesitated. His dad was gone. He didn't have to seek his approval. And although he'd talk to the rest of the family, it was ultimately his responsibility to make the best decisions for the ranch. "Animal sponsorship wouldn't be wrong in any way, would it?"

"Of course not. The campers and their families enjoy the horses in the summer, but you have to feed and look after those horses all year round." Beth's eyes were bright, and her expression animated. "You could also consider a hockey camp for kids of all abilities alongside the regular programming for kids with special needs. Your mom told me you coach her team in the winter. You must still have contacts. There are kids' hockey camps all over the US and Canada, including some at ranches."

"I coach a team of women between thirty and sixtysomething. I was gently pushed into it. My mom and her friends can be very persuasive." It was more fun than Zach expected, though, and the team had even taken home a trophy at a regional championship last winter.

"So? Between that and playing in Germany, you've had experience." Beth packed up the empty lunch containers and put them back in the cooler. "Think about it. You could start small with any of those things and grow. You have the space and most of the facilities. There's an arena in town, and your mom said that in the summer it's hardly used. How difficult would it be to build some extra cabins to house hockey kids?"

"Not hard at all." Not with the skills he

and his brothers already had, and they'd have time because the winter months were slower. Zach's heartbeat sped up. "Those are all great ideas. Thank you."

"No problem." Beth wedged the lid back onto the cooler. "Everybody's working again, so we should leave, but I'll be back with the dinner run. Ellie and I have a drama class tonight but not until seven."

Zach glanced across the field. While he and Beth had been talking, everyone except his mom had gone back to haying. She sat on a blanket, knitting needles flashing in the sunshine and a bundle of red wool on her lap. Even though his mom was never idle, she also never sat in a field knitting in the middle of the day. He and Beth had been set up—again. Yet, although he'd only planned to stop for a quick lunch, maybe he'd needed this break, and not only for the free business advice. "You don't have to come back with dinner."

"No, but I want to. When else will I see you on the last day of haying?" Beth waved away his offer to help her with the cooler, whistled to the dogs, who'd fallen asleep, and walked back toward his mom. Like everything about her, from her cuteness to her kindness, she was way too distracting.

And as Zach got back to work, replenished in soul even more than body, Cole's words echoed in his head. His brother was right. Out here, Beth did look like she belonged on a ranch, and a few kids would only complete the picture. Zach's chest burned. Beth had as good as told him she wanted kids, but he couldn't be the one to have them with her. So no matter how much he might want Beth to stay here, he'd have to let her go.

"YAY, ELLIE!" AT one edge of the outdoor basketball court, Beth jumped up and down as Ellie wheeled toward the net at the far end and lobbed a ball through it.

"She's good." At Beth's side, Zach cheered too.

"She sure is." Beth grabbed her water bottle and took a drink. "Apart from swimming, Ellie didn't have a chance to try a lot of sports before coming here." It was one of the many ways that Camp Crocus Hill had been life-changing, and Beth needed to focus on all the positive changes in Ellie's life. Not on how good Zach looked in tan cargo shorts, a blue T-shirt and his hair still damp from a shower. Or how times like this, when the two of them and Ellie weren't doing anything special, only hanging out together, felt a lot like being a family.

"One of our goals here is to help kids have fun with sports, and music, drama and art too. That's why we introduce them to such a wide range of activities. For Ellie, though, if she got the right kind of training, she might be able to take her interest in sports further, either in a recreational league or competitively."

"In wheelchair basketball?" Beth cheered again as a kid from the opposite team made a basket. In this kind of game, it didn't matter which team won, only that everyone enjoyed taking part.

"Maybe, but from the little I've seen, she's good at all the sports she's tried. She was already a strong swimmer, but along with basketball she's great at table tennis. When we played yesterday, she beat me twice and gave me a good workout too. She seems to like horseback riding the most, though." Zach gave Ellie a high five as she scored more points.

"Lauren says that in only a few weeks,

Ellie has made the kind of progress on horse-back that some kids don't make in a couple of summers." Beth's gaze darted from one end of the court to the other as the game continued, a blur of wheelchairs and excited kids. "Lauren's also put me in touch with a riding teacher she knows in Chicago. She thinks that Pam would be a good fit to teach Ellie so she can build on the learning she's done here."

"That's great." Zach's voice was flat.

The game ended with Ellie's Blue Team the winner by two points. Beth moved to congratulate Ellie where she sat in the middle of a group of kids and parents—people that until Camp Crocus Hill had been strangers but had become close friends, some likely lifelong.

"Mrs. Joy said we can make ice cream sundaes in the dining hall." Breathing hard, Ellie wheeled to Beth's side. "With as many flavors of ice cream as we want."

"Wow." Beth's breath caught at the expression on Ellie's face. Although she still grieved for her mom, and a part of her always would, the sullen girl who'd arrived at camp was almost gone, replaced with one who had new interests, along with new determination and purpose in life.

"Good game, El." Zach fist-bumped Ellie, and she returned the gesture before reaching up to pull him into a hug. "I took your advice about shooting." She grinned before hugging Beth too.

"You coach basketball?" Beth turned to Zach.

"No, at least not officially." He spoke to several other players, and Beth joined him. "Ellie and some others were playing a pickup game here a few days ago, so I gave them a couple of tips. I played basketball in high school and learned from a great coach, my dad." His smile softened as Bryce's daughter, six-year-old Paisley, gave him a Winnie-the-Pooh toy to hold while she tightened the straps on her pink sneakers.

Zach's family was close, connected and loving. Beth didn't have to look any further than this basketball court to see that. His whole family was here, not because they had to be—there were plenty of camp counselors—but because they wanted to. Like the ranch, this camp was part of who they were, a tight-knit unit who looked out for each other.

"Come help me make my sundae." Ellie tugged Beth's hand, standing now and balancing on the back of her wheelchair. "I texted Lily, and she and her mom are on their way. They might as well not have left camp at all. They're still here so much."

"True." Although Kate paid for all the activities she and Lily participated in, the two of them were almost part of the Carter family, a family that seemed to be expanding to include Beth and Ellie too.

Ellie tugged Beth's hand again. "Mrs. Joy says that after our sundaes we can have a fire in the firepit and tell scary stories."

"Not too scary." Real life was frightening enough, so stories shouldn't be. Although Jilly had sometimes made fun of Beth for reading romance, there was a lot of good to be said for books where a happily ever after or happy for now was guaranteed.

"If you get scared, Beth, I'll hold your hand." Zach's teasing grin had a more intimate edge that was new.

"Beth gets scared really easy. When the wind caught our inside cabin door last night

and slammed it shut, she jumped a mile."
Ellie rolled her eyes.

"Don't exaggerate." Beth tried to smile
and join in with the teasing. "Only half a
mile."

"Some people startle more easily than
others." Zach's grin slid away, and he put
a hand on Beth's back to guide her toward
the dining hall beyond the basketball court.
"It's nothing to joke about."

"Sorry." Ellie sobered. "When we first got
here, I was scared when that door banged
shut too. I thought it was a bear. Have you
ever seen a bear?"

"Lots of times, but not much around here."
Zach ruffled Ellie's hair. "The closer you
get to the mountains, in places like Glacier
and Yellowstone Parks, you might see black
bears or even grizzlies, but most of the time
bears want to avoid humans as much as we
want to avoid them."

"But if you met a bear—"

Beth's phone dinged with an incoming
text, and she reached for it in her tote bag,
one with a dream-catcher motif she'd bought
at the craft center. "It's probably Kate. I'll
catch up with you. Ellie wants to hear about

bears." She waved away Zach's offer to wait for her and stepped aside, still trying to find her phone.

Zach was kind, a man whose good manners were part of who he was and not surface polish. Was it because he'd had his own heartache, or because of the family he'd grown up in that he was so considerate of others? Maybe both, but whatever it stemmed from, Beth appreciated his thoughtfulness.

Beneath an extra pair of socks for Ellie, an apple she'd saved from lunch and a hair clip, Beth's hand finally closed around her phone case.

Not Kate. Two long-distance numbers she didn't recognize, so probably spam. She swiped the screen to unlock the phone. Since she didn't have consistent network coverage here, texts often arrived in bunches. She opened the first message, glanced at it and stilled. Then she scrolled to the next one, and her stomach flipped.

"Beth?" Zach sounded concerned. "Ellie and I didn't want to get ice cream without you so we waited. Are you okay?"

"I'm fine." The words echoed from a distance, not like her voice. She dropped the phone back into her bag. Her world spun, the basketball court, dining hall and sky blurring together. She couldn't let herself think about that message from her dad right now. However, all she'd have to do was type a reply to the one from a headhunter about a new job at a bigger company, and she'd be on track to have everything she'd thought she wanted. Except, maybe she'd been wrong and she didn't want it after all.

CHAPTER TWELVE

THE WARM WIND stung Zach's face as Scout galloped across the meadow. Tall grass brushed Zach's boots, and Scout's hooves thudded on the dry, level ground as his long mane rippled.

At a shout behind him, he patted Scout's neck. "Ease up, boy." As Zach circled back, he slowed Scout to a canter and finally a walk before they stopped at the edge of the open field behind the camp.

Cole drew alongside them on a bay horse. "Honey's an older girl. She can't keep up. Who were you showing off for?" He gave Zach a slow, sideways grin. "Performing like a rodeo cowboy is my style, not yours."

"I wasn't showing off for anybody." Zach set his hat more firmly on his head. "Scout got bored moving all those cattle. He did his job, so since he likes to run, I let him have his head. With the rain coming, he wasn't going to go anywhere except back toward the barn." He gestured to the dark clouds piling up in the west.

"We'd have gotten back before the rain without you running like you were being chased by who knows what." Cole let out a breath. "What's up?"

"Nothing." Zach fiddled with Scout's reins. Dani didn't mean anything to him and hadn't for more than three years. It didn't matter what was going on in her life. As for Beth, whatever was up with her, he wanted to help, but she'd been distant ever since the basketball game two nights ago. Maybe he should give up trying to understand women and stick to horses.

"Growing up, we had to share a bedroom for fifteen years. I know when something's bugging you."

"*You're* bugging me." Zach eased Scout into a walk, skirting the rear of Meadowlark cabin to follow the path along the creek. The same creek that meandered through the ranch, narrower here than near the campsite where he'd kissed Beth. He couldn't stop thinking about that night and didn't want to.

"Like that's anything new." Cole grinned.

"Mom says I've been bugging you since the day I was born and took away your status as the youngest."

"You didn't get to be the youngest for long." Bryce had been born fourteen months after Cole.

"No, but then I became the middle child. The family peacekeeper."

"Family wild child, more like it."

"I keep life interesting for the rest of you." Cole's cheeky expression was identical to the one Zach remembered from childhood.

"Not only interesting. Having you back home to help this summer eases the load on the rest of us. I appreciate it. We got the haying done faster thanks to you, and those cattle moved quicker too." He hesitated as the horses climbed the small hill that separated the camp from the main ranch property. "You should think about sticking around."

"Maybe someday." Cole's shrug was too casual. "I'm not like you. I don't want to settle down to ranch life." He gave Zach a meaningful look. "You and Beth are getting on well."

"I guess so."

"Don't you want to stop at her cabin?"

Cole gestured with his thumb to Meadow-lark, its roof poking out behind the hill.

"She's busy with Ellie in the afternoons." Except, Zach hadn't seen Beth at all today, and when he'd dropped by her cabin for their usual early-morning chat on the porch, the curtains had been closed and both the inside and screen doors shut.

"Trouble in paradise?"

"No." Beth wasn't Dani. She said she had feelings for him, and Zach believed her. They'd both agreed that what they were going to do about those feelings was a problem for another day.

"The only time I've ever seen you like this was after Dani." Cole shook his head. "And she's long out of the picture."

"She is, but…" Zach bit his lower lip.

"You hear from her?"

"No, but I heard from Jochen, a guy I used to play hockey with, that Dani has a kid with another one on the way."

"So? You've moved on." Cole opened a gate to let Zach and Scout into the field nearest the barn before following with Honey and closing it behind them. "Haven't you?"

"Yes." Zach tasted bile as Scout resumed

his slow walk. "When Dani walked out on me, she swore there was nobody else."

"And?" Cole's expression was puzzled.

"I did the math. Her son will be three in February."

"What? She was already…?" His brother's eyes widened, and his mouth fell half-open.

"Seems that way." Zach clenched his hands around Scout's reins. "Before you ask, there's no way that kid is mine. Dani must have gotten pregnant while I was back here. Dad passed, and I came home to the ranch in March just before the hockey season ended. I didn't go back to Berlin, so until a week before what was supposed to be our wedding in June, Dani and I were apart."

"That's bad. You going to call her on it?"

"No. There's no point." But the extra betrayal still stung.

When the email from Jochen, a goalie who'd always been way too full of himself, had landed in his inbox, Zach had barely glanced at it. It was a *Where Are They Now?* update along with details of a team reunion he didn't plan to attend. Yet, as he'd been about to hit Delete, he'd spotted Dani's name. And although he hated himself for looking, the details weren't hard to find. The dad of her two kids was a guy who'd joined the team a few months before Zach left and had soon gone on to play for a top professional team in California. Now he was the newest hotshot CEO of a Silicon Valley tech company, his face and net worth plastered all over the internet. Not only had Dani not wanted to live in Montana, she'd never planned to settle for a rancher either. A hockey player had more status, especially if he still had a chance of going to a North American team in the top league. However, when Zach's dad died, Zach had become a former hockey player and Dani hadn't waited to toss him aside.

"People." Cole shook his head as they neared the horse barn.

"Not everyone." The first icy raindrops stung his shoulders as Zach swung off Scout, opened the barn door and led the horse inside.

"A lot." Cole followed him into the barn with Honey. "You think you know folks, but you don't."

Zach grunted as he loosened Scout's cinch. His brother's track record of reading people didn't qualify him to judge. There *were* good people—women—out there. His mom and Molly, Bryce's late wife, Alison, Rosa and Kate. Beth too. His stomach lurched. He'd thought he'd known Beth before, but he hadn't. Was she telling him the truth about why she'd broken off contact? And more importantly, did he know her well enough now to trust her?

"Do you want to go into town later and shoot some pool? We could grab a burger and make a night of it." Cole took off Honey's saddle and patted her neck.

"I guess." After removing the rest of Scout's tack, Zach checked the horse for rubs or sores.

"I'll see if Bryce wants to come along and ask Mom if she could babysit his kids. We could invite a few of the cousins too. It's been ages since all of us guys got together."

"No, only you and Bryce." Zach had been made a fool of not once, but twice by Dani, and he didn't want the whole family knowing. He gave Scout water before feeling his legs. The horse loved to run but sometimes didn't know when to stop.

"Sure." Cole picked out Honey's hooves. "You can't run from your past, you know."

"I wasn't. Like I told you, I wanted to get home before the rain set in." Zach gestured through the barn-door opening. "Look at it coming down out there. We'd have gotten soaked if I'd let you set the pace."

"Maybe." Cole focused on Honey's left foreleg. "But if you're bothered by some rain, you've gotten soft."

"I haven't." He'd gotten sensible. No reason to get yourself or your horse drenched if you didn't have to. "As for the past, I've dealt with it. Dani is ancient history."

"If you say so." Cole straightened and eyed Zach. "I'm not saying you still have feelings for her, not after what she did, but now finding out there's more?" He let out a low whistle. "That kind of cheating is a reason for a guy to stay single."

"Speak for yourself." Zach checked Scout's hooves before walking him around the main area of the barn. The horse was fine. They'd both had a good run, and Zach wasn't running away from anyone or anything, his past least of all.

"I've always been the good-time guy, the

joker." His brother's mouth twisted. "With Paul being sick, Molly a girl and so much younger than the rest of us, and you and Bryce so perfect, it was the only way I could get attention. Not that I was happy when Dani dumped you, but finally I wasn't the one who hadn't had things work out for them. For a few months there, the town had something else to talk about besides how I mess up."

"I'm not perfect, and you don't mess up. Not really." Zach's response was genuine and heartfelt. "Like a lot of people, it's taken you time to find your way."

"That's a nice way of putting it, but before you find your way, you have to want to. And no matter how fast you run that horse, you have to deal with what you're leaving behind, and you have to be running to something too." Cole's expression softened. "Or to someone who loves you no matter what."

"Personal experience?"

Cole shrugged. "I was talking about you."

"*Love*'s a big word." It was too soon, Zach reminded himself. What he'd thought was love for Beth as a teen was a crush, albeit a serious one, but lasting love was deeper and more durable. It was also there in good times and bad, as well as all the ordinary days in between. Although he kept trying to deny it, what he felt for Beth now might be that lasting love if they could give it time to grow.

"Those four little letters aren't so big when love is real." Cole tossed fresh straw into Honey's stall and led her into it. "All I'm saying is don't get so hung up on what Dani did that it's all you can see. I'm not ready to settle down, but despite those years at college and in Germany, the biggest part of you has been settled since the day you were born. Just because one woman did you wrong doesn't mean the right one won't come along. Maybe she already has."

If only it were that simple. Zach studied his brother's broad back before he turned to get Scout stabled in the stall next to Honey's. What Dani had done *was* bad, and the email from Jochen had thrown Zach for more of a loop than he wanted to admit. However, he still couldn't tell Cole why he'd steered clear of relationships, that is, until Beth had broken down his defenses.

"You're sure you're okay?" In the gray light that filtered through the horse-barn window,

Beth studied Ellie's pale complexion. "We could have stayed at the cabin and watched another movie." Anything to bring a smile back to Ellie's face.

"It's only a pain flare. I forgot to pace myself. I should have taken it easier after the basketball game, but I didn't. Yesterday I swam and went riding and played tag and went bowling." Ellie's expression was pinched. "I have to keep moving. That's what my physiotherapist always says." She balanced herself against the barn wall. "This kind of pain doesn't go away no matter how much I rest. I don't have any spoons today, that's all."

Beth's heart squeezed. She should have remembered about pacing, but between thinking about Zach and getting those texts from her dad and the headhunter, Beth had almost forgotten that Ellie couldn't do the same things as other kids, or at least not as many of them in such quick succession. And now all she wanted was to help Ellie feel better, but she couldn't.

"Maybe Princess will distract you." And distract Beth as well. For most of the time she'd been in Montana, she'd been able to forget about her life in Chicago, but now things from that life had intruded, and she didn't know what to do. Yet, no matter how much she tried to avoid them, or how many holding messages she sent using the excuse of lack of network coverage, those things wouldn't go away. Instead they loomed over her, casting long shadows over this last week at camp.

"It's rained so hard all afternoon that Princess has been stuck in the barn. I bet she'll love your company. I bumped into Molly in the dining hall when I was getting your lunch, and she said you could help with feeding all the horses later." A lunch that Ellie hadn't eaten, even though Beth had said she could have whatever she wanted.

"Yeah." Ellie winced as she put one foot in front of the other and shuffled along the wall.

"We should have brought your wheelchair from the car." Beth hovered at Ellie's side to catch her if she fell.

"I don't want to use it." Ellie reached the stall on the end of the row, several away from where Princess nickered in welcome. "Not in the barn."

"But…" Beth pressed her lips together. When they'd first arrived at Camp Crocus

Hill, all Beth wanted was for Ellie to get out of her wheelchair, but now, when it could make her life easier and safer, Ellie wanted nothing to do with it.

"You can't fix everything, okay?" Ellie leaned against the closed stall door, sweat beading on her upper lip. "For once I want to be a normal kid and do whatever I want. Not be the sick one who has to rest and pace herself like an old lady."

"You *are* normal. There are all kinds of *normal*. You're normal for you, top to bottom, inside and out, and that's what matters." Would Jilly have said that? What would one of the camp counselors or Ellie's psychologist say? They weren't here, so Beth had to do the best she could. Her throat clogged as she put an arm around Ellie's thin shoulders. "Tomorrow will be better." At least she hoped so. "All you have to focus on is getting through today, even if it's only a few minutes at a time."

"Yeah." Ellie made her way along the row and stopped as Princess nickered again and stuck her head over the front of her stall to nudge Ellie's shoulder. "Look." Ellie gasped and pointed into the stall beside Princess's.

"Puppies. It's like Princess wanted to show me. Can we go in and see them?"

Beth looked over the open top half of the stall where four black, brown and white bundles of canine cuteness played in the straw. These must be the puppies Zach had told her about, offspring of his brother Bryce's rescue beagle. "I guess so. I don't see the mom, and these aren't newborns." Not that she was an expert, but a friend at work had gotten a beagle puppy last year, and Shaundra had shown Beth pictures at each stage of the dog's development.

Beth unlatched the bottom half of the stall door to let Ellie squeeze through and followed her, shutting the door quickly behind them.

"They're so adorable." Ellie sat in the nest of straw, and the puppies tumbled over her lap.

Beth agreed and sat across from Ellie, her back against the stall wall, a sinking feeling in the pit of her stomach. The puppies *were* adorable, but if Ellie wanted one, driving all the way back to Chicago with a puppy who wasn't yet house-trained didn't bear thinking about.

"Where did they come from?" Ellie's expression was animated, and she giggled as the smallest puppy tried to climb up her chest. "They weren't here yesterday when I groomed Princess."

"Zach mentioned his brother's dog had pups around the time we got here. They were likely at Bryce's house until now."

"Do you think he's looking for homes for them?"

"I don't know, but—"

"I bet he is. Please?" Ellie cradled the smallest puppy, a little girl, while its bigger brother tried to stick its head under Beth's rain jacket. The two other siblings rolled between them, yipping and playing.

"It's a long drive home, and we can't take a puppy with us." The boy puppy was soft and warm against Beth's stomach, nestling against her like she was a mother dog. "As soon as we get home, we need to get you ready for school, and I have work." The puppy nudged Beth's phone in her jacket pocket, where those texts about her career and family still needled her. Her stomach somersaulted as she cuddled the puppy closer.

"Details." Ellie stuck her bottom lip out.

"Those details are important." Although not to a thirteen-year-old girl who didn't yet have the maturity to think through actions and their consequences.

"What if we stayed here? Then we could adopt one of these puppies." Ellie's expression turned hopeful.

"Stayed here?" Beth swallowed, her mouth dry. "We can't stay at Camp Crocus Hill."

"Not here exactly, but in town. We could live in High Valley, and I could go to school with Lily where her mom teaches. I don't want to go back to Chicago, and I'm starting at a new school anyway."

As Ellie kissed the puppy between its velvety ears, Beth stopped herself from saying something about germs. When Ellie caught a viral or bacterial infection, her medical conditions meant she usually became sicker than others her age and also took longer to recover. "I know you like it here, but this is a vacation. Vacations end." They had to.

"I don't want this one to be over." Ellie's face got a sullen expression. "You like Zach, don't you?"

"Yes, but it's complicated."

"Why? He likes you too. I can tell." Ellie

picked up the other two puppies and cuddled them with the first. "That's another reason why we should stay here."

"I can't pack up my whole life, your whole life too, and move to rural Montana." Beth made her voice steady and logical, her work voice.

"My mom would have let me stay here. She was fun."

Jilly wasn't here, and whenever Ellie used what Beth thought of as the Jilly Card, she never knew what to say. Beth couldn't remind Ellie of her mom's death, but she also couldn't focus on what Jilly would or wouldn't have done. "I can't talk about this right now."

Especially with those text messages almost burning a hole in her pocket. In a way, her dad's message was the easy one. Apart from the pain he'd cause her half brother, him splitting up with his wife had nothing to do with Beth and was only another reminder, if she'd needed one, that her dad had never managed to sustain any kind of meaningful or long-term relationship.

But the text related to work was harder. From what the headhunter had said, the interview would almost be a formality. If she accepted that CFO job at a bigger firm with more responsibility, it would be a step up and give her experience she needed if she ever wanted to be a CEO. She should be flattered she'd been recommended by not one but two people in her professional network, and she was. Except, the job would involve more travel, even longer hours, possibly a move to Boston in the future and even less time for Ellie—and neither it nor the job she already had would allow her to live in Montana.

"We can't stay here, but I'll get you a dog when we're home." And she'd figure out dog daycare, training classes and everything else that went along with pet ownership as fast as she could.

"I don't want a dog from Chicago. I want this one." Ellie tucked the girl puppy into the folds of her hoodie. "And I want to call her Clementine."

"We don't even know if Bryce is looking for homes for these puppies." Beth hadn't used her work voice in so long it was almost a stranger's, but since she had to go back to the office in less than two weeks, she'd better get used to it.

"I bet he is." Ellie stood. "You don't know anything." Her voice stung like sleet in winter. "My mom would have let me have Clementine." She hugged the dog close. "So would my dad. You don't know what it's like to have no parents."

"I don't, and it must be horrible for you." But Beth knew what it was like to have parents you couldn't count on and who, when you thought you'd moved on, continued to disappoint you. "But since I'm the only one you've got, I have to make the best decisions for both of us. We have to go back to Chicago, and we'll look for a dog there." She'd talk to Shaundra at work. If Ellie truly wanted a beagle puppy, maybe they could get one from the same breeder Shaundra's dog had come from.

"I hate Chicago, and I hate you too." Ellie set the puppy in the straw and pulled open the stall door and slammed it behind her.

"Where are you going? Be careful, don't—" Beth stumbled to her feet.

"I'm going to feed the horses." Ellie jerked a hand toward the far end of the barn, where

Molly and one of the ranch hands had come in out of the rain. They were shaking water from their jackets and talking in high-pitched voices, their words indistinguishable above the rain drumming on the metal barn roof. "*They* like me."

"I don't only like you, I love you." Beth's voice cracked, but Ellie was gone.

Beth sank into the soft straw where all four puppies crawled into her lap, their warm bodies an antidote to the chill that enveloped her. She'd wanted to distract Ellie and make things better, but instead everything was much worse.

CHAPTER THIRTEEN

"WE GOT THE government agricultural grant money." Behind his desk in the barn office, Zach scrolled to the email on the computer screen and showed it to Beth. "Thanks to you."

"Not entirely." Beth's smile was strained. "I found the grant information, but you were the one who applied for it."

"With your help." Zach hugged her as she sat in a desk chair beside him. "I'd never have found that grant without your research, and you checked all the paperwork before I submitted the application too."

They made a good team. The thought skittered through Zach to lodge in a lump at the back of his throat. Beth and Ellie were only here for another week, and after they left his life would go back to the way it used to be. He could focus on the ranch, work on his house when he wanted to, sand and repaint his mom's front porch and only drop by the camp when they were short-staffed and needed him. His life would be his own again. He'd built that life after Dani dumped him, and it was a life he liked, so why did it now seem so empty?

"I'm glad I could help." Beth's words were stilted.

"We have to celebrate." Something was still off with Beth, but each time he tried to talk to her about it, she put him off. "Mom will likely want to have a big family dinner, but you and I should celebrate together too. My treat." His chest got heavy. Although neither of them would call it that, it would be more a goodbye meal than a celebration, one of the few times they'd have alone together before Beth and Ellie left.

"Okay."

"What's wrong?" Even with the good news about the grant, Beth seemed distracted, clicking a pen and staring out the window at the morning mist that hung over the fields.

"Nothing. What progress are you making on some of the other ideas we talked about?"

He got the message. She didn't want to

talk about herself. He wouldn't give up, though. "The animal sponsorship is a go. After she finishes college, one of the camp counselors wants to work in marketing and fundraising, so she's looking into that kind of sponsorship, as well as advertising opportunities, to use the ranch as a case study for her senior project."

"That's great." Beth clicked the pen again.

Anything that helped get Camp Crocus Hill and the ranch on a better financial footing was good news, and Beth had been a big part of that. Zach took a deep breath. "Something's sure up with you." He wasn't the best at sharing his feelings or even figuring out how he was feeling in the first place, but he needed to be able to trust Beth, and trust didn't come without talking. "Is it Ellie?"

"Sort of." Her shoulders hunched. "We had a big argument yesterday, and she's barely talked to me since."

"Have you tried talking to her?"

"Yes, but she's mad at me because I said we couldn't take one of the beagle puppies home with us." Beth brushed at her face.

"You saw them in the barn?"

"Yes." She grimaced. "They're so cute, and Ellie fell in love at first sight."

"Bryce left them there when he had to take the mom and two other little ones to the vet. He's looking for homes for them. There were six in the litter. The two that were at the vet are already spoken for, and my mom and Cole are taking one each, but that still leaves the last girl and boy. They'll be ready to be adopted in three or four weeks."

"Ellie wants the girl puppy. But even if the pups were ready to be adopted now, I can't drive to Chicago with Ellie and such a young dog." Beth's body folded in on itself. "And I can't..." She sniffed and grabbed a tissue from the box on Zach's desk.

"This is about more than Ellie and the puppy, isn't it?" If Ellie wanted the dog, he could ship it to her. He'd shipped cattle to Texas so there had to be a way to ship one small beagle pup to Chicago. Or he could take it to Chicago himself. Zach winced. He always tried to solve everyone's problems, but sometimes there were problems that couldn't be fixed.

Beth's chin jerked. "I have a lot of things going on. My dad's getting divorced again.

Usually, he only contacts me on my birthday and Christmas, but now, after not being in contact for months, he's texting multiple times a day. He wants me to find him a lawyer and pay for that legal advice because his latest business venture is in trouble. He also wants me to help make sure he gets visiting rights to see my half brother, who doesn't want anything to do with him. It's a mess."

"Are you going to help?"

"When it comes to recommending a lawyer, paying legal costs or a custody arrangement, no. Those are things he has to figure out himself." Beth's voice was firm, and Zach glimpsed what she must be like at work. Confident, in control and focused like she'd been with her ideas for the ranch—the kind of woman a man wanted to have on his side. "I'm worried about Alex, my half brother, though. He lives in Los Angeles, and I've only met him twice, but he's almost the same age I was when my folks split. I want to help him, but if I get in the middle of my dad and stepmother, I might make things worse."

"You won't know if you don't try." Zach studied Beth's bent head, her face half-hidden by a curtain of dark hair, today ironed straight like when she first arrived. "Why not text Alex or give him a call? The worst he can do is ignore you."

"You're right." Beth twirled a strand of hair around her fingers. "I remember how I felt when my dad left my mom and me. I also know what my dad's like. Alex might need a friend."

Like Beth had needed a friend but had been too scared to reach out to Zach. Only Jilly had been able to be there for her. Although regret punched Zach's chest, there was something else that Beth wasn't telling him. Like horses, Beth was good at hiding what was truly going on, but she was giving off enough subtle signs that if she'd been Scout or Daisy-May, he'd have had the vet on speed dial. Her eyes were dull, and she was quieter than usual like she'd retreated into herself. But most of all, his intuition told him that something else was bothering her.

"What do you think about taking a picnic for an early supper at the kissing bridge? This mist will soon clear so the weather should be great this afternoon, and I want to take you back there." With Dani, Zach had ignored his gut feeling until everything had imploded at the last minute. He wouldn't make that mistake again.

"That sounds fun." Beth's eyes brightened. "I could make those date squares and—"

"Nope." He shook his head. "It'll be my treat, so I'll take care of the picnic. All you need to do is show up at the horse barn around four thirty. We can ride out."

"What about Ellie?"

"Leave her to me." If Ellie wasn't already doing something at the camp, he could ask his mom or Molly to hang out with her. He had to get to the bottom of what was wrong with Beth so she wouldn't shut him out. If their feelings for each other were real, they had to be able to talk about real things, no matter how hard. And if they couldn't talk that way, well, that told him something important too.

SADDLE LEATHER CREAKED, and Beth held Daisy-May's reins loose as she rode beside Zach on Scout. As he'd predicted, the morning mist had cleared. Now, in late afternoon, it was a golden August day, ripe with the scents and sounds of this last month of summer. After leaving the barn, they'd ridden across the pasture and now meandered along the narrow, grassy path to the willow-shaded creek, the soft-red boards of the kissing bridge ahead in the distance.

She wanted to tell Zach the truth about the job she'd been invited to interview for, but how? Elizabeth had been headhunted for that job, not Beth. And Elizabeth in Chicago was a different person than Beth in Montana. Elizabeth wasn't the person Zach knew. She'd asked the headhunter for time to consider before fixing an interview date. If the interview was truly a formality, and she was the person the company wanted to hire, they'd wait until she returned to Chicago. At the moment, whether or not to take that job if it was offered to her was all Beth could think of. Before Jilly got sick, Beth would have jumped at a job like that, but almost without her noticing, her priorities had changed, despite the fear of disappointing the colleagues who'd recommended her.

"Here we are." Zach reined Scout to a stop near the bridge where willow branches dipped low over the slow-moving water.

Like Ellie, who was still giving Beth the silent treatment, Zach had barely spoken two words since they'd left the stable. While he'd always been someone she was comfortable being quiet with, this silence was different.

At work, Beth was confident, in charge, driven and decisive. But when it came to her own life, was she too ready to go along with what others wanted, instead of focusing on herself? When she'd stood up to Ellie about the puppy, it had all gone wrong, and although she'd told her dad she wouldn't help him, he hadn't stopped texting. And with each message, he tried to guilt her into doing what he wanted. She pressed her lips together. As the list of her worries got longer, she only got more confused, especially when it came to Zach, what she felt for him and what she was going to do about it.

"Do you need help getting down?" Zach tethered Scout to a post beyond the willow and came back to Beth carrying saddlebags.

"No, thanks. I was distracted." She slid off Daisy-May and led the horse to another post.

"You're looking more comfortable on horseback these days." As he eyed her up and down, the ever-present attraction sparked between them.

"I've had practice with Ellie. She has a

daily riding lesson, and afterward we usually go for a short ride." While she'd never be as comfortable on horseback as Zach, riding was another thing Beth would miss when she was back in Chicago. "Does your family picnic here often?" She took off her riding helmet, still conscious of his gaze.

"It's been our favorite spot since my great-grandparents' day. Hence the hitching posts." Zach took a red plaid picnic blanket out of one of the saddlebags and spread it on a grassy patch of shaded, flat ground. "Every two summers we have a family reunion here. Last time, we had almost two hundred people, even some of my dad's distant cousins from Wyoming and up in Canada came."

"It must be fun." As an only child, whose parents had come from small families, Beth could count her relatives on the fingers of both hands, and although she had several cousins, they were older and had never been close. She joined Zach at the picnic spot and smoothed her hair.

"Did you get in touch with Alex?" He took food containers out of the other saddlebag and gave them to Beth, his movements quick and efficient.

"Yes." Warmth bloomed in her chest. "I texted and then called him earlier. We talked for half an hour. He's a good kid." Although she wished she'd reached out to her half brother before, maybe now Beth had a chance to have a real relationship with him. "I told Alex he can call me whenever he wants, or if he needs math help. He'll be a freshman in high school this year, and math isn't his favorite subject." Except, it was about more than math help. Beth understood what it was like to be caught between warring parents, and if she could help Alex get through that, she wanted to.

"Good for you." Zach eyed her over a container of potato salad. "I'm proud of you."

"Thanks." Some of the tightness in her chest eased. "I'm proud of me too. When my dad finds out I'm talking to Alex instead of him, he'll be mad, but that's his problem." Despite the argument with Ellie, standing up for herself in her personal life could be good.

Zach gave her a fist bump, and her knuckles tingled. "What do you want?" He gestured to the food spread around them.

"Everything looks great." Beth took a soda and pulled on the metal tab. Zach wore his usual well-worn jeans with a pale blue Western snap shirt, and he'd left his hat on the edge of the blanket, crown down. His hair caught the light that filtered through the tree, and golden strands glinted in the brown. "How did you put this picnic together so fast, and how did you get all these things into only two saddlebags?"

"I called in a picnic order to the Blucbunch Café and picked it up when I went into town to get wire to fix a cattle pen. As for only two saddlebags, it's like that carpet bag in *Mary Poppins*. Magic."

Although Beth laughed at his teasing, she felt a special connection again when she took the picnic plate he held out and her hand brushed his tanned forearm. "You were there when Ellic watched that movie with Bryce's kids."

He laughed too, smile lines crinkling around his clean-shaven face. "Lots of companies make saddlebags to hold picnics. We have some for the camp, so I borrowed from their stash."

"Very handy." Beth sat cross-legged on the blanket and filled her plate. "Thank you." She couldn't remember the last time a guy had done something so kind and thoughtful for her. It was easy to make a restaurant reservation or buy a bottle of wine or a bunch of flowers, but this picnic was so sweet it tugged at her heart in a way that was new.

"I hope I got the things you like. I asked Kristi at the café about your favorites."

"I've eaten at the Bluebunch so often this summer that Kristi knows me well." And the café owner had become a new friend Beth would keep in touch with. She eyed the picnic spread, a selection of the café's pressed Italian sandwiches, several deli salads, a fruit cup, a cheese board with New York–style soft pretzels and, to finish, Kristi's frosted lemon sugar cookies and s'more crumb bars. "These are all my favorites. It's wonderful."

"So are you." Zach took a sandwich and stared at the creek, his expression unreadable. "Without your help, I don't know what I'd have done about the ranch. You gave me new ideas, and now, with that grant money, we have a fresh start. Have you thought about becoming a business consultant? You could have charged a lot of money for the advice you gave me."

Beth moved a pretzel from one side of her

plate to the other. "No money could compensate for what Camp Crocus Hill has done for Ellie and me, so I wouldn't think of charging you." Besides, she'd wanted to help, and after years of working for a technology company, it had been surprisingly interesting to apply her skills in a different sector. "As for consulting, I'm happier working inside a company." Or was she?

"If that suits you, okay, but you're great at what you do. I hope you recognize that."

Did she? Beth chewed on the pretzel, tasteless now. And what did she want to do? "Tell me more about the ranch and your plans."

"You're really interested?" Zach raised an eyebrow over his can of soda.

"Of course." She wanted to know more about Zach's work. Not only from a business perspective but also his life and what had made him the man he was.

"I want to know more about your work too." He gave her a teasing grin. "As well as your condo, that sporty car you zip around in and the famous Chicago pizza you order most Friday nights."

"Ellie told you?" She leaned forward and

her heartbeat sped up. He was interested in her life too.

"Yep." His smile widened. "She might not say so, but Ellie loves you. She respects the rules you set for her too, even though she sometimes fights against them."

"Like with the puppy?"

"I didn't say anything to her, but if Ellie wants that puppy, and you're okay with it, I can ship the dog to you."

"That would be nice, but I don't want Ellie to think she's gotten her way simply because she demanded it. She's desperate to have that dog, though."

"You could also make her work for it." Zach gave Beth a sideways look. "My folks used to do that with chores. Among other things, it taught me responsibility."

"Thanks." Beth had a lot to learn about being a parent, but maybe everyone did, not only people whose families were as messed up as hers. "What do you want to know about my job and Chicago?"

"Whatever you want to tell me."

And because Zach was truly interested, as they ate she told him funny stories about work, deep-dish pizza from Mr. and Mrs.

De Luca's family restaurant in her neighborhood, the car she'd saved up to buy and her favorite painting at the Art Institute.

As the early evening shadows lengthened across the creek, he told her how he worried about the ranch, his mom living mostly on her own, and what his life playing hockey in Germany had been like.

"Do you miss hockey?" Beth brushed cookie crumbs off her leggings.

"Sometimes." He leaned back on his elbows. "But then I remember that I got to follow my dream for a while, and now I'm following another one. Life might not have happened like I planned, and I miss my dad and Paul, but life can still be good. What about you?"

"What do you mean?" She packed up the picnic detritus, putting lids on containers and folding fabric napkins. Zach had given her an opening, and it was up to her to take it.

"Where do you want to go in life from here? From the sounds of it, you've got a great career."

"Yeah." Life hadn't happened like she'd planned either, but she'd made the best of it, and she'd do the best she could for Ellie. "I have to tell you something."

He stilled, holding a saddlebag. "What?"

Above the bank where they sat, the wooden bridge rattled as several men on horseback clattered across it. They fanned out on the other side of the creek, and red-brown dust billowed in their wake.

Zach sprang to his feet. "The neighbor's cattle must have gotten through a fence. I have to—"

"Go." Beth waved him away. "I'll finish packing up and ride Daisy-May back to the barn. It's not too far."

"You're sure?" Zach had grabbed his hat and was already halfway to where he'd left Scout tied.

"Of course. There's still plenty of daylight left, and I know the way. Daisy-May does too."

"Thanks." Zach blew her a kiss. "I'll make it up to you. I have to bring you back to the kissing bridge like I promised."

"Sure." Beth put the picnic supplies in the saddlebags. She might not have been saved by the bell, but she'd sure been saved by the cattle. Except, at what cost? Once she told

Zach about that job, she'd be Elizabeth again and maybe not the kind of woman he'd want to take to the kissing bridge—or anywhere else.

CHAPTER FOURTEEN

"DOES EVERYONE HAVE their time capsule?" The museum guide, a white-haired woman in her seventies who'd taught fourth grade to Zach and his siblings, gathered the tour group from Camp Crocus Hill near the gift shop.

Although Zach had visited this natural history museum many times before, seeing it with Ellie and the other campers had made the experience both different and new. It had also reminded him it had been too long since he'd taken Saturday, or any other afternoon, off from ranch work.

As the kids clustered around the guide and camp counselors, Beth joined Zach where he stood in a small, flower-filled courtyard outside the museum's glass entrance doors. "If I didn't say so before, it was good of you to step in and drive the bus. You must have had other things to do this afternoon."

"They could wait." Besides, after having to cut out on their picnic to help round up those cattle, he wanted to take every chance he had to spend time with Beth and Ellie. "I didn't want the kids to be disappointed they couldn't go on the museum field trip because the bus driver got sick."

"Well, thank you." Beth gave him a dimpled smile. "I thought Ellie might be a bit too grown-up for such a small museum, but the displays the guide spoke about were a hit, especially the dinosaur ghost story. I remember that one from when I was here."

"That story's been around since my dad was a kid, maybe even earlier. An older cousin told it to Paul and me when we were little and scared us half to death. We insisted on sleeping with the bedroom light on for weeks afterward." Now, perhaps because of talking about his brother to Beth, he could remember the fun times they'd shared too and not only how sick Paul had been at the end. "You don't want to go to the gift shop, Ellie?" He turned as the museum doors slid open, and she rolled her wheelchair to a stop beside Beth in the shade.

"I already went." She grinned and waved a paper bag. "Here. I got something for you."

"You did?" Zach took the bag. "You already gave me a super birthday present at our party. That cowboy tumbler with my name on it is amazing. I'll think of you each time I use it." And he'd miss her too.

Ellie's face went pink. "I wanted to get you something else. Open it. I chose it, but Beth helped me buy it."

"Okay." He glanced at Beth, who seemed to be trying to hold back a smile.

"It's…" Zach's throat worked "…perfect." He cradled the soft green dinosaur in the palm of his hand and smiled at the chocolate bar from High Valley Treats with it.

"I knew you'd like it because you love chocolate and you showed me and Lily dinosaur fossils the first day I was here. See?" Ellie fiddled with the toy. "It has a place to hold your phone so you don't lose it when you're working in the barn. Your mom says you always lose it there."

"I do." The gift was so simple and yet so thoughtful, Zach truly appreciated the gesture. "Thank you, Ellie." His gaze slid to Beth. "And thank you too."

"You're welcome." Beth's voice was low.

"Along with a list of my favorite things, I put a drawing of those fossils in my time capsule." Ellie showed him the paper tube on her lap. "When I get back to camp, I'll add one of the beads Mrs. Rosa gave me, a postcard and some other stuff."

"That sounds good." Zach nodded.

"When Beth gets her new job, I want to go to Hawaii for spring break. Maybe I could get shells there, and—"

"What new job?" Zach stared at Beth over Ellie's head.

"Nothing has been decided yet." Beth's face flushed. "Ellie, you shouldn't eavesdrop."

"I didn't. You weren't exactly talking quietly on your phone yesterday."

"Even so, you shouldn't…" Beth drew in a breath and focused on Zach. "I meant to tell you, but you had to go after the cattle, and it got late and… A headhunter contacted me a few days ago. I've been recruited for a new job, but it's contingent on an interview."

"I bet you'll get it," Ellie said. "Two people recommended Beth, and she said jobs with that company and salary don't come around often. I want to stay in Montana, but Beth said we couldn't, which is totally unfair. I'm going to come back here to live as soon as I'm old enough, though. I can go to college where Molly does and work at the ranch during vacations."

"I see." Why wouldn't Beth have told him about the job right away? It wasn't as if her going back to Chicago was a surprise, but if this job was as important as Ellie made out, why the secrecy? "Congratulations." He made himself smile. "It sounds exciting."

"It is, but I haven't even decided if I want to interview yet. Ellie got ahead of herself." Beth fiddled with her phone case.

"Is the job still in Chicago?"

"To start with, but after a year they might need someone in Boston."

Which was even farther away from Montana than Chicago. "If you want the job, I hope you get it."

"Really?" Beth's expression got tight.

"Sure, if it's such a good opportunity you wouldn't want to pass it up." *Liar.* It wasn't like he could ask Beth to stay here. Although Zach's chest was in a vise, he pushed the words out. "You're smart and dedicated. It's not surprising people recognize that." He was a fool to have talked to her about consulting work when she must have her career sights set much higher.

"Do you want your picture taken?" The female voice was perky and had a pronounced Southern drawl. "When our kids were young, we could never get a photo of us all together. I'd be happy to help y'all out."

"What?" Beth half turned.

"Your phone." The woman, in her fifties, had shoulder-length blond hair, bright blue eyes, and with cropped jeans wore a white T-shirt with *University of Alabama Mom* in red lettering. "I have the same phone. It wouldn't be a bit of trouble."

"I…" Beth darted a glance at Zach.

"Such a fine-looking family. You two get on either side of your precious daughter. With those big brown eyes and gorgeous face, she could be a model." Somehow the woman had Beth's phone and was directing the three of them into position, zeroing in on Ellie.

Ellie winked and nudged Zach's arm. "Thank you." She gave the woman a wide smile. "I'll frame this picture and put it on a shelf in my bedroom."

"Ellie." Beth's voice came out in an anguished squeak.

"That's a great idea, honey." The woman pointed Beth's phone at them. "You need to treasure family photos."

"We're not—" Beth stopped.

"Smile." The woman moved closer. "Lean more toward your daddy, Ellie. That's such a pretty name. I had an Aunt Eleanor, but you don't hear that name so often these days."

"Thank you." Beth retrieved her phone.

"My pleasure." The woman patted Beth's hand. "Family is everything, isn't it? My three boys are grown, but I still say to them that they can be rich in money, but if they don't have a family, they'll be poor in the end. Y'all have a good day now." With a little wave, she bustled back to a distinguished man with steel-gray hair, who waited for her near the museum's ticket booth.

"I'm sorry. I couldn't seem to stop her." Beth smoothed her already smooth hair.

"It's fine." Zach scrubbed a hand across his face.

"That lady was nice." Ellie looked up at him. "I wish we could be a real family."

"Ellie, we're already a family. You and me." Beth stuck her phone in her bag and avoided Zach's gaze.

"I still—"

"It's okay." Zach patted Ellie's shoulder as his belly knotted. "You and Beth can be an adopted part of my family, like Kate and Lily. What do you think?"

"I guess." Ellie studied him, her brown eyes shadowed. "But can we still be part of your family if we don't live here?"

"Of course you can." His mouth went dry. "Geography doesn't mean anything to true family. We'll always keep in touch."

Geography made a difference to a lot of things, though, like him and Beth.

"Zach's right." Beth's voice was tight, and her smile forced. "You and your mom were the family I chose, and we're closer than a lot of people who are family by birth. As for geography, we'll come back and visit too." She glanced inside the museum. "Here's the rest of the group. We need to get back to the bus."

As she and Ellie turned away, Zach fumbled in his pocket for the bus keys with the dinosaur toy and chocolate bar Ellie had given him in his other hand.

Although he'd tried to fight his feelings, he loved Beth and Ellie. Beth hadn't seemed as excited about that new job as he'd have expected, so maybe her career wasn't as important to her as he thought. If it wasn't, what would it mean for him to let himself think about being a real family with her and Ellie? A family he never had to say goodbye to.

"THIS IS ZACH on his first day of school. He was so proud of his little cowboy boots." In the spacious family room at the ranch house, Joy sat beside Beth on a comfy beige sofa piled with cheery red-and-white gingham throw pillows and pointed to the photo in the old album.

Beth fixed her face into a polite smile. Being invited to a Sunday buffet lunch with the entire Carter family wasn't a big deal. Kate and Lily were here too, as were the ranch hands. Yet, being with Zach in his family's home was also somehow significant, as if she and Ellie had indeed been adopted, like Zach had said at the museum yesterday.

Beth had never been surrounded by so much family, biological or chosen, or had this kind of family meal before. Previously, a *table groaning with food* was only a figure of speech, but Joy's buffet had proven to Beth that such a thing existed.

"He was cute." From Joy's other side, Ellie studied the picture of Zach. "Is that his horse?" She pointed to a brown pony beside him.

"Yes, Zach wanted to take Billy Bob to school. When he couldn't, he cried all the way to the end of the lane until the bus picked him up." Joy's smile was infectious. "He didn't believe me when I said Billy Bob would be in the field waiting for him when he came home."

"How many more embarrassing stories are you going to tell about me?" Zach sat on the arm of the sofa beside Beth.

"That's not embarrassing, it's sweet." Joy reached around Beth to pat Zach's arm. "You were such a sensitive little boy. You always thought of others. I never had to teach you to be kind and compassionate. That's who you were and still are."

"Mom." He shook his head and made an annoyed face.

"What? Kindness is a virtue. Each little drop of kindness adds up to become a bucket full of goodness." Joy turned back to Beth. "Zach will make a wonderful dad. He was so good with his brothers and sister." Her voice quavered as she pointed to a group photo of the kids, Zach's arm around Paul's shoulders.

"Paul's death must have been so hard." Parents weren't supposed to outlive their kids, but parents weren't supposed to die when their children were still young either. Beth glanced at Ellie, who helped Bryce's daughter, Paisley, dress a baby doll. "I can't imagine what that time was like."

Zach stiffened, but his face was impassive.

"It was terrible, but I try to focus on the good years we had Paul and not how he died. He was a blessing in all our lives, and in some ways, his death taught me how to live." Joy brushed at her face and hugged Ellie. "That's what your mom would want for you, Ellie. Jilly was the happiest girl, always smiling and laughing. She went at life full tilt and never wasted a moment. Even though she's gone, she'd want you to live your life to the fullest."

"You think so?" Ellie's voice trembled.

"I'm sure of it." His mom took another photo album from the stack she'd pulled off the shelf earlier.

"I found this picture last week and wanted to show it to you." She flipped through the plastic-covered pages. "See?"

"It's Jilly and me. Zach too." Beth drew in a soft breath. "I remember that day."

Over time, the picture had faded, the colors now muted instead of sharp, but Beth's memories of that day had never dimmed. The three of them had been in the camp stables. While Zach cleaned out stalls, Beth and Jilly had fooled around, singing pop songs and eating chocolate Jilly had bought the last time they'd gone into town. When Zach's mom had come with the packed supper he'd forgotten, she'd taken a picture and told Zach to get back to work. But while Jilly had gone to play tennis, Beth had stayed with Zach and helped him until the chores were done. Afterward, they'd climbed the ladder to the hayloft to eat the last of Jilly's chocolate and talk. And there in the clean straw, afternoon sunlight filtering through the gaps in the weathered barn boards, he'd kissed her for the first time.

"Your mom and Beth were so pretty." Joy traced the plastic-covered image. "Like you, Ellie. Looking back now—" She stopped. "Those were happy times."

"They were." Beth's voice caught. "Could I make a copy of that picture? It would be nice for Ellie to have." It would be nice for her to have too, a tangible reminder of that special day etched in her memory.

"Sure." Joy slid it out of the slot. "I'll put it aside, and you can take a picture or scan it before you leave."

"How old was my mom then?" Ellie's tone was reverent.

"Almost sixteen. So about three years older than you are now." Beth held the photo by its corners. "I was almost sixteen too." And Zach had just turned seventeen. Unlike her, he'd kissed girls before, but she'd never kissed a boy and had worried she'd done it wrong. He'd laughed and told her she was great, but maybe they should practice some more, so they had. Although she'd kissed her fair share of guys since, none of them had ever kissed her like Zach did—then or now.

"I want to show you photos of my wedding and Zach as a baby." Joy pulled out more albums. "Apart from when my kids were born, my wedding was the happiest day of my life. I didn't think it was possible to be so happy. My childhood sweetheart was my forever love."

Joy was lucky. Not many people married their childhood sweetheart and lived happily ever after until death parted them.

"Zach is the image of his father. Here they are at Zach's college graduation."

Beth looked at the photo Joy pointed to and many more. Pages of pictures documenting a happy family life: Christmas, Easter, Thanksgiving, birthdays and sporting events, year after year. Ranch life too with photos of horses, cattle and even a few chickens.

When Joy reached the last album, Ellie was building a farm out of wooden blocks with Bryce's kids and Lily, and except for Zach, Molly and Cole, who sat on the other side of the room watching a rodeo event on the flat-screen TV, everyone else had gathered around the dining room table to play Monopoly.

"You have a lovely family." Beth hoped her expression didn't betray the fact that her own family experiences had been so different.

"Thank you. I'm proud of them, but I'm sorry if I talked your ears off." Joy's laugh was embarrassed. "I didn't realize it had gotten so late. It'll soon be time for evening chores."

"It's fine." All of a sudden it was. Although it hurt to see such a happy family, it also gave Beth hope. The Carters weren't perfect, and they'd had sorrows along with joys, but they loved and cared for each other and had helped make Zach the fine man he was.

"You and Ellie are a family, and I'm sure you'll have a husband and other children someday." Joy's smile was warm.

"I...don't..." Could Joy read Beth's thoughts?

"You want children of your own, don't you?"

"Yes." But wanting children and being scared to have them were very different propositions. However, since Ellie had come into Beth's life, she'd begun to figure out the mom thing. Maybe there was no such thing as a perfect mom, only mothers doing the best they could, even her own.

"In some ways, I envy you."

"Why?" Beth looked at Joy in astonishment.

"You went to college and have a career. I never did that. Although I'm happy with my choices, part of me regrets not having much of my own life before I became a wife and mother."

"You could go to college now and take classes online or locally, part-time. It's not too late."

"That's what Rosa says, but I'm not sure." Joy shook her head. "You're only as old as you think you are, but wouldn't it be silly to try for a college degree at my age?"

"Never." Beth made her voice firm. "With college or whatever else you want, you should go for it."

And maybe she should take her own advice. Zach's gaze locked with Beth's. If she had a child, she wouldn't be on her own. And if she had a man like Zach by her side with a family like this one, she'd have all the love and encouragement she'd need.

When it came down to it, trusting in love and family was about the right time and the right man. And maybe, like Joy, if she was lucky, a first love could be a forever one.

CHAPTER FIFTEEN

"I'M GLAD YOU could ride out with me today."
On Scout's back, Zach smiled at Beth and
gestured to the panorama in front of them—
the golden-green fields dotted with red-and-
white cattle, and the distant mountains a
blue-gray ribbon against the misty horizon
and undulating terrain. "From the top of this
hill, it's Carter land as far as we can see."
The family legacy his dad had entrusted him
and his brothers to maintain.

"It's beautiful. Some of the pictures your
mom showed me after lunch yesterday must
have been taken from here." Beside him on
Daisy-May, Beth sat relaxed in the saddle.

"My folks came out here a lot. A cabin a
mile or so to the east was their special place."
A place that, as far as Zach knew, his mom
hadn't been to since his dad passed. "I'm
sorry about Mom monopolizing you with
those photo albums and family stories." His

mom might as well have put Zach's history on an online dating site the way she'd thrown him and Beth together.

"Don't be." Beth grinned. "Your mom's proud of her family, and rightly so. Besides, you were cute when you were little."

"Only when I was little?" He moved closer and snagged one of Beth's hands.

"No." She leaned over and gave him a quick kiss."

He cupped her jaw and pulled her closer, fitting his mouth to hers. Kissing Beth was the best, but between the ranch, the camp and Ellie, they were rarely alone long enough for him to do it.

"You're even cuter now." She drew back, her face a pretty pink. "And you're a great kisser. Happy?"

"With you? Always." Except, although they hadn't talked more about Beth's job opportunity and why she hadn't told him her big news soon after the headhunter called, it hovered between them.

"Me too." Beth smiled before her expression clouded. "Ellie was disappointed not to come with us, but she was so interested in that art workshop with Rosa, she couldn't say no."

Although Zach liked spending time with Ellie, he was enjoying this time alone with Beth. He wanted a chance to test the new feelings he had for her. The new and unexpected love which felt so right. Yet, maybe it wasn't new at all. Maybe that love had always been there and this summer had helped old feelings deepen.

"To be honest, it's too far for Ellie to ride all the way out here and back. She needs to pace herself on horseback. Besides, she loves Rosa, and she'll love the art workshop."

"True." Beth squeezed Zach's hand. "When I told Ellie that we could only adopt the puppy if she could prove to me she was responsible enough to have a dog, she came up with a list of things we'll need and has researched the best vets in our area. Thank you for suggesting she put effort into working for the puppy."

Zach nodded. "Ellie's had a tough time, but she's a good kid. That puppy might bring her out of her shell more."

"It's not *puppy*, it's *Clementine*." Beth chuckled and moved away as Daisy-May pawed the ground. "I don't know where Ellie got the name Clementine, but it's stuck. It's going to be a long month until Clementine is old enough to travel to Chicago. I'm grateful to you for figuring out how to ship her to us."

Zach's skin chilled. It would be an especially long month without Beth unless he figured out a way to tell her how he felt before she left. Now that she had Ellie, maybe she wouldn't want a child of her own. She'd been sympathetic when his mom had shown her pictures of Paul, so possibly she'd understand where Zach was coming from.

"While Ellie waits for Clementine, I promised to send daily pictures. We can set up video calls as well." Zach stiffened as Scout raised his head and swished his tail. "What is it, boy?"

"Is something wrong?" Beth straightened in her saddle.

"It looks like there's bad weather coming." Zach patted Scout's withers and studied the dark clouds massing above the mountains.

"Apart from that one day of rain, it's been beautiful the entire time we've been here. Sunny and warm but not too hot." Beth's voice shook as heat lightning flashed in the distance.

"Summer *is* beautiful here, but..." Zach studied the sky again. He'd checked the weather before they left, and a storm hadn't been forecast until early evening. He'd thought they'd be okay to head out, but he'd been wrong. "Sometimes things can change fast." He wheeled Scout around and gestured to Beth to follow with Daisy-May. "We should be able to outrun it." If he'd been on his own with Scout he could have, but Daisy-May didn't have Scout's speed, and Beth didn't have Zach's skill on horseback. Today was also the first time she'd ridden so far from the camp.

"If we don't?" Beth kept pace with him as the two horses trotted into a gully. "This isn't the way we came."

"The ground is lower here, and it's a quicker route back. We also have a better chance of finding shelter." But the ground was more uneven too. Zach glanced at Beth from under the brim of his hat. "We'll be fine." He glanced at the sky again, the dark clouds closer now. Lightning danced, and thunder rumbled in the distance.

"Okay." Beth adjusted her riding helmet. "Lead the way."

"First we need to cross the creek. Although it's water, it's lower, so it's safer than riding along the ridge." He pointed to the narrow strip of water in front of them at the base of the gully. Like the creek near the camp, it was another tributary of the river that spilled from the mountains. "The creek bed is rocky, but Daisy-May is steady on her feet." Although, unlike Scout, the mare was sensitive to storms.

"Okay." Beth set her mouth in a firm line and spoke softly to her horse.

"Right, here we go." He led Scout into the shallow water, the horse sturdy beneath him. "Good boy." He glanced over his shoulder as Beth and Daisy-May followed. "Almost there." Zach leaned low in the saddle as Scout scrambled up the creek bank.

"You can do it, Daisy-May." Beth continued to talk to the quivering horse as they edged across the creek. The wind rose and slapped water against protruding rocks.

"Come on, girl." From the bank, he encouraged both the horse and Beth. "There you go." He slid off Scout to grab Daisy-May's bridle and lead her up the bank. Atop the horse, Beth's brown eyes were huge in her pale face.

"Which way now?" Her hands were tight on the reins, and she shivered in the hot wind that buffeted them.

"Up and over the hill." He pointed ahead of them and swung back into the saddle and rubbed Scout's shoulder. "We'll have to keep the horses to a walk until we get to grassland again."

"Okay." Her voice shook as lightning lit the purple-gray sky and thunder cracked, closer now.

"You're doing great." Zach gave her an encouraging smile. "If we have to, we can shelter in my folks' cabin. It's not far." Except, they'd have to cross open grassland to reach it, and if the storm came closer as fast as it had blown up... He swallowed hard. "Stay near me, and hold Daisy-May to a walk."

Beth nodded.

"Okay, boy. You know what to do." Zach kept his voice calm and guided Scout across the rocky terrain, the sound of Beth and Daisy-May behind him muffled by the wind that whipped up dust and cried like a child in pain. Like Paul. Zach pushed the thought away.

"How much farther to the cabin?"

At the top of the rise, Zach turned at Beth's faint voice. "Across the field and the other side of the next hill." Hot air swirled around them as Zach scanned the mass of towering, greenish-tinged clouds. "Be sure to stay away from the barbed wire fence line. It can conduct electricity and make you more vulnerable to a lightning strike."

"You sound like a Boy Scout." Beth's smile was grim.

"I was one." He'd helped with a few Boy Scout camping trips too but never in weather like this. "There's no place to shelter before the cabin so we need to head across the field in a diagonal direction. The cabin is in a hollow beyond it in a stand of trees. Ready?"

Daisy-May snorted, tossed her head, reared and pawed the ground.

"What's wrong with her?" Beth hung on to the reins and saddle horn to keep her seat.

"She's scared." Zach glanced at the sky again. They didn't have any time to lose. "Here." He jumped off Scout and steadied Daisy-May. "Get behind me." He'd have to ride Scout and lead Daisy-May and trust in the horses to trust him and remember their training.

"On Scout?" Beth already had her feet out of the stirrups.

"I won't let you fall." He settled Beth on Scout's back. Then, holding both horses in check, Zach clambered in front of Beth as she locked her arms around his waist. "Hold on tight." He calculated the distance across the field and urged Scout forward, all the while talking to both horses as Beth clung to him.

They reached the far edge of the field as lightning sizzled around them. The roof of the cabin peeked out from the trees at the bottom of the hill.

Thunder crashed as he drew Scout along the hilly, rock-gouged track. Zach's muscles strained to hold both horses as the cabin came closer through the patch of trees, their branches meeting overhead.

"I can't..." Beth's voice wobbled.

"Yes, you can. Hang on. Only a few more minutes." As they reached the compact log cabin, there was a sulfur smell, lightning sizzled, and a clap of thunder shook the ground. Both horses cried out and stood still. Zach dismounted, tied the horses to the rings on the covered porch, and lifted Beth out of the saddle.

She stood frozen in place. "Beth." He pulled on her arm as lightning illuminated the small clearing, wood cracked, and thunder roared. With Zach following right behind her, Beth sprinted onto the porch just before a pine tree swayed and then came down, narrowly missing both the horses and cabin roof.

"Hold on." Instinctively, he tried the door handle first as the wind shrieked and the trees almost bent double. *Sorry, Dad.* He mouthed the words as he kicked in the locked door. "Hurry. Get inside." He half pushed Beth through the open doorway. "I have to see to the horses. There's a stable out back."

He left Beth then and went back out into the storm to soothe the terrified horses and lead them to the stable.

Lightning split the sky in tandem with a barrage of thunder. Zach's stomach knotted as wind whipped the tree branches into a frenzy. "Almost there." He grabbed for his hat, and as he reached the stable, another tree came down, its branches brushing the stable wall. He turned and glimpsed Beth's frightened face framed by one of the cabin's small windows.

He pushed open the unlocked stable door, the horses almost knocking him over in their haste to get to shelter. "Here you go, boy. You too, Daisy-May." He settled the horses in the two stalls, the familiar activity soothing them and him.

He'd almost forgotten that Beth was a city girl, but the storm had sure reminded him. Although Montana was fun for a vacation, he worried that she could never truly come to terms with life in a wild place like this. Thunder cracked again, and rain arrived in a gray cloud to envelop the small clearing. The backs of Zach's eyes burned, and he buried his face against Scout's warm side. He'd already made a fool of himself once and learned a lesson in front of the whole town. He wouldn't make the same mistake twice.

RAIN DRILLED AGAINST the tin roof of the log-beamed cabin, and an oil lamp cast a golden light across the wooden floor topped with colorful scatter rugs. Wrapped in a forest-green afghan, Beth sat on the striped sofa and cradled a mug of instant coffee.

"No tea, but at least there's water to boil, and I found a few cans of stuff we can cook if the weather doesn't clear soon." Zach shut one of the cookstove's doors with a clang and picked up a toolbox.

"It's fine." Beth drew in a shuddery breath. He must think her an idiot to have been so scared. "Thank you for everything. I've never experienced a storm like that."

"It was a bad one." He carried the toolbox to the door he'd had to break down and used a screwdriver on the bolts. "We're lucky it's raining, though."

"Why?" She stared at the back of his head, his hair flat on top from where his hat had been and tousled and damp on the ends.

"Dry thunderstorms, the kind where it doesn't rain, can spark wildfires. They're a big hazard here."

"Oh." She glanced at their phones on the rustic coffee table in front of the sofa. "We still don't have cell service. What if Ellie needs me?"

Zach turned and gave her a half smile as he indicated the battery-powered wall clock in the small kitchen area. "Ellie will still be in town at Rosa's studio, along with several camp counselors and a bunch of other kids. She'll be fine. She's probably having too much fun to miss you."

"That's supposed to make me feel better?" Beth huddled in the afghan, her body still chilled.

"Yes, because you're doing a great job of helping Ellie be independent." Zach set aside his tools and came to sit beside Beth on the sofa. "It's okay. She's safe, and we are too."

"We almost weren't. When those trees came down…" Beth buried her face in Zach's warm chest as his arms encircled her. "I was terrified, and you protected us, but you could have…"

"I didn't." He stroked her hair, his touch soothing. "Don't think about what could have happened. Besides, those trees will give us firewood for winter once my brothers and I get out here with chain saws. It's part of the cycle of life."

She knew what he said was true, but still, she felt the fear deep down. "The day my dad left my mom and me, there was a big storm. I've always been scared of storms, and Dad would comfort me. He'd make jokes or tell me stories, but that time he walked out the front door and never looked back." The steady thump of Zach's heart against her ear gave Beth the courage to continue. "Since then, whenever there's a storm, I remember that day and how my world ended. Silly, right?"

"Not at all." He rubbed her back until the rain lessened, and Beth relaxed again.

"Your shirt hadn't dried from the rain, and now I've gotten it even wetter." She fumbled for a tissue from a box on the coffee table.

"It's fine." His voice was soft and gentle.

"Thanks for listening to me. It feels better to get that out." Surprisingly, it did. The storm had sparked things she'd buried but had needed to share. She picked up her mug of tepid coffee, dark sludge in the bottom.

"That looks awful." He patted her shoulder. "I just remembered something better."

"What?"

He got up and went to a cupboard in the kitchen, opened it and came back to her hiding something behind his back. "Close your eyes, and hold out your hands."

Beth did as he asked, and something heavy dropped into her palms.

"Open."

"Milk chocolate with almonds from High Valley Treats." She glanced at the bar and back at him. "My favorite."

"Cole's too. He and I rode out to check the cabin for Mom last month. I brought chocolate and left a few bars here because we planned to come back." Zach's smile widened, tenderness, teasing and something that looked a lot like love all mixed together. "Dig in. The sugar should help you feel better too."

"Trust you to have chocolate for any occasion. Thank you." She tried to smile back as she tore open the packaging. *Love*. She glanced at Zach as the emotion slid through her to lodge near her heart, and her hands shook.

"Here, you're still upset." Zach took the package and broke off several squares.

She took a piece of chocolate and popped it into her mouth, the sweet, rich taste exploding against her tongue.

Love. She tested the word under her breath. She loved Zach. It wasn't a crush. It was real.

When he'd pulled her against him to protect her from the falling tree and even before that, he'd thought of her before himself. He was a man she could count on for always. The kind she hadn't thought existed. Beth took another chocolate square and stared into Zach's face and gentle blue eyes—the man she wanted beside her for the rest of her life.

"Your color's coming back." His tense expression eased. "The rain has almost stopped too. Most of that water is from the trees." He gestured to the roof where raindrops pattered in a soft, infrequent staccato. "Once I fix the door as much as I can for now, we can head back. You'll be at the camp in time for supper with Ellie."

"Great."

That new job didn't matter. Even her current job wasn't as important as it once was. She could find work here, maybe even consulting like Zach had suggested to give her the flexibility she needed for Ellie. Excitement stirred at the thought of other possibilities.

"Are you sure you're okay?" Zach moved away from the sofa to the toolbox.

"Yes, never better." Beth ate the last piece

of chocolate and gave him a wide smile. Zach already loved Ellie, but could he love her too?

There was only one way to find out. Beth had to tell him how she felt before she and Ellie left Montana. That she wanted the three of them to make a family and future together, for always.

OUTSIDE THE MAIN BARN, Zach rested his forearms on the top rail of the pasture fence. The first stars glimmered in the evening sky, and a crescent moon nudged the western horizon. The air was infused with sweet scents of clover and damp grass, and a light breeze ruffled his hair.

The afternoon storm had rolled away almost as quickly as it had come. Apart from a strip of shingles the wind had torn off the hen house roof, everything was the same as it had been before.

Storms were part of life here. He accepted and respected them as a reminder of nature's power. Yet, unlike Beth, even as a child, he'd never feared them. Her terror today had reminded him that despite their similarities, they were still much different. Maybe too different. Even when they'd reached the shelter of the cabin, and although she'd tried to hide it, Beth was still shaken. And when they'd finally made it back to the ranch, leading the horses around fallen tree branches and a place where the creek had burst its banks, she'd hugged Ellie tight as if she'd been afraid she was never going to see her again.

"I thought you'd gone home over an hour ago." Molly joined Zach by the fence. Her curly blond hair was in a messy ponytail, and she wore old jeans and a plaid work shirt with a pair of brown cowboy boots.

Zach shrugged. "I decided to stop by the office to take care of a few things." Except he was restless. He couldn't focus on work and the prospect of going home to an empty house held even less appeal. "It's sure a pretty night."

"It is. You wouldn't guess the weather had been so bad earlier. Although I'm excited about going back to college, I miss the ranch when I'm in Bozeman. Especially this kind of sky." Molly tilted her head to the stars too. "Remember when Dad brought us all out into this pasture to look for a meteor shower?"

"I sure do. We didn't see any meteors, but Dad showed us stars and constellations instead." Zach smiled at the memory. "You were real little. Cole and I lifted you up to sit on top of this fence and we each held one of your arms so you wouldn't fall off."

Molly chuckled. "In this family, I'll still be *real little* when I'm forty."

"True." Zach laughed with his sister. Although Molly was the baby of the family, he needed to start treating her like a grown woman. "Dad would be proud of you. A college senior and almost a nurse."

"I hope so. I still think of Dad and miss him every day." Molly's voice wobbled. "I never thought he'd wouldn't be here for my high school and college graduations or to walk me down the aisle when I get married."

Zach's chest got tight as emotion rolled over him. Their dad had been taken too soon. Out of all the kids, Molly was the one who'd miss sharing some of life's biggest milestones with him. "I know it's not the same, but when the time comes, I'd be honored to walk you down that aisle."

"Thanks." She gave him a grateful smile. "After I finish my nursing degree and take my licensing exam, I want to get a job in a big city hospital alongside doing a part-time graduate program in pediatric nursing. I love all of you and the ranch, but I need to spread my wings. I'll still come home for vacations, but as a nurse, I can get a job almost anywhere. New York City, San Francisco or maybe even Australia."

"No matter where you go, you'll do well. I'm proud of you too." It wasn't surprising that Molly wanted to make her life elsewhere. She was like Beth in that way. "Have you told Mom yet?"

"No." Molly's smile slipped. "Mom's all for me getting as much education as I want, but I need to work up to the leaving Montana and moving to a big city idea. I talked to Beth, though. She gave me lots of tips about city life."

Of course she would because Beth was at home in a city. Zach stared at the stars again.

"I can't wait to go to all kinds of different restaurants, and concerts and shows. I also want to live in a place where people don't remember every embarrassing incident from my childhood and remind me of them." Molly's voice was wry. "I can still be connected with horses in the city too. Beth's found a fabulous equestrian center for Ellie in Chicago."

"Super." Zach's mouth was dry. He'd had those years in Germany, but playing hockey was temporary and he'd come home each summer. Unlike Molly, he'd never yearned for a different life than the one he had on the ranch. Although he didn't doubt that Molly meant to come back on vacation, once she experienced the options of city life, she'd likely want to travel to other places too. "When you do come home, I'll even let you off chores. At least most of them." He tried to make his voice light.

"Thanks, but I won't expect to be treated any differently. I'll always help out here because we're family, but I won't miss early morning chores two weeks out of every four. Especially in the winter, they're brutal." Molly grimaced. "I don't mind hard work, but I'd be happy to never muck out a stall, ride after cattle or help with haying again. Ranch life is nice if you can sit on a porch in the summer and admire the crops growing and animals in the fields. It's not so nice when you have to work from dawn until dusk to keep the ranch going every day of the year. Even when I was little, I never wanted that life. I'm lucky Mom and Dad didn't try to change my mind."

"They wanted us to live our own lives." Except, Zach's life and future had always been on the ranch because that's what he wanted.

"I should get back to the house. Mom bought some new clothes and asked me to help her clear out her closet." Molly stepped away from the fence. "You should go home too. I already settled the horses for the night."

"Thanks. I'll miss you when you go back to college." And not only because of how much his sister helped out around the place. "But I understand why you need to leave." Like Beth, Molly didn't belong here. "When you get that big city job, I'll come and visit."

Molly wrapped her arms around him in a hug. "I'll hold you to that promise. No matter how far away I go, I'll miss you too."

Zach hugged his sister back. "Go have your exciting adventures. Home will always be here waiting for you."

He'd be here too, but Beth wouldn't. He loved Beth but, like Molly, he had to let her go. With one last look at the stars, Zach turned away, his heart heavy. No amount of wishing on stars or anything else would change one fundamental fact. Both Beth and Molly wanted city life and he wouldn't stand in their way. If he tried, it would only end badly—for him perhaps most of all.

CHAPTER SIXTEEN

ZACH PATTED PRINCESS as she nuzzled his head. "Although it was your last ride with Ellie for a while, she'll be back." She and Beth were returning to Montana to spend Thanksgiving with Kate and Lily. Except, it wouldn't be the same. He tried to avoid the thought as he checked the other horses and gave them hay.

Outside, through the half-open barn door, purple evening shadows lengthened across the pasture, and the air was cool and crisp. Although it was still August, fall was coming. His mom's garden was heavy with produce, and Zach counted hay bales and checked winter forage inventory. Even the cows were restless, sensing it would soon be time to graze nearer home. All things that signaled the change of seasons.

And tomorrow morning he'd have to say

goodbye to Beth, Ellie and most of the other campers.

"Zach?"

At Beth's voice, he stopped sweeping loose straw from the barn's center aisle.

"I'm by Daisy-May's stall."

The horse's ears pricked, and she gave a soft whinny in welcome. Like Princess would miss Ellie, Daisy-May would miss Beth.

"Hi." Beth stopped beside him, out of breath as if she'd been running. "Your mom said you'd still be here. I'm glad I caught you. We finished packing, and Ellie wanted to watch a movie with friends, so I was able to leave her." With her hair in a sleek ponytail, and in cropped jeans and an off-the-shoulder white eyelet blouse with red canvas sneakers, Beth wore clothes Molly called *trendy country casual* but that were rarely worn by anyone who actually lived in the country.

"What's up?" He gave Beth a half smile and swept up the last of the straw. "Did Ellie forget or lose something?"

"No, I did." She followed him to the far end of the barn, where they kept tools and other things that didn't go in the tack room.

"I didn't find anything in here." He hung the broom on a wall hook. "Did you lose whatever it is in the paddock?"

"No, Zach, I..." She drew in a sharp breath. "This summer has been great for Ellie and me too. Camp Crocus Hill has changed both of us, and now, although we'll always miss Jilly, I feel like Ellie and I will be a real family."

"That's wonderful." One of the reasons they'd set up the camp was to give parents, kids and caregivers space and time to *be* families and go back to their everyday lives better equipped to face challenges. "I'm happy for you both."

"I'm happy too." Beth stepped closer and laid a hand on his arm.

Zach froze. Her hand was warm and filled the empty spaces inside to make him whole. "Montana makes lots of people happy."

"It's special. It always has been, but it's not only Montana. You're special too, and it's *you* who makes me happy. Ellie wants to stay here, and so do I. When I said that I lost something, what I meant was that I lost my heart. To you." She gestured with her free arm. "I don't know how I'll work out the details, and I have to go home to Chicago for a while, but I want to come back to High Valley to stay. I love you, Zach, and I've never felt this way before. Along with Ellie, you're my family too." Her cheeks were pink, and her eyes shone.

"I… You…" Zach's heart gave a painful thud. Beth wasn't like Dani, and maybe she could build a life in Montana, but no matter how much he loved her, that life and family couldn't be with him. Taking her hand from his arm wasn't easy, but he made himself do it and step away. "I care about you, Beth. You and Ellie both." He grabbed for the broom again so he wouldn't touch her. "But it's complicated."

"How is me loving you complicated? I thought…maybe you might feel the same way." Her voice caught.

He did have those feelings, but he couldn't let them go any further. Once Beth left, she'd forget him like she'd done before. "We've had a great summer, but that's all it was. You have your life in Chicago and a wonderful new job opportunity and—"

"My life in Chicago *is* my job. I don't

want to live that way anymore. And now, especially with Ellie, I want a different life. A life with you. Here." Her chest heaved. "Forget about that job. Along with Ellie, you helped me see there are other things in life beyond work. More important things like family, being part of a community and letting myself be open to love." She drew in a harsh breath. "Before this summer, I was too scared to fall in love, but you helped me believe I deserve a happily ever after and children of my own."

A tractorlike weight settled in the middle of Zach's chest. "You'll get all that, Beth. You're smart and beautiful, and you're a wonderful mom to Ellie. Some guy will be lucky to have you in his life."

"*Have* me?" Her voice sharpened. "I see relationships as equal partnerships. I thought you did too."

"I do." His mouth was dry, his tongue thick, and he gripped the broom handle tight. "I said it wrong, but what I meant is that some guy will be lucky to have a life with you in it. To share it. And you'll be lucky too because he'll be able to give you…" He stopped. The more he said, the worse he made things. "A better life than on a struggling Montana ranch. You visited on vacation, but ranching is hard work, and the winters are harsh."

"So?" She eyed him, her gaze assessing. "I'm not Dani, and I won't be put off by weather. Besides, I can help with the ranch. Maybe not mucking out stalls or herding cattle, although I can learn, but from what I've seen this summer, ranching is a big business. To run a ranch like this one and make it a success, you need someone with business expertise. Someone like me."

They did, but he couldn't ask her to make that sacrifice. "I can never repay you or thank you enough for what you did for us this summer." And he could only hope that Beth had given them enough of a start that he could figure out how to carry on by himself.

"So why are you so opposed to me staying in Montana and seeing where things go between us?" The hurt in her eyes winded him.

Because he knew where things would end, and they'd both be hurt even more than they were now. "I can't let you stay." No matter how much he wanted her to.

"I don't understand." She hugged herself, and Zach's heart broke a little more, but if he let himself comfort her, he'd be lost. "Tell me."

"You know that Paul had cystic fibrosis."

"Yes. I don't understand, though, what that has to do with me staying in Montana and us being together." The concern in Beth's voice almost broke Zach's resolve to not take her in his arms and forget about what he had to tell her.

He took a deep breath and made himself say the words that would change everything. "Cystic fibrosis is a genetic disease, and I carry the gene." The truth he'd never told anyone but Dani left a bitter taste in his mouth, and his heartbeat seemed to stop before it sped up again and his thoughts swirled. Honesty and being true to yourself were good. That's what his folks had taught him. But instead, Zach had never felt worse.

BETH'S ADRENALINE SPIKED, and she tensed. Out of anything she might have expected Zach to say, it wasn't that. "How do you know you carry the cystic fibrosis gene?"

She landed on the only question she could make sense of amidst her fuzzy thoughts.

"I got tested. Dani, she…" He stared at the barn floor.

"That's why she left you?" Beth reached out, but Zach stepped away toward an empty stall.

"Along with not wanting to live in Montana. She didn't want to get tested, but I said I would and… Well, she cheated on me and had a child with someone else. I can never risk having kids of my own. Even if my wife wasn't a carrier and our kids were fine, what if I passed on the gene and my grandchildren got sick? What happened to Paul almost destroyed my folks and our family too. I couldn't live with myself if I put anyone I loved through that."

Beth didn't know anything about cystic fibrosis, but there had to be a way she could make Zach see reason. "Have you talked to anybody else about this?" Given what she knew about Ellie's medical situation, there had to have been some kind of counseling after he'd gotten his test result.

"No." He still didn't look at her. "What

good would talking do? I know I'm a carrier, so I don't want kids."

"There are other ways of having a family." Her mind whirled. "Look at Ellie and me."

"You said you want your own children, so you should be able to have them." His voice was low.

"That's in the future. Whether or not you carry the cystic fibrosis gene, or I do too, doesn't change me loving you. Besides, since I've never tried, I don't know if I can even have children." Deciding not to pursue a relationship on the basis of hypothetical future children didn't make sense.

"I can't be with you, Beth." Zach went into the empty stall and closed the bottom half of the door behind him.

"*Can't* or *won't*?"

"It's the same thing."

"No, it's not." She hugged herself again. What she felt for Zach she'd never felt for anyone before, and now that she was ready to take a risk and seize a chance of happiness, he'd thrown it back in her face. "What we have is special and wonderful."

"It is. It was." He corrected himself. "But you need to go back to Chicago. You'll meet someone else there." His voice was flat, stripped of emotion.

"What if I don't want to meet anyone else?"

"You have to." He fiddled with the latch on the stall door, the metal click echoing above the roar in her ears.

"There's nothing I can say to change your mind?" She leaned against the barn wall to steady herself.

It was like her parents when she'd come home from camp all those years ago. They'd decided to divorce, and it didn't matter what she thought or wanted. Her dad had already moved out and only one suitcase, the black one with the red trim he took on business trips, sat in the front hall on the tiled floor at the foot of the stairs.

"No." Zach's voice was clipped. "It's better this way."

Better for him, maybe, but not for her. "I see." She made herself stand tall and keep her voice even to hide how much he'd hurt her. "That's it, then?"

"Yes. I'm sorry."

"I'm sorry too." She bit her lower lip hard. Her mom and dad had said they were sorry as well, but words were easy. "Mostly, I'm sorry for you. You're missing out on life. You told me that Paul lived his life, even though he knew it would be limited. You don't have those limits, but you're hiding out because of him, and Dani." She stared at Zach's stiff shoulders under the blue University of North Dakota T-shirt he'd worn for barn chores. "Take care."

"Yeah." He turned toward her, and she sucked in a breath at the pain in his eyes. "Safe trip home." His expression became a careful blank. "Say goodbye to Ellie for me."

"You'll say goodbye to Ellie yourself." The emotional armor Beth had cloaked herself in since that terrible day her parents told her their marriage, the family she'd counted on, was over slid back into place. "I'm not letting you break Ellie's heart by not being there when we check out tomorrow. She's counting on you having Clementine there too."

"Of course, I didn't think." His voice was gruff. "I'll be there with the puppy."

"Good." Somehow, Beth would hold herself together until she got back to Chicago, where she could be Elizabeth again—and where Zach would be a part of her life she'd never let herself think about. She'd done that once before, and no matter how hard, she could do it again.

CHAPTER SEVENTEEN

JOY ROLLED HER chair from behind the desk in the camp office to let Zach use the computer. "This machine is even slower than usual this morning." She studied his bent head, hunched shoulders, tousled hair and the dark circles beneath his eyes. The office computer *was* slow, but it was merely an excuse to get him here.

"We need a new computer system, but you shouldn't use the desktop for filing." He clicked a few keys.

"I use those files every day. I keep them on the desktop so they're easy to find."

A new computer system would cost money, and although the grant money Beth had helped them apply for was a boost, it wouldn't solve every problem, including whatever was bothering her son. Zach hadn't turned up for breakfast after early chores, and since Joy had called him to help in the office, he hadn't said more than a few words to her or anyone else who'd come in and out. Although she wasn't a betting woman, she'd wager that whatever was up with Zach had something to do with Beth.

He squinted at the screen and clicked more keys. "Which file do you want to open and print?"

"The spreadsheet attached to the first email in this week's check-out folder. I worked on it yesterday, and it was fine."

Zach grunted.

"Didn't you sleep well?" Joy made her tone casual.

"I'm fine." He stared at the screen.

"No, you aren't. I'm your mother. I know when something's wrong." But he was a grown man, and even though Joy wanted to, she couldn't solve his problems like she once had.

"Why do you have a folder labeled *Jilly and Beth*?" Zach swiveled to look at her, his expression puzzled.

"It's nothing." She put her hand over his on the computer mouse and scrambled to find a logical excuse. "All I need is that spreadsheet. The campers will be checking out soon, and—"

"Mom." His voice sharpened. "This folder has messages from Jilly Grabowski. Messages from earlier this year." He kept his hand on the mouse, clicking and opening emails.

"They're from when Jilly booked the camp for her and Ellie. Remember? She booked first, and then after Jilly passed, Beth emailed to change the booking." Joy gave Zach her most innocent smile.

"Jilly made the original booking, but..." He grimaced as he stared at the screen. "You were interfering again. You and Jilly—"

"I wanted to help you." Joy realized she should have made a plan about how to tell him. Now it was too late. "And Jilly wanted to help Beth. Anything we did was out of love."

"You set us up." Zach's voice was ragged. "I suspected you had, but I thought it only started when Beth was here. But you asked me to check Beth and Ellie in without telling me... Everything was a setup." He pushed Joy's hand away and stood.

"Not everything." Joy should have filed

those emails in her personal account, but at first, they'd only been about the booking, so she'd saved them like she'd have done for any other prospective camp family. "I asked you to help Beth and Ellie get checked in, and I might have encouraged you and Beth to be in the same place at the same time, but everything else was up to the two of you." As soon as Zach and Beth had begun spending time together, and except for inviting Beth and Ellie to that Sunday meal, she'd stepped back. "All I want is for you to be happy."

"Then, you need to let me figure things out for myself." His body was stiff, and his expression tight.

"But you're hurting." When Zach was little, she'd fixed his hurts with a kiss, a fresh-baked cookie and a glass of milk, but as kids grew older, their hurts got deeper, and no matter how much you wanted, sometimes you couldn't fix them. "You care about Beth, don't you?"

He shrugged. "She's great, but whatever was between us was only a summer thing."

"Summer things can last a lifetime if you want them to." Anyone who saw Beth and Zach together knew they shared something important, but was her son too scared to admit it?

"Beth's got a great job opportunity in Chicago. She's busy with Ellie too." Zach grabbed his hat from a corner of the desk. "She'd never be happy with life on a Montana ranch or a guy like me."

"From what I've seen, Beth could be happy with both the ranch and you. If you give her a chance, she'd be there for you until you're my age and beyond. *Who* you are and what you feel for each other is what's important, not where you live."

"Happily ever after is only in those books the two of you read." Zach's tone was short, and he fumbled in his pocket for his phone. "I have to get to the barn. The vet is coming out to check on that mare who is due any day now, and—"

"Isn't that appointment this afternoon? Besides, I thought Cole was handling it." With five kids, Joy had a lot of practice in knowing when one of them was avoiding an issue—or lying to her—and Zach was doing both.

"Yes, but…" He blew out a long breath.

"I have to get the puppy to say goodbye to Ellie."

Joy glanced at the time on the computer. "You have a while yet. I thought things were going well between you and Beth."

"They were, but we're different people. We want different things."

"From where I sit, it seems as if you want the same things, at least the important ones. Love, a family with children and building a life together. Beth is so good with Ellie, and she'll be a great mother to her own little ones too. Since she's smart and efficient, she'll juggle whatever paid job she has with motherhood no problem."

"Sure, she will." Zach rubbed a hand across his face. "But she'll have to find someone else to have that family and build a life with because it won't be me."

Joy worried her bottom lip. If she pushed Zach much further, he'd shut her out, but if she didn't still push him a bit, he might spend the rest of his life alone and live with regrets. "I always pictured you as a family man. Just because things didn't work out with Dani doesn't mean they won't work out with someone else. Beth isn't anything like Dani." Although Joy could finally say the woman's name, she still got a bad taste in her mouth.

"Beth isn't like Dani, but she wants a home and a family, and I can't…" He twisted his hat between his hands.

"So you're going to let Beth drive away today and go on with your life like she was never here?" If he did, Zach was a bigger fool than she thought. There had to be something else going on.

"Pretty much." He edged toward the door.

"But—"

"Drop it, please? And no more interfering. Whatever scheme you and Jilly cooked up to get Beth and me together is over."

Joy slid behind the desk again and stared at the check-out list without seeing it. She'd riled him, but none of her other kids would have been as understanding if she'd tried to fix them up behind their backs. None of her other kids needed the kind of help he did, though.

Her gaze drifted to the picture of Ellie riding Princess that Ellie had given her yesterday. Ellie's smile was as wide as the Montana sky in a frame she'd made of green-painted popsicle sticks and decorated with silver sequins and pink, flower-shaped buttons. Joy still owed it to Jilly, and now Ellie, to make things right.

IN THE PARKING area outside the camp office, Beth folded Ellie's wheelchair, put it into the back of the SUV beside their suitcases and closed the hatch. She only had to get through the next few minutes, and then they'd be on the highway with Camp Crocus Hill, the Tall Grass Ranch and High Valley all firmly in the rearview mirror.

"I don't know how I'm going to wait a whole month until Zach ships Clementine to us." Ellie leaned against the passenger-side door wearing jeans, a green camp T-shirt, and the white cowboy hat Molly had given her for her birthday.

"Clementine will be with us before you know it." Before Beth knew it too. As soon as they got home, she had to puppy-proof the condo, look for obedience classes and a dog daycare and get everything on Ellie's list, including puppy food, toys and a heated bed. "All set?"

"Yeah." Ellie's smile slipped. "I still don't want to go."

"That's the sign of a good vacation." Beth made herself give Ellie an encouraging smile.

"I want to say goodbye to Zach and Clementine one more time."

"Okay." Beth had to say goodbye to them for the first time, something she'd avoided by busying herself with returning the cabin keys, signing the check-out paperwork and saying goodbye to the other campers until she and Ellie were the only ones left.

She followed Ellie to where Zach stood on the path by the wagon wheel Welcome sign and flower-filled barrels. Apart from Clementine, who wriggled in his arms, everything looked the same as it had when they'd arrived five weeks before, but it wasn't.

Beth had changed in ways nobody could see on the outside, and Ellie was different too. For Ellie, though, the changes were good, and that's what Beth had to focus on. And although she'd as much as thrown herself at Zach in the barn the night before, she'd say goodbye with dignity and claw back some of her self-respect. Luckily, Joy and Molly, Kate and Lily, and Rosa were here too, so Beth could shake Zach's hand and that would be it.

"We'll miss you." Joy's blue eyes were shiny. "You weren't only campers. You became part of our family. You helped me buy all those new clothes too." She gestured to her dark jeans, floral blouse and sandals. "And you encouraged me to register for that online psychology course at the college this fall."

"Helping you was a pleasure, and you'll do great in your course. We'll miss you too." Beth stepped into Joy's embrace, and her throat got scratchy. "We'll also keep in touch." Except, apart from Christmas cards, and the occasional visit when they came to High Valley to see Kate and Lily, it would be hard to be friends with Joy when Beth wanted to be so much more than friends with Zach.

"You'll be back at camp next summer, won't you?" Molly hugged Beth in her turn.

"I don't know yet." Returning to Camp Crocus Hill would be awkward. She'd have to find another camp—and disappoint Ellie.

Rosa enveloped Beth in a tight embrace. "I won't say goodbye because you'll be back. In the meantime, wear your butterfly necklaces and remember what the butterfly means. It's a sign of hope too." She touched the matching necklace to the one Ellie had given Beth that now nestled at Beth's throat. Beth had bought it at the craft gallery the day before, along with a raven pendant for Shaundra at work.

"Thank you." Beth's voice was choked and she could hardly look at Rosa for fear she'd start crying and wouldn't be able to stop.

"Rosa's right. We'll see you at Thanksgiving." Kate pulled Beth close. "That man has less sense than his pack mule out there in the field." Her voice was a low hiss in Beth's ear.

Beth fought for control. She'd planned to tell Kate what had happened with Zach once she was safely back in Chicago but not before. "How do you know?"

"It's written over both your faces." Kate hugged Beth tighter.

"I'll be fine." Beth stepped back and darted a glance at Zach, engrossed with Ellie and the puppy. His expression was shuttered, and his smile forced.

Kate sniffed. "Call me tonight?"

"Okay." Beth straightened. "We need to hit the road, El. Say goodbye to Zach, and give Clementine a last cuddle." She hugged

Lily and made herself walk past Joy and Molly to reach Zach. "Thanks for everything you've done for Ellie. It's been great." Beth kept her tone even and stared over his shoulder at a teenage maintenance guy watering plants outside the office.

"You're welcome." Zach's voice hitched as he hugged Ellie. "I'll be in touch about Clementine."

"Yes. You have all my numbers and our address." Along with her heart.

"I do. Beth, I…" He stopped and glanced at the others. "Take care."

He held out a hand, and Beth took it, her palm brushing against his before she took it away. "You take care too." She had to get out of here before she let her emotions show.

"Keep up with your horseback riding, kiddo." He gave Ellie another hug.

"I will, but it won't be the same as with you and Lauren." Ellie held Zach as if she never wanted to let him go.

"Ellie already has a lesson booked with the teacher Lauren recommended." Beth dug in her bag for her sunglasses, stuck them on her face and manufactured a smile. "Come on, Ellie. We need to make tracks. I've got a hotel

room booked for us tonight in North Dakota."
Beth gave Zach a wave meant to be breezy
and walked to the SUV, her legs leaden.

Even if they didn't get as far as that hotel,
as long as Ellie was up for it, Beth would
drive until they reached the North Dakota
state line and find somewhere else to stay:
anything to get out of Montana.

She fastened her seat belt and made sure
Ellie was buckled up too. Then she started
the SUV, swung around the looped parking
area and pointed the vehicle toward the east.

Home. It wasn't where she wanted it to be,
but somehow, she'd make it work. It would get
easier in time, and even when she talked to
Kate later, Beth would be more herself again.

And if she wasn't? She blinked away tears
as the SUV bumped along the driveway to the
camp, and Ellie waved out the window until
they got to the main road and Camp Crocus
Hill had disappeared behind a low rise.

Beth flipped the signal on to make a left
turn onto the highway. Like she always
did, and as her parents had taught her, Beth
would fake it until she made it, with Zach
and everything—and everyone—else.

CHAPTER EIGHTEEN

"COME ON." ZACH'S NIECE, six-year-old Paisley, tugged his arm. "I want to see the bunnies."

"Okay." He made himself smile and tucked his cold hand in her warm, sticky one. Beth and Ellie had left almost two weeks ago and were back in Chicago. Knowing they were almost halfway across the country should make him feel better, but instead, the dull ache in his heart was even worse. And each time his phone pinged, he caught himself, half-expecting it to be Beth before remembering he was the one who'd sent her away. Although Ellie messaged him several times a day, she only asked about Clementine, Princess and the ranch and never mentioned Beth.

"Where did Grandma, your dad and the others get to? They were here a minute ago." He scanned the packed county fairgrounds for his mom and Bryce. Trying to keep track of his family was harder than herding cattle. As always, they'd come to this fair together but split up into smaller groups to do different things before meeting up again for lunch and when the prizes for livestock, arts and crafts and other classes were announced.

Paisley hopped from foot to foot beside him. "My brother had to go to the bathroom, so Daddy took him, and Grandma said she had to go too, so Lily and Ms. Kate went with her. The bunnies are right there." She gestured to an enclosure on their right. "Daddy will see us when they come back, or you can text him."

"Good idea." Zach tapped at his phone. "Then we can go see the rest of the junior livestock. In a few years, you'll be old enough to enter that division."

"Daddy says that when I'm seven I can raise a rabbit for 4-H like he and Mommy did." Paisley pulled him toward the bunny enclosure. "I wish Ellie and Ms. Beth were still here. They were fun. Ellie was great at doing my hair too."

"Your hair looks fine." He patted the top of Paisley's blond head as they made their way through a crowd of excited 4-H kids and parents.

"You're a guy. You don't know anything about girls' hair." Paisley grinned. "Ellie did my hair in a special way. Like Mommy used to." Her lip wobbled as her smile slipped. "And Ms. Beth reminded me of Mommy. She gave the same kind of hugs."

"I know you miss your mommy." Zach gave Paisley a one-armed embrace. "But you have your dad, Grandma, me, Uncle Cole and Aunt Molly to give you hugs too."

"None of you give hugs like Ms. Beth." Paisley crouched in front of a rabbit pen and stuck her hand through the wire to stroke a Havana bunny's ears. "I wish Ms. Beth and Ellie could have stayed longer to come to the fair with us."

"They had to go home, sweetheart." Zach's breath hitched as he crouched beside Paisley. He'd thought that once Beth and Ellie left, he could get back to the life he'd had before, but that life wasn't the same. When he was in the barn, he expected to see Ellie near Princess's stall. And each time he rode past Meadowlark cabin, his heart gave a dull thud because Beth wasn't on the front porch or anywhere else on the campsite. He couldn't escape the memories in town either because whenever he passed the Bluebunch Café or craft center he half expected her to be there, chatting with Kristi or Rosa.

He had to move on without Beth, but with memories of her everywhere, he couldn't. And even Daisy-May had given him what was for her a displeased look when he'd mucked out her stall yesterday, as if to ask where Beth had gone and when she'd be coming back.

"I thought you liked Ms. Beth." Paisley's expression was as accusing as Daisy-May's. "Daddy said you did and that's why you were kissing her behind the barn. We saw you one day before my riding lesson."

Great. Although Zach loved his family, he could never get a moment's privacy. "I do like Ms. Beth." No, he loved her, but he'd sent her away for her own good.

"Daddy said you should only hold someone so close and kiss them like that if you're going to marry them." Paisley's tone was prim. "And that I shouldn't kiss someone like that until I'm grown-up."

"Your dad's right." Zach would have to have a word with Bryce later.

"So, you're going to marry Ms. Beth?" Paisley's eyes sparkled. "Can I be a flower girl? My best friend at school was a flower girl when her uncle got married, and she had a pink dress and got to wear a wreath of pink and white flowers in her hair."

"No, I'm not marrying Ms. Beth. I meant you shouldn't kiss someone until you're much older." This here was another reason why he was right not to have kids of his own. No matter how careful you were, kids saw stuff they shouldn't and led you into conversational mazes you couldn't find your way out of.

"I think you should marry Ms. Beth. You'll be forty in a few years. That's what Grandma said to Mrs. Rosa when Mrs. Rosa came to help Grandma with quilt sewing and they didn't know I was there. Grandma also said that Uncle Cole needed to find a nice woman like Ms. Beth. What's he supposed to do with the lady once he finds her?" Paisley glanced at the rabbits again.

"Well, get married, I suppose…but like I said, I'm not marrying Ms. Beth." Zach stopped. He couldn't tell a six-year-old about the complications and nuances associated with romantic relationships. Hopefully, Paisley would forget they'd ever had this conversation or he'd have some explaining to do the next time he spoke to Cole.

"Oh." Paisley stared at him with trusting brown eyes almost the same color as Beth's. "How come you and Uncle Cole don't want to marry nice ladies?"

"Uh…" The more Zach waded into this conversation, the worse it got. "Tell you what. Why don't we get corn dogs and cotton candy? It's almost lunchtime, so you must be hungry." He'd make some excuse about not waiting for the family lunch.

"I'm starving. Can I have fried cheese curds and a huckleberry shake too?"

"Sure." Anything to distract Paisley from Beth and marriage.

"Great." Paisley squeezed his hand. "I love fried cheese curds, but Daddy never lets me have them because I was sick after the fair last year. He also says cotton candy will rot my teeth." Her smile was smug.

"No cheese curds and forget the cotton

candy. Also, we'd better share the shake. It's too big for you to drink all by yourself."

"But you said—"

"There you are." His mom bustled up with Kate and Lily, followed by Bryce, and Paisley's younger brother, Zach's four-year-old nephew Cam. "What's wrong?"

"Nothing." Apart from missing Beth and trying to convince himself he'd done the right thing by letting her go, and being grilled by a savvy six-year-old who was way too observant for her age. "Paisley and I were going to get something to eat."

"Yes, and Uncle Zach promised—"

"I didn't promise. I only mentioned—"

"Paisley strikes a harder bargain than most livestock dealers." Bryce ruffled his daughter's hair, and Zach's gut pulled at the fatherly gesture.

"I look forward to the corn dogs here every year." His mom studied Zach, her gaze shrewd. "I want to take a picture to send Beth and Ellie. Do they have corn dogs in Chicago?"

"They must." Most places had corn dogs, but they wouldn't have the kind they had here, hand-dipped and made to a special, secret recipe that had been the same since Zach's parents were teens.

"You miss them, don't you?" As Paisley ran ahead with Cam and Bryce, and Kate and Lily stopped to talk with a teacher from the local high school, Zach's mom put a hand on his arm to hold him back.

"Corn dogs? Sure." He pulled the brim of his hat farther over his forehead.

"No, Beth and Ellie." His mom looped her arm through his as they left the bunny enclosure and returned to the fairgrounds. At almost midday, the sun shone high overhead, and combined with the raucous midway noise, a headache throbbed behind Zach's temples.

"They had to go home."

"You didn't answer my question." She tugged him away from the crowd, sat at an empty wooden picnic table shaded by a green umbrella and patted the seat beside her.

"Of course I miss them." Zach sat too and stared at the Ferris wheel rising above the midway. He missed Beth and Ellie so much it was like a hole inside him, as big as the steep, arid gully that marked the eastern edge of the Carter property.

"So what are you going to do about it?"

"There's nothing to do." He dug his boot heels into the ground.

"Not even if you're making yourself miserable and likely Beth too? Paul and your dad are gone, but they lived their lives while they had them." His mom's mouth quivered. "You rarely smile, you haven't laughed since Beth and Ellie left, and you sure aren't living. You're only existing, because you're shutting yourself off from the possibility of happiness. You can't live your life always worrying about what *might* happen. Just because you carry the cystic fibrosis gene doesn't mean you'll pass it on. Although we didn't know it until much later, your dad and I were both carriers, but we still had four healthy kids. Besides, nowadays there's more treatments and therapies for CF too."

"You... How did you guess?"

His mom pulled him close into a hug. "After you and Dani got engaged, and you brought her home to meet me and your dad, there was a call for you at the house. The woman said it was urgent, and she couldn't reach you on your cell. She didn't give me any details, only her first name and telephone number, but from the number I knew she was from the medical genetics program in Billings. Paul talked a lot to a counselor there, and your dad and I did too, so the number was familiar. Then, with the way you acted, and Dani breaking your engagement, I put two and two together."

And made four. Zach swallowed.

"It took me a while to figure things out, but that's why you pushed Beth away, isn't it?"

"Yes." The fair noise blurred.

"I take it that Dani wouldn't get tested for the CF gene?"

He shook his head as memories pressed in on him. Dani wouldn't take a chance on him or Montana, but what he hadn't known then was that she'd already taken a chance on someone else.

"If I'm right about Beth, she'll not only get tested, but even if she's a carrier too, she's already made a family with Ellie. There's nothing to say she wouldn't be open to making a new kind of family with you. There are lots of kids who need a loving home, and you don't have to give birth to a child to love them."

Beth had said almost the same thing, but Zach had been so set on what he thought would happen he hadn't listened. He'd also been so sure that every woman would, in the end, be like Dani he'd ignored all the ways that Beth was different.

"You love Beth, don't you?"

"Yes, but I didn't think I could ask her to be with me. I thought she'd be better off with someone who doesn't carry the CF gene."

"Lots of people carry that gene and go their whole lives without knowing. Or they pass something else to their children. Life and children don't come with guarantees, so if Beth loves you too, you need to give her and yourself another chance."

Could Zach do that? And more importantly, would Beth give him that second chance?

"There's only one way to find out, isn't there?" As if she'd read his thoughts, his mom's smile was gentle.

"I don't know how to be a dad or a husband."

"You think your dad knew? Or I knew how to be a wife and mom? You learn on the job."

Her soft chuckle gave Zach a familiar, bone-deep sense of comfort, security and unconditional love. "Thanks, Mom." Some of the pressure he felt eased. Beth had left, but that didn't mean he couldn't go after her. And he'd get there faster if he caught a flight. He could even take Clementine to deliver the dog in person.

"You're welcome." She still held him tight. "Right back since you were little, you always thought about everyone else instead of yourself. I worried it was because of Paul that you had to grow up too soon. But now it's time for you to think of yourself, as well as Beth."

Zach's eyes burned as he returned her hug, the kind of embrace they'd shared when he was a boy and his mom could make everything right in his world.

"A little tip, though." She drew back and gave him a sideways glance. "For a kid, never mix those cheese curds with corn dogs and a huckleberry shake, followed by a turn on the big slide. That's what made Paisley sick after last year's fair. As for that talk about marriage and your brother, you

did fine. Paisley's so quiet I sometimes forget she's there."

"You heard?"

"Moms hear everything. Grandmas do
too." She waved at two women from her
quilting circle. "Bring me back a Chicago
snow globe for my collection. Beth and Ellie
can help you choose one."

"I will." He tried to smile. But first, and
if it was the last thing Zach did, he had to
make things right with Beth.

On a sunny Sunday afternoon in mid-
September, Beth rested her elbows on the
top rail of the white-painted paddock fence
as Ellie, riding a golden-colored horse with
a white mane and tail, completed another
circuit of the outdoor arena. This top equestrian facility in a Chicago suburb was suited
to riders of all ages, abilities and disciplines,
from beginners like Ellie to serious competi-
tors aiming to be national and international
champions.

She couldn't fault the training facility or
Ellie's teacher, Pam, the one who'd been per-
sonally recommended by Lauren. Everything was great, but Ellie had only smiled

once in the hour they'd been here, and as she rode around the arena, it was as if she was going through the motions with none of the joy she'd had at Camp Crocus Hill.

"Good job, Ellie." With a warm smile, Pam helped Ellie off the horse near where Beth stood. "I'll see you at the same time next week."

"Yes, thank you." Ellie's voice was soft.

"You looked wonderful out there." Beth thanked Pam too and opened the paddock gate to let Ellie through.

Ignoring her wheelchair, Ellie moved slowly to the seats in the nearby viewing gallery. She sat, took off her riding helmet and set it beside her. "Pam said I could watch the dressage class. Can we stay? I've never seen dressage, but Lauren told me about it."

"Of course." Anything that might get Ellie to smile. "I brought a packed lunch. I thought you'd be hungry after your lesson." Beth took the lunch bag from a bigger tote.

"Thanks." Ellie opened the bag and removed a plastic sandwich container. "Pam's great, and Venus—that's the horse—is a dream. It should all be perfect, but it's not."

Her voice cracked. "I miss Lauren and Princess and the ranch and everything."

"I know you do." Beth did too, more than she could tell Ellie. "But we have to make the best of things where we are." Or did they?

What if, instead, you fought for what you wanted?

She glanced at her e-reader poking out from the top of her tote. The heroines in her favorite books didn't give up at the first setback. They persevered and overcame obstacles to earn their happily ever after in life, as well as love.

"I have to make the best of some things. Like math, at least, until I'm old enough not to have to take it." Ellie grimaced.

"Math isn't so bad. I'm tutoring you, remember?" Like Beth was tutoring Alex too, a connection with her half brother she hadn't expected but which, she felt certain, would make both their lives better.

"Apart from math, Mrs. Joy said you should look for all the joy in your life that you can. Isn't that funny? Her name is Joy, and she told me to look for joy."

"Mrs. Joy is right." The realization rocked through Beth. All summer, she'd focused on making the most of the moments with Ellie, but those joyful moments didn't have to stop because summer had ended. Beth needed to build a life of moments filled with joy to store up like a reservoir and balance the hard days. That new job she'd interviewed for last week would bring her even less joy than the job she already had—and, as she'd feared, less time with Ellie too. She'd always vowed she wouldn't be like her parents, but by working all the time she'd followed their example. That pattern had to stop now.

"Lily sent me more pictures from the county fair. See this one?" Ellie showed Beth her phone and took another bite of sandwich.

Beth shaded the screen with one hand to focus on a group photo of Lily and Kate, Joy, Bryce and his kids, Cole, Molly, who held a giant plush purple unicorn, and Zach. Except for Zach, they all made funny faces. Even half-hidden by the unicorn, Zach's smile was forced, and his eyes sad. Beth pressed a hand to her stomach. Did he miss her like she missed him?

"It looks fun, doesn't it?" Ellie's tone was wistful. "I wish we could have gone to the fair. I don't know how I'm going to wait until

Thanksgiving to see everybody again. November is ages away. Anything could happen. Like an asteroid could hit us or we could get sucked into a sink hole and boom, gone."

"Don't think like that." Beth passed the phone back. Since losing her mom, it was natural for Ellie to think that bad things would happen, so part of Beth's job was to get her to see that life had good things too. Yet, what was she showing Ellie?

Beth had convinced herself she had to get over Zach, like she'd convinced herself she had to interview for that job. But she'd been listening to her head instead of her heart. She had more of a choice about where she lived and how she earned her living than she'd thought. And now, thanks to late-night online research and a friend from college who was a pediatrician, she knew more about cystic fibrosis as well. If Beth truly loved Zach, she shouldn't let him go without trying again to make him see how good they could be together.

"You're right that anything could happen, but what if it was something good?"

"What do you mean?" Ellie crunched one of the carrot sticks that Beth had packed.

"I need to talk to Zach." Although Beth didn't have any more vacation time and now, after Labor Day, there were no more holidays until Thanksgiving, she could fly to Montana on a Friday night and come back on Sunday.

"On the phone?"

"No, in person." Beth could travel in early October, after Ellie was more settled in her new school. Zach would either listen to her or he wouldn't, but she had to swallow her pride or she'd always regret it. Kate had said her guest bedroom was theirs whenever Beth and Ellie wanted it, but this was a trip Beth had to take alone. Ellie could stay with Jilly's cousin. While the cousin was in her seventies and couldn't raise Ellie, she'd love to have her for a weekend.

"I'll come with you." Ellie packed up her lunch.

"Although I'd love that, honey, it's too far for only a few days. With school and pacing and your spoons—"

"I have the rest of my life to pace myself and a whole lot of spoons. This is more important. It's about our family, isn't it?"

"Yes, but—"

"Then, I'm coming." Ellie's anxious expression softened. "If Zach won't listen to you, maybe he'll listen to me. I always wanted a dad, and he'd be a great one."

"Ellie, I—"

"Paisley told me she and her dad saw you and Zach kissing by the horse barn, and her dad said you should only kiss someone like that if you were going to marry them." Ellie grinned, and all of a sudden, it was as if Jilly was there, teasing Beth like she used to. "Go get him. Like that Lady What's-her-name did with Lord What's-his-face in that book you read. The one with a horse on the cover where the girl's dress is so big you can hardly see the horse."

Beth couldn't stop her burst of laughter. "I thought you only read fantasy and mysteries."

"Mostly, but you always say I should be open to new things." Ellie's expression was demure.

"True." Beth pulled Ellie into a hug. She'd been wrong. She didn't have to do everything on her own. "I love you, El, so much."

"I love you too." Ellie's voice was muffled against Beth's shoulder. "I'm sorry I gave you such a hard time before. That wasn't fair. I'll always miss my mom, but I'm really glad you're here."

Beth drew in a shaky breath. *Really glad* was fine, better than fine, and if Zach... No, she wouldn't let herself think too far ahead. Even if it was only she and Ellie, Beth would have plenty of joyful moments and a family to cherish.

CHAPTER NINETEEN

ZACH PAID THE cab driver, got out of the taxi and stared at the high-rise building on the corner. September sunshine glinted off the wall of glass that reached to the crisp blue sky. It wasn't as if he was a stranger to cities—he'd lived in two when he'd played hockey in Germany—but Chicago was a different world. He straightened his hat and lifted the soft-sided pet carrier with Clementine inside onto his shoulder.

As he moved away from the cab, his phone vibrated, and he pulled it out of his pocket to answer the call. "Hey, El."

"Are you there with Clementine?"

"I'm almost at Beth's office. Aren't you in school?" He held the pet carrier closer to his body and dodged pedestrians to move to the other side of the sidewalk beneath an awning for a restaurant that advertised Puerto Rican food. His stomach rumbled, a reminder he should have eaten at the airport or the pet-friendly hotel he'd booked where he'd left his luggage. He needed to see Beth, though, before he thought about a meal.

"I'm between classes, so I can use my phone." A bell shrilled in the background. "Don't forget what we talked about."

"I won't." He could herd cattle, calm an angry bull and rope a steer faster than anyone in his family except Cole, but facing Beth was harder than all of those things combined.

"I should have come with you."

"You're thirteen." And making things right with Beth was something Zach had to do on his own.

"So?"

"I can't show up at your school and take you out of class. You have to have permission to pick up somebody else's kid."

"But you're family." Another bell rang.

"Thanks, anyway. Better get to class, El." Zach took a deep breath and turned toward the building where Ellie had told him Beth worked.

Ellie's voice got low. "Remember, Beth

likes romantic stuff. In this book she's reading, the guy—"

"I can figure that part out. You helped me get here, but the rest is on me." And Beth too with maybe a little help from Clementine.

"Good luck." Ellie giggled before disconnecting.

Despite what Zach's mom had said about Beth loving him, Zach needed all the luck he could get. But between his mom and Ellie, he'd already had all the advice he needed and some he didn't. Now he was on his own. Zach scanned the busy street. "Ready, Clementine?"

The puppy nosed Zach's hand through the carrier's mesh panel.

"Here goes." Zach stepped into the crush of pedestrians. People walked faster here than they did at home, and they dressed differently too, but most of them probably had the same worries. How to pay their bills, care for their loved ones and live the best life they could.

He dug in his pocket for change to give to a street busker, and his face heated as a group of women in high heels and dark business clothes stared at his cowboy hat and boots. Overhead, a subway train screeched, and as he ducked into the entrance to Beth's office building, Zach grabbed for his hat as a gust of wind caught it.

The massive glass doors slid open, and he walked into a sunny atrium with seating, towering greenery and more people. Beth's office was on the twenty-second floor, and the elevator was across from the security desk.

Clementine whined, and he patted her through the carrier. "Almost there, girl." Ignoring the stares, he waited for the elevator, entered when the doors opened and pushed twenty-two.

A gray-haired man who'd stepped into the elevator after Zach gave him a wide berth, as did a younger, bald man, both in suits and carrying briefcases.

The elevator dinged, and Zach stepped into a carpeted hallway that led to a glassed-in area with the name of Beth's firm on the outside door. He set his hat on top of Clementine's carrier, smoothed his hair and pushed the door open.

A fortysomething woman, with shoulder-length curly black hair and wearing a tailored burgundy dress, skyscraper heels and square glasses, met him by the empty reception desk. "May I help you?" She stared at him for a moment before her mouth curved into a professional smile.

"I'd like to see Beth. Elizabeth Flanagan, please."

"Do you have an appointment?" Her gaze centered on the pet carrier.

"No, but I've traveled a long way."

"I…" She hesitated. "Do you have a dog in there?"

"Yes."

Clementine vocalized her version of *hello*.

"Apart from service dogs, this building has a no-pets policy, but…it's a beagle puppy, isn't it?" She bent to peer into the carrier as Clementine thumped her tail.

"She's part beagle. Her name is Clementine."

"I love beagles. I have one of my own." Her voice softened. "You shouldn't have gotten past the security desk, but seeing as you have, and since our receptionist is off sick today, I'll see what I can do. Take a seat. What's your name?"

"Thanks. I'm Zach Carter. From Montana." Zach let out a breath and sat on the upholstered chair she indicated near a table stacked with business magazines. Ellie hadn't told him about the security desk.

"You *have* come a long way." Dimples indented her round cheeks. "If Elizabeth is busy and can't see you right away, I assume you'll want to wait?"

"Yes." He'd wait for Beth as long as it took.

"I'm Shaundra Robinson. Elizabeth and I work together." Shaundra studied him. "We're friends as well as work colleagues, and Elizabeth hasn't been the same since she came back from Montana. She won't tell me what's wrong, but something sure is. What with Jilly passing and taking on guardianship of Ellie, Elizabeth's had a tough year. I don't want to see her hurt."

"I don't want to hurt her. I need to explain some things."

"You mean grovel?" Shaundra's voice held a smile.

"You could call it that."

"I've been married twenty-six years, but when my husband messes up, there's nothing like a good grovel to fix things."

Zach hoped so. "What if you've messed up so bad you don't know if someone will ever forgive you?"

"You won't know unless you try." That was pretty much what Zach's mom had said. "My Tyrone is an economics professor and the smartest person I know, but when it comes to our relationship, he can still get it wrong. He's not afraid to admit when he's vulnerable or scared, though, and that makes all the difference. Admitting you're wrong is the first step for all of us. A lot of guys think if they show up with flowers or chocolates, all will be forgiven, but gifts don't mean anything unless someone has truly changed. Now, a cowboy with a puppy…" Shaundra pressed a hand to her mouth. "I'm ready to forgive you, and I don't even know what you did."

"Clementine is for Ellie." But Zach hoped the dog would help him connect with Beth too. "And I'm a rancher, not a cowboy."

"You still herd cattle and ride horses, don't you?"

"Yes, but—"

"In a city where a lot of people have never seen a horse outside the movies, let alone ridden one, you've got the hat and boots, so you're a cowboy." Shaundra grinned. "Own it. Wait here while I look for Elizabeth." This time, her smile warmed him like a hug. "If anybody asks, Clementine is your emotional-support animal, and I okayed you having her here."

"Thank you." Although Shaundra was at least fifteen years younger and didn't look anything like Zach's mom, she had the same inherent kindness.

"Don't thank me until you've seen Elizabeth. I'll tell her you're here, but what happens next is up to her."

"Okay." Zach would do anything that would help put things with Beth the way they needed to be—for him and, if he was lucky, for her as well.

BETH CHECKED THE budget projections again. Something in the figures was still wrong. She turned away from the computer, rubbed her eyes and stared out the window. Twenty plus floors below, some of the trees in the small park two streets over were tinged with yellow leaves, and the sky had the clear blue of fall. Were the trees turning color at Camp Crocus Hill too?

Her gaze drifted to the framed picture propped beside her computer of Ellie riding Princess. Why didn't Ellie want to book flights to Montana? At first, she'd been so keen, but as soon as Beth wanted to set a date, Ellie made excuses about school or not wanting to miss a riding lesson.

She grabbed her phone and scrolled to the calendar. Enough delaying and avoiding. She'd pick a weekend to go see Zach, and Ellie could come if she wanted to or stay with Jilly's cousin.

"Elizabeth?"

She looked up at a knock on her half-open office door followed by Shaundra's voice.

"I've checked these figures three times and can't find the problem. I need to go back to the… What?" She stared as Shaundra came into her office and closed the door. Except for human-resources meetings, the company had an open-door policy, and apart from senior staff, nobody had offices with doors, anyway. "Is something wrong?"

"No." Shaundra sat in the chair across

from Beth's desk. "There's someone here to see you."

"Oh?" Beth glanced at her calendar again. "The internal-marketing meeting with you isn't for an hour, and I don't have anything else scheduled this afternoon."

A smile played around Shaundra's mouth. "We can reschedule our meeting."

"But this was the only time this week you were available." Beth stared at her friend. Since Shaundra was the chief marketing officer, Beth worked closely with her, and before Jilly's illness, they'd often gotten together outside of work.

"It can wait. This new meeting is more important." Shaundra's smile broadened.

"Okay." Shaundra was talking in riddles. "Is it a client?" Beth grabbed the navy pin-stripe blazer that matched her trousers from the back of her chair, shrugged into it and smoothed the front of her cream blouse.

"No." Shaundra paused. "It's Zach Carter from Montana. I was on my way to security to get my badge replaced when I met him in reception. He's sitting there right now."

"Zach's here?" Beth's mouth went dry. "Why?"

"He wants to talk to you. I get the impression you're important to him."

Beth gripped the edge of her desk. "He… I… Ellie and I stayed at the camp his family runs." She wanted to see Zach, but she needed time to plan. "He's a rancher, and his family's ranch is nearby."

"I see." Shaundra studied her. "You talked a lot about that camp, the ranch, the woman who designed the silver raven pendant you gave me, and that small town with the great café, but you didn't tell me about him."

"No." Beth hadn't told anyone about Zach. "It's complicated."

"Is he why you turned down that job you interviewed for?"

"Of course not. The job didn't fit with Ellie." Beth pressed a hand to her face. Whenever she'd imagined seeing Zach again, it was in Montana, not here. And especially not at work when she was Elizabeth.

"I don't think it was only because of Ellie." Shaundra's smile was knowing. "If Zach came all the way from Montana to see you, he must have a good reason. If I was you, I'd listen to what he has to say."

"I will but…" Beth checked her reflection

in the small mirror atop her computer. No food or lipstick on her teeth, and in preparation for tonight's family evening at Ellie's school, she'd gone to a blow-dry bar at lunch.

"You look great." Shaundra followed Beth's gaze.

"Great for Chicago but not Montana." For a start, she was dressed in a suit. Beth shrugged out of the blazer and dug in her desk drawer for the sweater she kept there for chilly days.

"Zach came to see you, not what you're wearing." Shaundra stood. "Do I have to push you out to reception? I would, you know." Despite her smile, her tone was firm.

"I can't meet Zach there. Everybody will talk." Beth stood and shoved her arms into her sweater, a dark blue cardigan that buttoned up the front.

"Everybody will talk no matter what. The important thing is that *you* talk to him. He wasn't sure you would."

"He wasn't?" Beth's heartbeat kicked up a notch.

"Nope." Shaundra shook her head.

"I'll bring him back to my office." Her heart squeezed. She'd counted on going to

Montana to see him, and now she wouldn't be able to do that. "But it's the middle of the working day. Billable time."

"So? You'll work tonight after Ellie goes to bed. You always do. Besides, today is the first time this week you took a lunch break. You work harder than anybody else here, so get out there and lasso your cowboy, or whatever people do in the West, but catch him, woman."

"Cowboys lasso cattle." Beth stifled a laugh. She might not know much about Western life but she knew that. "Besides, I'm not trying to catch him."

"Why not?" Shaundra's grin was impish. "He's a sight better than any other man you've dated."

"You spoke to him for, what, five minutes?" Beth moved out of her office with Shaundra following.

"I can tell a bad man in a lot less than five minutes and a good one too. Besides, the dog likes him. Dogs are excellent judges of character."

"He brought a dog?" Beth walked along the row of cubicles, where heads popped up like prairie dogs from a burrow.

"Oh, yes." Shaundra's laugh rolled out as they turned the corner and went into reception.

Beth stopped so suddenly that Shaundra bumped into her. Zach. Recognition sizzled. And Clementine. The puppy was curled up on Zach's lap, asleep and paws twitching, a pet carrier on the floor by his chair. Her vision blurred. "You're here."

"Yeah." He got to his feet, still holding Clementine, and with his hat under one arm.

Beth had forgotten how tall he was and how big and safe. With the cowboy hat, boots and the dog, he should have been out of place here, but he wasn't. Zach was the kind of man who'd fit anywhere. But would he fit with her?

"I want to make things better, not worse." His voice was low and rasped as if he'd pushed the words out from someplace deep inside. "Can we talk?"

"Yes." In Beth's world, talking was the easy part. Finding solutions was much harder.

CHAPTER TWENTY

BETH'S OFFICE DOOR clicked shut behind Zach. He sat in the chair Beth indicated, and she pulled another chair, one on wheels, around her desk to sit beside him. "Nice view." He gestured to the bank of windows that encircled her office on two sides, the city skyline spread out in front of them. "You've got a corner office, so you must be important."

She shrugged. "It's a small company. When the former CFO got a job at a bigger firm, and I was promoted to fill his role here, everyone else was happy where they were."

"It was good of Shaundra to ask one of her team to walk Clementine. I don't want her to have an accident on the carpet." Was Beth happier to see the dog than him?

"Everyone probably wanted to walk that puppy. You showing up with Clementine is the most exciting thing that's happened here in ages. Ellie will be thrilled. She's been counting the days until Clementine was old enough to be shipped." Beth stared out the window. "Given you planned to ship Clementine to Ellie next week, why are you here?"

One of the things Zach loved about Beth was that she got straight to the point. However, even though he'd practiced what he wanted to say all the way here, the words, except the most important ones, were gone. "I came to say I'm sorry."

"You could have apologized in a text or email. Or called me." Beth's jaw was tight, and she still stared out the window, avoiding his gaze.

"I could have, but I wanted to make sure you knew how much I mean it." He drew in a breath. What had Shaundra said about a good grovel? "I'm so sorry about how things ended between us, sorrier than I've ever been about anything."

"I see." Beth turned to look at him, and he moved his chair around to face her.

"No, I don't think you do." Beth had never been this stilted, but Zach guessed he deserved it. And here in her fancy office, wearing those dressy pants and buttoned up sweater, her hair ironed into submission in a style that looked fresh from the salon, she'd never seemed so far away. "The thing is even though I couldn't admit it then, you were right. I *am* missing out on life. After you and Ellie left, I saw that, and I want to change." The back of his throat hurt. "I made a mistake, a lot of mistakes, but now I want to make things right."

Beth hugged herself. "That's good. That you want to change your life, I mean, and you admit you were wrong." Her voice was still cool, but there was a little hitch in it that gave Zach hope. Maybe she wasn't as indifferent to him as she might want to seem.

"It is, yes, but the thing is, I need help to change."

"I'm sure your doctor could recommend a counselor. Ellie sees someone, and it helps her a lot. We're doing some family therapy too. The camp was great, but we still have a long way to go." She tucked a smooth strand of hair behind one ear, and a diamond stud earring glinted in the light.

"My doctor already recommended someone." Zach had been a fool not to take up the offer of counseling after the genetic testing. If he had, maybe he wouldn't be in the mess he was in now. "I had my first appointment yesterday."

"Really?" Beth nodded and gave a weak smile. "That's great."

"I figure it's something I need to do." He swallowed. No matter how hard it was or how much it scared him.

"I'm glad for you." One of Beth's knees bumped his, and heat shot through Zach at the brief contact before she rolled her chair away.

"Thank you, but you see, I hoped you could also help me and you meant what you said that night in the barn."

"About what?" She fiddled with a button on her sweater.

"You said you'd fallen in love with me."

She turned at a knock on the door and moved to open it and take Clementine from a tall dark-haired guy in his midthirties wearing black jeans, shiny black shoes, a yellow-striped shirt, black blazer and rimless round glasses. His gaze skittered from Beth to Zach and back to her again.

Zach tucked his booted feet farther under his chair. He was messing things up big-time. Not that he'd expected Beth to fall into his arms, but he'd hoped she'd show some kind of emotion. Even yelling at him would be better than this coolness. He'd had more heated conversations about the weather.

Beth closed the door again and sat with Clementine on her lap. "I'm sorry, you were saying?"

Zach got it. He'd interrupted her workday, and no matter what he said or did, he could hardly make things any worse. "When you said that you loved me, I didn't say it then, but I love you too. I was afraid to let myself be vulnerable to tell you the truth, so I pushed you away. I used living in Montana and me carrying the cystic fibrosis gene as excuses. Since Dani didn't want to be with me because of those things, I convinced myself you wouldn't either, but I was wrong. I also convinced myself I didn't want children because I was scared, so I didn't listen when you said you'd be open to having a family in other ways." He gulped in a breath. "What I'm trying to say—badly—is that I want to have a life with you, and a family."

"Oh." Beth leaned toward him. "I—"

"Wait, I have to finish." If he didn't, Zach might never tell her everything. "I thought I was doing you a favor because if you didn't know I loved you, you'd go home and forget about me. You have a great life here with museums, concerts and all kinds of restaurants to choose from. You can also go out with men like him—" he jerked his chin toward her office door "—and have kids too without worrying."

"Bryan?" Beth raised her eyebrows, and a corner of her mouth twitched. "I don't date men I work with, but even if I did, Bryan is *so* not my type. Besides, he got married last year, and his wife works in the building next door."

"Oh." Now Zach was an even bigger fool. "Well, I meant generally."

"First of all, what makes you think I need museums, concerts and different food every day of the week?" Her voice had an edge Zach couldn't identify.

Sweat trickled down the back of his flannel shirt. "You're a city girl, and High Valley is a small town. Molly said she talked to you about city life, and she wants those things. Ruby's Place is our definition of fine dining, and the High Valley Players and school band are all we can offer for theater and music. As for museums, you've been to the only one, so you know how small it is. And in Montana, snow can come in September and last until June. It's cold and windy too."

"So is Chicago." Beth rubbed Clementine's floppy ears. "As for the rest of those things, I'm not Molly. Maybe she wants city life because she's never experienced it. She's also younger and at a different point in her life than me. I enjoy seeing plays and going to concerts and museums, and it's fun to go out for a nice meal, but even before I had Ellie, I didn't do those things all the time. And now? My big outings are going to a school event with Ellie or our favorite pizza place, and I'm okay with that. As for worrying about a child, I'd worry about having one no matter what. Like I worry about Ellie."

When Beth put it that way, Zach's reasoning had been even more flawed than he'd thought. "Yes, but—"

"When I told you that I loved you, I meant it." Beth's cheeks got pink. "And when I told you I didn't care about you carrying the cystic fibrosis gene and there were lots of ways to have a family, I meant that as well. But now I'm not sure if I know you or you know me. Or if you even know what love is."

Zach sucked in a breath. Although fair, it wasn't easy to hear, and Zach had to prove to Beth that he'd do anything to get her back. "I'm a Montana rancher whose life is cattle, horses and earning an honest living. I also want to leave my corner of the world a better place than I found it. I love my family and my community, and I love you too." He cleared his throat. "I love you most of all. If the only way I can be with you is to move to Chicago, I'll do that."

"You couldn't!" Her head jerked up. "The Tall Grass Ranch and Camp Crocus Hill are your life. They're more important to you than anything. You couldn't leave."

"Before my dad passed, I never thought the ranch could go on without him, but it did. Nobody is irreplaceable. My mom and my family want me to be happy. I don't want to leave the ranch, but if it's the only way I can be with you, I will. I'll find a job here." He leaned forward. "When it comes down to it, the ranch and the camp are things. You're more important." He couldn't live without her. He'd make it work in Chicago if he needed to, anything for her.

"And Ellie?"

"Ellie comes with you." He smiled. "I love her, and I want the three of us to be a family. What do you say?"

BETH COULDN'T LOOK at Zach. Instead, she got to her feet and, still cuddling Clementine, went to the window. The ranch was too important to him to sacrifice. Besides, Beth wanted to move to Montana. As did Ellie, who'd be packed within a day of the decision being made.

Zach said he loved her and wanted to be a family with her and Ellie. Why was she hesitating? She stared into the blue haze, sunlight reflecting off the windows of the skyscraper opposite. Apart from work, she didn't have any real ties in Chicago, and in Montana with Zach she'd have love, a family, a community and a whole new life. Interesting work too, if she set up a consulting business in between keeping the ranch on a sound financial footing.

She finally turned to face Zach, her heart hurting. "I still love you, but I grew up in a

family where we avoided talking about problems until we weren't a family anymore."
The backs of her eyes stung. "I don't want
that to happen to us." And until now, she'd
wanted a family but had been too scared to
take a risk to get one.

"Okay." He scraped a hand through his
hair and joined her by the window. "What
do you want to talk about?"

"You say you love me and want us to make
a life and family together, but whether that's
in Montana or here, we need to talk about
how we'd have that family." She paced in
front of the window, not seeing the familiar skyline.

Zach folded his arms over his chest. "I
always wanted kids, but when I found out
I carried the CF gene, I was scared, so—"
he stepped closer "—I convinced myself I
didn't want children. When Dani left me,
and a while ago I discovered she'd found
somebody else to have children with when
we were still together, those things hurt." His
voice was ragged.

"I'm not Dani. I wouldn't cheat on you."
But Dani had betrayed Zach twice.

"I know." He brushed a hand across his

face. "In all the ways that matter, you're not like Dani at all, but when you've been stood up in front of the whole town like I was, you get wary. And stupid." He gave her a crooked smile.

"I have a friend who's a pediatrician, and she helped me research cystic fibrosis." Beth put a hand on his forearm, the corded muscles tight. "I'm willing to get tested, and once we get the results, whether I carry the gene or not, that's another conversation."

"You'd risk the uncertainty of maybe never having a biological child of your own?"

"Of course. Life is about risks." Her muscles tightened as she acknowledged a truth she'd never admitted to herself, let alone anyone else. "I've tried to keep myself safe, but like you, I haven't been living either. I used to think that a great job would make me happy. Or having my dream car or my condo decorated exactly how I wanted it. But those things didn't mean much because I wasn't happy inside myself. *You* make me happy. Ellie does too. And I want a different kind of life and work, and a real family. The kind of life I could have in Montana with you."

"You'd do that for me?"

"Yes, but I'd do it for me too." Beth's mouth trembled, but she refused to give up. They'd come so far. "If we want to make things work between us, we have to talk about genetic testing and kids and everything else and not be scared. If we don't feel comfortable trying to have a child of our own, we can adopt. I'm not related to Ellie by blood, but I couldn't love her any more if I'd given birth to her."

Zach put a hand on her shoulder and then opened his arms. Beth set the puppy on the floor to move into his embrace.

"And even if we had a child with CF, it would be okay." She spoke into his shoulder, enveloped in the love and warmth he offered. "Having Paul in your life made it richer, didn't it?"

"Of course. He taught me so much."

"Exactly. Like Ellie teaches me." Beth batted away her tears. "Besides, life doesn't come with guarantees. Jilly's death, summer at the camp, Kate, Lily and everyone else taught me to be grateful for what I have when I have it. So no matter what happens, I want us to face it together."

"Me too." Zach's voice cracked.

"We can't think too far ahead." Beth squeezed him tight and took a step back to see his face.

"My mom says that." Zach gave her a watery smile. "I love you so much, Beth, and I've been a fool."

"True." She gave him a small smile in return. "But we all have things we believe about ourselves that are wrong. Sometimes we can't see that until someone else points it out." She looked into his face and clear blue eyes. "I was scared to have a family because when my parents split up, it almost destroyed me. We were supposed to be a happy family, but that was a lie. So I shut myself off from everyone, including my half brother, because I thought I could keep myself safe. I couldn't, though, and when I finally got the courage to open up to you, you rejected me, and all those old feelings came rushing back."

"I'm sorry." He pulled her closer and kissed the top of her head. "I hurt you even more."

"You did, but you also made me realize something important." She looped her arms around his neck. "For most of my life, and except at work, I haven't fought for what I wanted or stood up for myself. I'm tired of being that person. If you hadn't come here, I planned to book a flight to come to see you."

"Oh, Beth—"

"I wanted to come to Montana because I didn't want to give up on you or us. Ellie wanted to come with me, but I couldn't pin her down to a good time for travel. She always said she had something at school or riding."

"You know why?" Zach tilted Beth's chin, and his face held all the love she'd ever need and more. "Ellie knew I was coming here. She and my mom wanted to get us back together, so the two of them have been messaging each other since you left. I found out about that last night when I asked Ellie for your work address." His laugh rumbled against her ear.

"I should be mad, but I'm not." Beth laughed.

"There's more." Zach's grin was sheepish. "Come sit, and let me grab Clementine before she chews your office to bits." Zach scooped up the puppy from beneath Beth's desk.

"What?" Beth sat close beside Zach.

"Before you came to Camp Crocus Hill, my mom and Jilly emailed each other. I found out by accident the day you left. Jilly wanted us to meet each other again, and my mom went along with it." Zach kept hold of Clementine and looped his free arm around Beth's shoulders. "I told my mom she shouldn't have interfered, but she loves me, and Jilly loved you. They both wanted us to be happy."

Beth's eyes watered again. "Jilly never said a word, and apart from once, I never mentioned you to her after that summer." But Jilly was her best friend, and she'd known Beth better than Beth had known herself. "Jilly's gone, but in a way, it's like she's still here with us."

"Yeah." Zach's voice was gruff. "Like Paul and my dad."

"They'll always be in our hearts." Beth grabbed a tissue. "I thought I had to be independent, but it was because I was scared to trust or rely on anybody, even Jilly. But Jilly knew I needed someone, and Ellie did too. They knew I needed you."

"Like my mom knew I needed you. I hope you believe me now when I say how much I love you." Zach pulled her closer.

"I do. And I love you." For the first time,

the words were easy and natural. "And although I appreciate your offer to move here for me, I don't want to stay in Chicago. I want to move to High Valley. It's the right place for all of us."

"Land of big skies and herding cattle, huh?" Zach's low chuckle took away the last bit of doubt from Beth's heart.

Zach cupped Beth's face and looked into her eyes, his expression as serious as she'd ever seen it. "Whether we have a child of our own or adopt, what we have right now—you, me and Ellie—is perfect. I want to spend the rest of my life showing you how much I love you, and Ellie too."

"Me too. With you." Happiness rippled over Beth like summer wind across a grassy Montana pasture. She tilted her face for Zach's kiss, Clementine between them, and out of all the moments in her life, this might be the one she'd cherish most.

EPILOGUE

Three months later

"SEE THAT FENCE LINE?" As Zach drove his truck along the winding Montana highway edged by snow-covered fields, he gestured to Beth in the passenger seat and Ellie with Clementine behind.

"Yes?" Beth looked where he indicated.

"That marks the start of Carter land. We're almost home."

"I can't wait to see everyone." From the back seat, Ellie's voice was high-pitched with excitement. "Thanksgiving was ages ago."

"Less than a month." A sweet smile curved Beth's mouth. "But now we're here. It's great of your mom to let us live with her for a little while. That helps a lot."

"You're helping her too." Zach smiled back. "Mom gets lonely on her own in that big house. She'll love your company. Since she enjoys cooking, she's also excited about having two other people to make meals for."

"And in January I get to go to school with Lily and Ms. Kate, and later today Clementine gets to see her brothers."

From where she was strapped in beside Ellie, the puppy gave a sharp yip.

"I still think we should be paying your mom rent," Beth told him.

"Forget that idea. None of us will hear of it. You're turning the ranch around, and with your encouragement, Mom did great in her college course and wants to study to become a counselor. The least we can do is give you a comfortable place to live. Besides, you're a part of my family." As soon as he could, Zach wanted to make it official so Beth and Ellie could move in with him.

"We are. You're the family I never thought I'd have." Beth stared out the window at the rolling fields framed by a pale blue winter sky. "I almost can't believe it. We only left Chicago this morning, and here we are. It's another world."

"A better one for you, I hope." Zach's pulse raced. After spending the last three months traveling back and forth between Montana and Chicago, he'd never have to say goodbye to Beth and Ellie again.

"It will be." Beth gave him a teasing grin.

"I haven't had a big family Christmas before." Ellie poked her head between them over the seat back. "I have presents for everyone, even Alex, when he gets here after Christmas."

"Thank you for including my brother, Zach." Beth's smile slipped. "My dad is going golfing the day after Christmas, and since Alex's mom has to work, he'd have been on his own."

"He's family too." Zach took one hand away from the wheel to pat Beth's parka-covered arm. "Besides, he'll get to see what ranch life is like, so if he comes here to work next summer, he won't be surprised. Thanks to the plans you've put in place, we'll need more staff." Although Zach knew Beth was smart, he hadn't appreciated what a business dynamo she was. With her help, on top of her consultancy work that she'd already lined up, the ranch and Camp Crocus Hill would soon be more profitable than they'd ever been.

"Aren't we going to your mom's house

first?" Beth turned to him as the entrance to the Tall Grass Ranch slid by on the right.

"Nope. I need to take care of something before we meet everyone." Zach gave her a sideways glance, but Beth's head was turned away looking out the truck window again.

"No problem. Ellie napped on the plane, and we had a snack before— Where are we going?" Beth turned back to him, her expression puzzled.

"Wait and see." Leaving the highway, Zach drove the truck along the narrow road he'd asked one of the ranch hands to plow, snow banked up on either side.

"It's a bridge with a roof. Are we stopping here?" Ellie's voice was threaded with excitement.

"Yes." Zach parked at one end of the bridge. The sun shining off the snow with the red-painted bridge in the middle could have come from a Christmas card. The creek below was partially frozen, only a trickle of clear water in the center. "Hang on until I get your wheelchair."

"I'm okay to walk. I have enough spoons today," Ellie said. "Can Clementine come too?"

"Sure." Ellie used her wheelchair when

she needed it, and he and Beth trusted her to pace herself. Although Ellie still had bad days, there were lots of good ones too. Together, they'd learned to focus on and make the most of each and every moment. "You better put your hat and gloves on. We aren't walking far but it's cold out." Zach hid a smile. Although Ellie was in on part of the surprise, Zach had kept this bit to himself. "You dress warm too." He grinned at Beth as he put on his hat. "A city girl like you isn't used to a Montana winter."

"A city girl like me will be just fine." She smiled back as she put a knitted hat with a snowflake pattern, purple and white to match her parka, over her dark curls and added coordinating purple mittens. "Where are we going?"

"Only to the middle of the bridge." Zach got out of the truck and opened Ellie's door to help her down. "All set?"

Ellie nodded, winked at him and waited while Zach unhooked Clementine's car harness and replaced it with her leash. The puppy bounced into his arms and then landed on the ground to follow her nose. He held out his other arm, and Ellie took it as they walked around the truck to join Beth, their boots crunching in the crisp snow.

"Last summer, I promised you that we'd walk or drive over this bridge but we never did." Zach passed Clementine's leash to Ellie.

"I remember. You had to herd cattle." Beth tucked one of her hands in his, her mitten fitting around his glove.

"Yes." Zach led Beth to the middle of the bridge and gestured to Ellie to stay with the dog a few feet away, where she could balance herself against the bridge rail if needed. "I always regretted I never got to kiss you here."

"Me too." Beth stopped, and her face went a pretty shade of pink as she glanced back at Ellie.

"But you see, when I thought about it, kissing you on this bridge wouldn't be enough."

"No?" Beth stared at him, her eyes wide.

"No, because we want to build a life together, and although we've talked about a lot of things, something important is still missing." He took off his gloves, put them in his coat pockets and clasped Beth's hands through her mittens. "I talked to Ellie, and she said it was okay to do this." He darted a glance over his shoulder, and Ellie's smile reached from ear to ear.

"Yes?" Beth's breath clouded in the frosty air, and Zach waited a beat. He had to get this right the first time. He knelt on one knee on the bridge floor, clear of snow. "You already know how much I love you and want to spend the rest of my life with you, but when we talked about getting married, we talked about doing something small and quiet."

"I'm fine with that. I don't need a huge wedding." Her expression was earnest but expectant too.

"You might not, but I want something bigger." He took a deep breath and put the last of the ghosts of the past behind him. "I want everybody to know how much I love you and for them to celebrate with us. And I want to do things formally. I talked to your parents."

"You did?"

"Yes." Although Zach might never be close to them, he wanted Beth's mom and dad to be as much a part of their lives as she was comfortable with. "They gave me their blessing." He cleared his throat. "I never thought I'd have this chance with you, and now that's it here, I'm so happy. I hope that you are too and that you'll do me the honor of marrying me. Beth?"

"Yes, of course." She tugged him to his feet and flung her arms around him. "I thought we'd already decided that."

Ellie cheered and clapped with mitted hands.

"We did, but I wanted to give you something special to remember. For us to remember." He kissed her lips, too briefly, but he would wait for more. "This bridge is important to my family and to me. So I wanted to mark the start of our new lives here. All of us." He gestured to Ellie and dug in his jacket pocket.

"I want you to wear this, and I hope I can add a wedding ring to it soon." He took out the small box he'd carried with him on all those trips to Chicago, waiting for the perfect time and place before realizing that he had to ask Beth to marry him here in Montana, where things had started between them. He opened the lid of the box, and the sunlight caught the three pale blue sapphires flanked by baguette diamonds in a platinum setting.

"It's beautiful." Her voice was soft, but the love in it, and on her face, mirrored the love in him. "Sapphires are my favorite stone. How did you know?"

"I told him." Ellie hugged Beth and Zach. "And see? He chose three stones because there's three of us. It's for our family. One of the little diamonds on the side is for Clementine, and if you have other kids, the others can be for them."

Zach grinned. Beth had been tested and she didn't carry the cystic fibrosis gene. However, they wanted to take things slowly to build a family with Ellie first before making any other decisions.

"It's perfect." Beth's voice was choked, and as Zach took off her left mitten and slid the ring onto her finger, his throat got tight. "It fits." She held out her left hand to admire the ring.

"I snuck into your jewelry box and got your ring size. I measured one of your rings against a size chart Zach sent me." Ellie's tone was smug. "Only because he wanted to surprise you. I'm not a snoop."

"I know you aren't." Beth cupped Zach's face with the hand that wore her engagement ring. "Thank you. I can't wait to marry you, but if we want a bigger wedding, it will take time to plan."

"I can help, and so will Grandma Joy, Ms. Kate, Mrs. Rosa, Lily and everyone." Ellie leaned against Zach's arm. "Like everyone is helping to finish the work on Zach's house and decorate a bedroom for me and Clementine for us to live there after the wedding."

"Grandma Joy?" His heart swelled.

"She said I could call her that. She also said I should ask if I can call you *Dad* since I never knew my real one."

"I'd love for you to call me *Dad.*" Zach's eyes smarted. "But what about Beth?"

"I chose a special name for her too. I can't call Beth *Mom* because I have my own mom, and I'll never forget her." Ellie's smile slipped. "I thought… I like *Mama B*. What about you?"

"That's great." Two tears tracked down Beth's cheeks.

"Good." Ellie still hung onto Zach's arm. "Can we go now? I'm freezing, and Clementine's wriggling like she needs a thick blanket to curl up under."

"Sure." Zach laughed and kissed Beth again.

"Love you." He mouthed the words to Beth as Ellie walked ahead with the dog.

"Love you too. I always did. Right back to when we were only a bit older than Ellie. And I always will." Beth gave him a dimpled smile. "But maybe I *am* a city girl, because Ellie and Clementine aren't the only ones who are freezing. Let's go home."

"Sounds good." He tucked his arm in hers as they walked to the truck.

Home. From this moment on, home would be with her. There was no other place he'd rather be.

* * * * *

HARLEQUIN SELECTS COLLECTION

19 FREE BOOKS IN ALL!

From Robyn Carr to RaeAnne Thayne to Linda Lael Miller and Sherryl Woods we promise each author in the Harlequin Selects collection has seen their name on the *New York Times* or *USA TODAY* bestseller lists!

#411 A DEPUTY IN AMISH COUNTRY
Amish Country Haven • by Patricia Johns

Deputy Conrad Westhouse has one job—protect
Annabelle Richards until she can testify. The best place to
keep her safe is his ranch in Amish country, but getting to
know the beautiful witness means risking his heart...

#412 THE COWBOY MEETS HIS MATCH
The Mountain Monroes • by Melinda Curtis

Cowboy Rhett Diaz is starting an outdoor adventure company—
with needed help from Olivia Monroe's family. He just has to
get her across the country first... Can the road trip of a lifetime
lead to lifelong love?

#413 TO TRUST A COWBOY
The Cowboys of Garrison, Texas
by Sasha Summers

Hattie Carmichael's brother is marrying her childhood bully.
Participating in the hasty wedding is one thing—doing it alone
is another. Thankfully, Forrest Briscoe plays along with her fake
relationship ruse...until neither can tell what's real from pretend.

#414 SECOND CHANCE LOVE
Veterans' Road • by Cheryl Harper

Marcus Bryant returns home to Miami—and to old friend
Cassie Brooks. Their friendship never survived his joining the
air force after graduation. Planning their high school reunion
together might help them unravel the past...and find a future.